PSYCOME

6

A MURDERER
AND THE DEADLY
LOVE AFFAIR

"SORRY TO KEEP YOU WAITING. ♪ HERE ARE YOUR GRAY MATTER CREAM PUFFS AND FRESH BLOOD SQUEEZED FROM SINNERS. ♪"

MAID CAFÉ HADES

"I'LL MAKE YOU FORGET ALL ABOUT HER!"

Pulse of the Prisoners

KILLING PRACTICE: LOUD PARK

TRACK ONE

"HEY, KYOUSUKE... RENKO DID ALL KINDS OF THINGS WITH YOU, RIGHT? IN THAT CASE, I'LL HAVE YOU DO THEM WITH ME, TOO! YOU WANT TO, RIGHT?!"

Life After Me, Death After You
HEARTBREAK DOWN
TRACK FIVE

"......MISS...
KURUMIYA—"

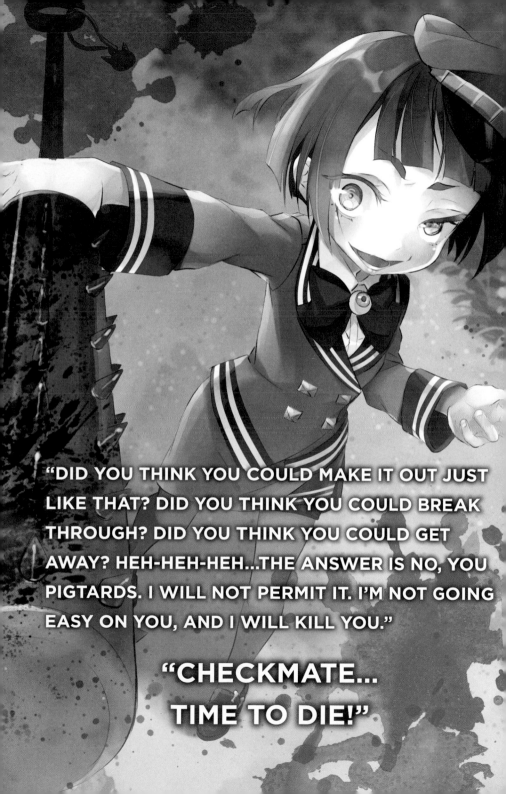

—She pressed her
lips against his.

Fall in Love, Equal KI

DEATHBED PROMISE

TRACK SIX

PSYCOME

6

A MURDERER
AND THE DEADLY
LOVE AFFAIR

Mizuki Mizushiro
X
Namanie

YEN ON
NEW YORK

PSYCOME, Vol. 6: A Murderer and the Deadly Love Affair
MIZUKI MIZUSHIRO

Translation by Nicole Wilder
Cover art by Namanie

PSYCOME
©2014 MIZUKI MIZUSHIRO
First published in Japan in 2014 by KADOKAWA CORPORATION ENTERBRAIN.
English translation rights arranged with KADOKAWA CORPORATION
ENTERBRAIN through Tuttle-Mori Agency, Inc., Tokyo.

English translation © 2018 by Yen Press, LLC

Yen On
1290 Avenue of the Americas
New York, NY 10104

Visit us at yenpress.com
facebook.com/yenpress
twitter.com/yenpress
yenpress.tumblr.com
instagram.com/yenpress

First Yen On Edition: February 2018

Yen On is an imprint of Yen Press, LLC.
The Yen On name and logo are trademarks of Yen Press, LLC.

Library of Congress Cataloging-in-Publication Data
Names: Mizushiro, Mizuki, author. | Namanie, illustrator. |
Wilder, Nicole, translator.
Title: Psycome / Mizuki Mizushiro ; illustration by Namanie ;
translation by Nicole Wilder.
Other titles: Saikome. English
Description: First Yen On edition. | New York, NY : Yen On, 2016–
Identifiers: LCCN 2016005815 | ISBN 9780316272339 (v. 1 : pbk.) |
ISBN 9780316398251 (v. 2 : pbk.) | ISBN 9780316398268 (v. 3 : pbk.) |
ISBN 9780316398305 (v. 4 : pbk.) | ISBN 9780316398329 (v. 5 : pbk.) |
ISBN 9780316398350 (v. 6 : pbk.)
Subjects: LCSH: False imprisonment—Fiction. | Science fiction. | BISAC: FICTION /
Science Fiction / Adventure.
Classification: LCC PZ7.1.M636 Ps 2016 | DDC 895.63/6—dc23
LC record available at http://lccn.loc.gov/2016005815

ISBNs: 978-0-316-39835-0 (paperback)
978-0-316-39836-7 (ebook)

10 9 8 7 6 5 4 3 2 1

LSC-C

Printed in the United States of America

PSYCOME

6

A MURDERER AND THE DEADLY LOVE AFFAIR

Contents

PSYCHO LOVE COMEDY

Biiiiiiiing, boooooong...
Baaaaaang, boooooong...

A normal chime rang out from an undamaged speaker.

At the sound of that electronic tone, reminiscent of normal school life, Kyousuke stopped working and raised his head to look at the clock hanging on the clean, graffiti-free wall. It was 12:50—third period was over, and it was time for lunch to start.

"......"

However, no class had been held. Their bored-looking homeroom teacher, Hijiri Kurumiya, had one elbow up on the lectern and was tapping her shoulder with an iron pipe as her irritated gaze swept around the classroom.

"Miss Kurumiya! We finished the picture to hang on the blackboard. The theme is 'Hell Screen'! It shows us, the students of first-year Class A, wantonly slaughtering men and women of all ages. Hch-hch."

"You're in it, too, Miss Kurumiya—look here, as King Enma! We drew you up like the demon king watching over the devilish murderers, see? It's a total masterpiece, if you ask me... What do you think, ma'am? Is it okay to do it like this?"

"...Sure. Don't bother checking with me. Do whatever you want, piggies!" Coldly shooing away two students who had approached the lectern, Kurumiya stood up and, without saying another word, left the room.

Shinji and Tomomi stared at each other.

"Yo, has Miss Kurumiya, like, totally lost her motivation or what?"

"Seems that way... Well, this isn't like the athletic festival—it's not a competition. Since we can do it however we please, let's do just that!"

With that, the two of them returned to their stations. In the spacious classroom on the second floor of the new school building's A wing, their jersey-clad classmates were scattered about, working in noisy groups.

Some were cutting stage settings out of cardboard, some were adorning the walls with finished decorations, some were spreading skull-patterned tablecloths over groups of desks that had been pushed together…and so on.

Normal classes had been suspended due to an upcoming annual event, and all the students in every class were being pressed into service to make the preliminary arrangements.

The Nineteenth Purgatorium Remedial Academy Purgatory Festival.

Held at the end of October, the event was a kind of culture festival. A festival where the murderous students would entertain dangerous attendees: killers and assassins, gangsters and fixers who pulled the world's strings from the shadows, and more—all guests from the criminal underworld.

Such guests would be more than capable of wiping out any person or thing that might offend them, so the reputation of the academy itself was on the line. For that reason, the students had been allowed to spend a whole two weeks planning and prepping in their class groups.

…Only one person, the unmanageable problem child Mohawk, had been locked away alone in the dungeon the day the preparations had started. Apparently he was to be strictly confined, forbidden from taking even a single step outside his prison until the Purgatory Festival had safely concluded.

Truly, no one had seen Mohawk for the past four days, and there was no way to contact him. Could Kurumiya's recent lack of ambition be somehow connected…?

"Kyousuke, do you want to take a little break and go to lunch soon?" Maina interrupted his thoughts. She had put down her pen and stood, stretching.

Kyousuke, who had been making a menu board out of paper pasted onto a cardboard cutout, also stood up from the floor. "Yeah, okay," he agreed. "That's good work, Eiri. You wanna come eat with us?"

"……Mm." Eiri, who was working at a desk in the corner, glanced up at the two of them. "…I'm at a good spot right now. Go ahead without me," she answered nonchalantly and then resumed stitching with thread and needle. One completed costume was already casually strewn out before her.

"Whoa!" Maina let out a shout of admiration. She rushed over and picked up the finished costume, her big eyes sparkling. "You finished it already?! Wowww, how cute... That's our Eiri!"

"Wow, I can't believe it's handmade! That's amazing, Eiri."

"...Eh, not really. Something like this is no big deal." The unanimous praise didn't seem to annoy Eiri as much as one would expect.

The black-and-white costume was supposed to be some kind of maid outfit. It featured plenty of lace and frills, and it was adorned with a crimson bow on the chest. Only on closer inspection were the more gruesome details apparent—the buttons were fashioned like eyeballs, for example, and the apron was decorated with bloody polka dots. The costume incorporated many grotesque touches.

Eiri, who had handled everything from the design to the actual sewing by herself, was obviously proud. "An ordinary maid outfit would be boring, right? Since I'm going to all the trouble, I tried to come up with a few clever touches... Isn't it perfect for the Maid Café Hades?"

—The Maid Café Hades. A cosplay café combining two themes (maids and the underworld) was first-year Class A's festival project. They were decorating their classroom to look like an infernal hellscape.

Oonogi, who was working on making a "Bloody Pool of Damnation" out of a plastic kiddie pool, looked up and raised his hand. "Yo, Eiri! I think the skirt oughta be shorter!"

"Hee, hee-hee-hee...," Usami chimed in. "At twelve inches above the knee, the chances of a panty flash go up substantially...hee, hee-hee..."

"...Just die already!" Eiri quickly shut them down before deliberately recrossing her legs. Rather than a tracksuit, Eiri was wearing her regular uniform, the skirt of which looked to be shorter than twelve inches above the knee...

"Say, Eiri—"

"What? I'm not changing the skirt length."

"No, no...we're going to lunch, is that all right?"

"Yeah. I'll go when I get to a stopping point. And don't forget to visit your sister, all right?"

"Sure. Though she seems pretty busy herself... I'll peek in on her just in case."

In addition to the class programs, the Purgatory Festival would include many other voluntary projects. Ayaka had come up with an idea of her own and had been given one of the classrooms in the new school building to pursue it. She hadn't told them what kind of exhibition she was planning, but it was probably hard work setting it up alone.

Maina finished looking over the completed costume and began to fold it up. "Um, won't you be lonely by yourself?" she timidly inquired. "Maybe you should come with us—"

"Uh-uh. I'm fine... I have him." Eiri smiled.

—*Right, Pooh Bear?* On the desk facing Eiri sat an enormous teddy bear. It was Eiri's prized possession, brought over from her dorm room.

"Poo-poo...Pooh Bear, poo-poo-poo!" Shinji burst out laughing, but a single bloody glare from Eiri quickly shut him up.

Three days ago, when Eiri had first brought Pooh Bear over, she had sent every boy who had laughed at him to the infirmary. The so-called Bloody Plushy Incident was still fresh in everyone's mind.

Kyousuke took a moment to shake off the image of the classroom painted in bright red blood before speaking. "All right, later then. We're headed to the cafeteria."

"Good luck with your costume making, Eiri!" Maina announced. "I'm looking forward to seeing the finished products."

"...Yeah, okay." Eiri waved them off.

Turning away from their friend, Kyousuke and Maina moved to leave the classroom when—

"*Kksshh?!* What the heck is this interior design?! It's super elaborate, wow! Our Purgatory-Style Massage Parlor is just beds lined up!"

—at the room's rear, a student from another class threw the door open and appeared in the doorway.

Wearing a thin blue hoodie, a tank top, oversized headphones, and a sinister-looking gas mask, the girl looked around the classroom with exaggerated surprise.

"Kyousukeeeeee!"

It scarcely took her a moment to identify Kyousuke's figure and run straight for him, leaping on him in a full-body embrace. In the process, she trod on the picture that Shinji and his group were working on, completely ignoring their screams of protest.

"I wanted to see you, Kyousukeeeeee!" she squealed, squeezing him tightly with both arms. "I've been busy with preparations, too, so I couldn't come see you for a while... I'm sorry! I'm sooo sorry I neglected you for more than half a day! Ohhh, I was getting so Kyousuke deficient that I was dangerously close to death...so I thought I'd better hurry up and replenish my Kyousuke supply! Hey, come on—you can also replenish yourself fully. —Ah, but in your case, you don't store it up; you have to get it out, right? *Kksshh...!*"

"Wha?! H-hey, Renko—"

"Eh-heh-heh. Are my hands okay? Or would you prefer my boobs? I can't use my mouth, because the mask is in the way, so I guess we should go with boobs. Okay, get your pants off!"

"Absolutely nooooootttttt!" Kyousuke shouted in panic as Renko continued fawning over him with no regard for their audience. Desperately defending his drawers, the young man looked around at the crowd of classmates staring at the two of them with exasperated looks and grumbling, "This again?"

One month had passed since the athletic festival. Renko had awoken after two days in a coma, and every day since then had been like this: her flirting with Kyousuke, regardless of the situation.

It was fine during breaks and after school, but she had even begun barging in on him in the dorms and in the bath, pouring all her energy into her romantic pursuit. Renko's goal was not—as it had been up until this point—to seduce Kyousuke. Rather, she was simply using her whole body and soul to express her rampant joy.

Perhaps it was because he had finally declared his true feelings for her. As lukewarm as he'd felt in the men's bath during the Summer Death Camp, he couldn't deny that there was a certain thrill to what she'd done there that was extremely appealing. Honestly, it was not all bad, but...

"D-dummy...think a little bit about where you are! Don't you care about people staring?! Are you into public humiliation now? If you have to do this, do it where there aren't many people—"

"...Hmm? A place without many people you say, hmmm?"

"Eh?! Ah, no...th-that's not what I—"

"Insolent! Impure! Shameleeeeeess!"

Eiri glared at him coldly, and Maina swatted at him with every accusation. Kyousuke felt as if he were being pressed down onto a bed of nails.

"Kyousuke, you're too easily embarrassed!" Renko cooed. "When we're alone together, you're so passionate. Earlier in bed, when you went inside, you were so—uaah?!"

Flustered, Kyousuke tried to hold Renko back as she chattered away about unsavory subjects. He tried to cover her mouth with both hands, but of course the gas mask was in the way, so all he ended up doing was hugging her head.

Renko let out an enraptured sigh. "Oh, Kyousuke..." She hugged him back with all her might.

Kyousuke's classmates started jeering "Ohhh!" as they watched the farce play out.

BANG!

—Suddenly, there was the sound of a chair falling over.

"Wahh?! Ei-Eiri—"

"......"

Dropping the costume that she'd been stitching, Eiri furiously clambered to her feet. She walked around to the other side of the desk and grabbed Pooh Bear from his chair. Gripping his collar in her left hand, she pressed him up against the wall, pulled back her right hand in a tight fist, and...

—*Boff! Boff! Boff!*

Without a word, Eiri began ramming her fist into the stuffed animal's soft belly.

Taking note of this strange behavior, Renko pulled away from her obsession and laughed a triumphant "*Kksshh!*"—and then immediately made her next outrageous move.

"Aah?! No, don't, Kyousuke, not heeere!" She grabbed both of Kyousuke's wrists and pressed his hands forcefully against her own breasts.

"Aah?!" she gasped again, melodramatically. "Kyousuke, you're so intense—*aaaaaahn*?! Oh, when you rub them like thaaat— I know my melons are attractive, but...ah, ah, aaah!"

"Stooop!! Hey, what do you think you're doing, Perv Mask?! Don't just move people's hands however you liiiiiiiike! Seriously, sto—"

"You can say what you like, but your face gives you away, doesn't it?

I only moved your hands, didn't I? So why are your fingers massaging me?"

"...Huh? I'm not moving them—"

"Just fucking die!" Eiri, who had taken this act seriously, gripped Pooh Bear with both hands and smashed him with a flying knee strike.

"...Kyousuke," Maina muttered disapprovingly.

"N-no...that's not right! I'm innocent—it's a false accusation!"

"Eh, is that really so, Kyousuke? *This part* seems to be telling the truth."

"Heeey?! Y-y-you idiot, watch where you're grabbing—!"

"What's this? So you are backed up after all...*kksshh*. There's no way around it—I'll put you at ease. Wait just a second, okay? I'll be ready soon—"

"No, stoooooop!" Kyousuke shouted at Renko, who wasn't paying the least bit of attention to anyone around them. Grabbing and holding down the kink master before she could remove her bra in public, he sighed heavily. "...Geez. You're so intense."

It was hard to believe that she'd slept for two full days after the athletic festival. As he watched the young woman's oblivious frolicking, Kyousuke couldn't help feeling that there must have been a mistake in what Reiko had said that day.

"Sometime in the near future, probably sometime very soon, Renko is going to die."

Renko's true age was three years old, and she had shortened her already short life expectancy by using her Over Drive power during the athletic festival. She was not supposed to have long. There was no time to waste.

That was why—

I've got to quit doing this and prepare myself...

Renko had nearly thrown away her life for Kyousuke's sake, and Kyousuke was determined to put his own life on the line and repay her.

Pulse of the Prisoners

KILLING PRACTICE: LOUD PARK

TRACK ONE

MAXED OUT: THE COMMON Man

01. Hopeless Slayer

02. My Adolescent Comeback

03. Shit Breaking Brain Breaking Lady

04. What's Up, Normal People?!

05. PUNCHING1000tOON

06. Megadeth of Love

KYOUSUKE KAMIYA 1st EP

"Welcome to the other side, our condolences. ♪"

Female students in maid costumes greeted the guests of Café Hades thus.

It was Purgatorium Remedial Academy's Nineteenth Annual Purgatory Festival, and the Maid Café Hades set up by Kyousuke and his class had seen constant traffic throughout the morning.

The students had been told that all the guests were members of the bloody criminal underground, but their outward appearances were not so different from normal, upstanding citizens. Men and women of all ages came one after another to their establishment.

A third of the classroom had been partitioned off by a curtain to serve as the café's kitchen, and it was incredibly busy. The girls took orders from the customers, and the boys prepared the sweets and juices.

"......Here."

Eiri returned with an order. She tore the page from her memo pad, which she was using as a sales book, and lined it up with the other orders on the desktop. Her exhausted voice and expression were just like a zombie's.

"Table five, two-top, they need two Gray Matter Cream Puffs and two tomato juices, plus a game of Burning Infatuation Inferno

Rock-Paper-Scissors and a Café Hades Souvenir Photo Shoot...*haa*."
A long sigh escaped Eiri's mouth like a soul escaping into the afterlife.

As he poured tomato juice into paper cups, Kyousuke smiled and said, "Good work out there. More orders from the special menu, huh? It's really popular."

"...I'm not happy about it. They should all just die." Eiri glared at him as she fixed the placement of her headdress. It seemed like putting on a professional smile and an ingratiating voice was really beginning to wear on her.

Oonogi, who was preparing the cream puffs, laughed lightheartedly. "Ha-ha-ha! Eiri acting sociable is something we almost never see, right? The first time I watched her play rock-paper-scissors, it was so cutesy I thought I would die of love!"

"Burning. ♪ Love. ♪ Rock. ♪ Paper. ♪ Scissors. ♪ One, two, three. ♪ ...Hee-hee-hee." As Usami imitated the words and motions of the Burning Infatuation Inferno game, Eiri's face flushed before their eyes...

"Sh-shut up! Do you want me to send the two of you to hell for real?!"

"C'mon, Eiri, try to control yourself," Kyousuke offered, keeping Eiri from grabbing the two boys. "You only have to put up with it for a little bit longer." He directed his gaze toward the clock on the wall.

The time was 10:20—their shift ended at 10:30, so these would probably be her last customers. Eiri clicked her tongue a little bit and picked up the tray bearing sweets and juice. "...That's right. I want to break free already." She turned on her heel. Her short skirt, fourteen inches above the knee, swished as she spun.

"Eiri," Kyousuke said behind her.

"......What?"

"The maid outfit really suits you! It's obvious why you're so popular."

"Eh—" Eiri stiffened, at a loss for words over the compliment. Kyousuke, for his part, had been holding on to the thought for some time. However, she soon had her sour look back. "...H-huh? Wh-what are you saying all of a sudden? St...stupid idiot!!"

She turned around and strode away. Before long—

"Sorry to keep you waiting. ♪ Here are your Gray Matter Cream Puffs and fresh blood squeezed from sinners. ♪"

The voice they could hear from the customers' table was bright and lively, without the slightest hint of its previous sullenness. Popping a misappropriated cream puff into his mouth, Oonogi muttered pensively, "She's hard to understand, that Eiri..."

× × ×

"A lowly bastard is killed by a demon of death, and it is a great sin not to kill someone of the same low rank!"

Each carrying a program emblazoned with this incomprehensible maxim, Kyousuke and Eiri navigated the crowds of Purgatory Festival attendees. The colorfully decorated school building was boisterous with festive merrymaking.

Still dressed in her maid costume as she walked the halls, Eiri turned and asked, "...Is there any place you want to go?"

Kyousuke opened up his pamphlet. "Let's see...there are places I definitely don't want to go, like the Snuff Film Screening and Bloody Torture Experience and Hangman's Bungee Jump, but...if I have to pick, maybe the Black Market Flea Market? I'd like to see what kind of things they're selling."

"Hmm. Where is that, anyway?" Moving alongside Kyousuke, Eiri peered at her own pamphlet. "...Ah, it looks like it's outside. Since we're already here, do you want to look around inside first? I'm interested in the Cursed Doll Show. And the nearby Shadow of Death Fortune-Telling seems—"

"Ah, um...Eiri?"

"What?"

"N-nothing...just that, um..."

—She was close. Ridiculously close. At a distance where their cheeks were nearly touching. Her silky rust-red hair was tickling Kyousuke's nostrils and had a sweet scent like candy.

Eiri snorted. "Hmph, what are you getting flustered for? You've gotten close to that girl Renko's various parts plenty of times...doing all kinds of things."

"Uh—"

Her scornful eyes turned on him at point-blank range, and Kyousuke was hard-pressed for an answer. After glaring silently at him for a short while, Eiri pouted. "...Hmmm? So you don't deny it. You sex fiend! Pervert! Corrupted youth!"

"Guh?! N-no comment..."

Eiri pulled away and grabbed Kyousuke's right wrist. "Come with me."

"Eh—"

Pulling the perplexed young man along by the hand, Eiri led them from the third floor of the A wing up to the fourth floor. After they had gotten away from the crowds, they turned toward the closed door to the roof.

"H-hey..."

"It's fine."

Eiri easily picked the lock with a bit of wire she pulled from her pocket. She opened the iron door with the words NO ENTRY painted in red. Kyousuke closed the door behind them as he followed Eiri onto the roof.

"Hey..." In an instant, the girl nimbly spun around and closed the distance between them. "...Are you an idiot?"

She peered into his face as she spit out the words. Her rust-red, upturned eyes were as sharp as knives. Eiri continued speaking in a quiet tone as Kyousuke listened, unable to respond.

"If you and Renko fall in love, she'll kill you, right? Knowing that, why—" Eiri's voice was trembling, and she bit her lip as if to try to control it. "What are you flirting with her for?!"

—Bam! The yakuza kick that accompanied Eiri's desperate shout grazed Kyousuke's left side before smashing into the iron door. He reflexively tried to back away, but the door kept him from going anywhere.

Still pressing her right foot into the iron slab, Eiri groaned. "...Kyousuke, do you want to die?"

Her question was as direct as her gaze.

Daunted by the menacing demeanor, Kyousuke let his averted eyes wander. "N-no...uh, ummm...that's...well..."

"......"

"O-of course I don't want to die...but..."

"......"

"Th-there's a good reason—"

"Like?"

"W-well—"

"Like?"

Kyousuke was stumped in the face of Eiri's silent pressure and the persistent repetition of her question.

She didn't know about Renko's condition—how Renko's life span as an artificial life-form was so short, how she couldn't live as long as Kyousuke and the others, how she had sacrificed so much of her life to save his own, how she was likely to die so soon...

As he ruminated on the secrets of the Murder Maids, Kyousuke recalled that Reiko had said, "Not a word to anyone." He clenched his jaw hard.

Eiri's piercing red eyes narrowed. "You can't say?"

"......Sorry."

"Tch—" Letting her gaze fall, Eiri lowered her right leg. However, the moment Kyousuke began to relax— "I see. If it's like that, I have no choice... I'll have to use my *full ability*."

—*Bam!* This time her palm thrust forth, grazing Kyousuke's right cheek as it slammed into the iron monolith. Deeply furrowing her brow, Eiri brought her face close to his without hesitation.

"Wha...?!"

Kyousuke tried to step back but found he had nowhere to go. He was blocked from behind by the iron door and from the front by Eiri's body, and any retreat to the right was blocked by the girl's left arm.

"I won't let you escape."

—*Bam!*

The moment he glanced left, Eiri cut him off with her other arm.

Now completely surrounded on all four sides, Kyousuke began to tremble. Feeling Eiri's strong gaze on his cheek, he slowly turned his head, and...

"Hey, Kyousuke...Renko did all kinds of things with you, right? In that case, I'll have you do them with me, too! You want to, right?! If you're falling for her extreme sex appeal and about to give in, then... I-I can't just stay silent, can I? I have to mount a full attack and, the circumstances being what they are, make you forget all about her!" Though her face was flushed, Eiri's eyes were as resolute as her shout.

I-I'm going to be eaten alive! Kyousuke's body stiffened instinctively with the sense of impending danger.

They were so close that their breaths mingled. Eiri's sweet scent traveled through his nostrils and excited him to his core, making his mind dizzy.

"〰〰〰〰〰?!"

Unable to stand it, Kyousuke found himself holding his breath. He could hear his heart pounding in his chest, and his face quickly grew hot. When he hung his head, unable to look straight at her with his wet, blurry eyes, his gaze passed over the girl's long, supple legs, stretching down from the short skirt of the maid costume...

Even though she had said, "I'm not changing the length of the skirt," she had in fact cut the skirt in question two inches shorter. He believed that by doing so, Eiri had revealed something of her true feelings. She had altered the skirt to show off her beautiful, sleek legs...

"...D-do as you... Do whatever you like...!"

"Huh?"

As she followed Kyousuke's gaze, Eiri's voice grew vanishingly small. Both of her hands were still pressed against the iron door, and she fidgeted bashfully, moving her dazzlingly white thighs back and forth—framed in the gap between the black skirt and her knee socks.

"D-do as you p-please, I said! I-I won't get angry, so...the th-things you do with Renko—no, more than you do with her—d-do them with me, too, you creep! If you don't, I'll—"

She took her right hand off of the door and moved it over the doorknob.

—*Kachink*. After locking the door, she placed both forearms against it, bringing her body even closer. The distance between them vanished, and her chest pressed against him. It was soft.

"......?!"

Deliberately, Eiri placed her chin on Kyousuke's shoulder and rubbed her cheek on his. Kyousuke's breath caught in his throat as she whispered nervously into his ear, "I'll have you do those things, and... I'll do more with you than Renko has."

"E-Eiri—"

All the thoughts swirling in Kyousuke's mind were blasted away in an instant. Eiri's hot breath, her seductive voice, her soft body, her sweet scent, her innocent feelings—all those things came together as one to overwhelm him and burst the bounds of his reason.

"Kyah?!"

Almost unconsciously, Kyousuke embraced Eiri's body and pulled her close.

"Noooooooooooooo~~~~~~?!"

Suddenly, a lascivious voice filled the air. It came from *right above* Kyousuke and Eiri.

"Eh?"

Separating their lips just before they could touch, the two of them looked upward in confusion, only to see—

"No, no, you tried so hard to contain yourself, but your voice slipped out! Damn, damn, stupid! Kurisu, you idiooooooot! If you had just watched them in secret, they definitely would have started, but...now you've ruined it, FUCK! Seriously FUUUUUUUUUUCK!"

On top of the doorway, peering down at them from an unexpected vantage point, was a female student who looked like she was about to tear out her brightly dyed hair in frustration.

"Geh?! Aren't you—?"

It was the third-year student who had been in charge of broadcasting at the athletic festival, Kurisu Arisugawa.

When she noticed Kyousuke and Eiri looking at her, Kurisu snapped back to her senses and quickly stiffened. "Huh?!" For a moment, she said nothing, glancing back and forth awkwardly. "D-don't mind me!"

"We do mind!" "Yeah, we do!"

Kyousuke and Eiri shot back at their upperclassman, who was grinning like a fool while trying to win them over.

"Ahh..." Kurisu, clearly at something of a loss, started frantically trying to explain the situation. "How should I put this, um...sorry? I wasn't planning to get in your way? I just wanted to hide from the teachers and Public Morals Committee and take a nap...and when I heard signs of people and then your voices talking, I thought *Shit!* and jumped up here. And then I secretly watched you to see what was up—"

She narrowed her lazy, catlike eyes and continued talking in an ever more excited voice. "And it turned out to be two underclassmen having a secret rendezvous! What's more, I felt like there was something even more suspicious going on, but I couldn't quite put my finger on it... So I thought to myself that it would be too good to miss and decided to hide."

...So that was it. She had been playing hooky from the festival and just coincidentally happened to be up on the roof.

Kurisu smiled, satisfied, at the pair below, who said nothing. Then her gaze fixed on Eiri, who was hanging her head in silence. "Whaaa, HA-HA-HA-HA! Excuse me, underclassman, but aren't you the bitch with the beautiful legs? That was some magnificent seduction—even I was getting embarrassed over here... It's dangerous stuff! Don't worry—he'll fall for it. He'll give in for sure. Was that the carnivorous style that's been popular lately? I tell ya, if I was a man, I'd've nailed you in an instant...especially when you said, 'Do as you please'—that was dan-ger-ous! Coming at him with a strong offense, and then flipping the table at the last moment... What a technique!! How many people did you have to do to learn that? And by 'do' I certainly do not mean 'kill,' if you catch my drift—"

"......I'll kill you," Eiri growled, interrupting Kurisu's frantic chatter.

"—Pardon?"

Looking up at Kurisu, who was playing dumb, Eiri pulled a small dagger out from who knew where. "After witnessing a scene like that, there's nothing to do but make sure to keep your lips sealed... If you want something to blame, blame your own laziness for leading you to play hooky in a place like this..."

"Fwah?! Wait, wait, wait, wait, wait a minute, waitress!" Kurisu panicked at the palpable bloodlust. "I'll seriously keep it a secret... I absolutely won't tell anyone! Not even Kamiya's *girlfriend*—that gas mask girl. I'll keep quiet about you *trying to steal him* from her—"

"Just die already!"

Eiri finally lost it. She clambered up after Kurisu with the dagger gripped between her teeth.

"Eeeeee?! I'm gonna die, killed by this bitch!"

"I'm not a bitch!" Eiri brandished the dagger as Kurisu retreated.

Barely avoiding the blade, their elder jumped down in a rush and brushed aside Kyousuke, who was still standing in front of the iron door. "Later, freshie. See ya in the mosh pit!"

"Ah?!"

Kurisu quickly unlocked the door and scrambled through it, escaping the scene. Eiri chased after her, yelling, "Wait, you!"

Left behind all alone, Kyousuke stood still for a moment, then let out a long sigh. As the tension left his shoulders, he sank down to the ground.

"I-I'm saved..."

X　　　X　　　X

"Chocolate bananaaas! Treat yourself to a nice, dark, thick, looong chocolate banana! Bananas so big they put black gentlemen to sha— Ah, Miss Arisugawa? You're looking rather out of breath—whatever could have happened?"

"Ohh?! Public Morals Committee Chair, it was awful! Truly awful! The state of public morality at this school has really gone out the window!! Listen here, just now I was relaxing and taking a nap upstairs, when two underclassmen showed up—"

"......A nap? You were taking a nap?"

"Ah, yeah! I was gonna play hooky from the festival and take a nap, so I went up to the roof—guah?!"

"Oh-ho-ho-ho-ho-ho-ho, Miss Arisugawa...it seems you really want to be disciplined, hm? Ho-ho, I understand. I'll take this chocolate banana and use it to violate your impertinent mouth! And not just the mouth up here, either...oh-ho-ho-ho!"

"Mbwah—ah?!"

Kurisu was quickly restrained by the Public Morals Committee chair—Saki Shamaya, who had been selling chocolate bananas as she patrolled the school—and was promptly dragged off down the corridor.

Eiri, hiding in the shadows nearby, clicked her tongue—"...Tch"— and put her dagger away. "I missed my chance to kill her, but she'd better not go mouthing off about anything."

"Eiri..."

"...What?" Eiri whipped around, voice still thick with bloodlust.

Under her withering, half-lidded glare, Kyousuke averted his gaze. "Nothing... What should I say, um...sorry? I—"

"It's fine."

"...Huh?"

"I said it's fine! You don't need to make a point of bringing it up again—it's fine!" Eiri shouted, bright red all the way out to her ears. "I-it was stupid of me... How I feel about you...ah...aaaaaargh!! What am I doinggg, grrraaaaaaaaagh?!" She doubled over, holding her head in apparent agony. "Wh...when I think about it, I'm so embarrassed I want to die... Please, Kyousuke, forget all about what just happened? Forget iiiiiit!"

"O-oh..." Kyousuke scratched at the side of his face as if he was stumped by Eiri's desperate pleas.

If Kurisu hadn't interfered, what might he have done to Eiri...? As he imagined it, guilt filled his chest. And not just guilt toward Eiri but also toward Renko, who truly always had him in her thoughts—

"Ah, big brother!"

A bright, bouncy voice called out just as Kyousuke fell into dark musings. He looked up to see a girl in pigtails leaving the nearby bathroom, smiling and waving at him.

"Ayaka..."

"Tee-hee. What a coincidence, big brother...," she said as she scampered over to him. "...And, Eiri, what are you doing?"

Eiri, who was still clawing frantically at her hair, looked up and blinked her red eyes in confusion. "Huh?!" Quickly she regained her senses and, smoothing her hair back down, she stood up. "...N-nothing? I'm n-nnnn-not doing anything!"

"Su-spi-cious..." Ayaka's eyes opened wide, and she stared at Eiri's face.

"...Wh-what?" Eiri winced as Ayaka brought her nose close and *sniff-sniff-sniffed* her.

She frowned and grumbled. "—The smell of a female in heat."

"Eh?" Eiri quickly stiffened.

"What were you doing with my brother?" Ayaka inquired, scowling at her with upturned eyes. "What were you doing *to* my big brother? Taking advantage of Ayaka's fondness for you? Don't tell me you were trying to take him by force—"

"Hey, Ayaka! Is your exhibit popular? It was in a classroom right around here, right?!"

"...Hm?" The girl turned her head and looked at Kyousuke. Sure enough, the light of reason had vanished from her eyes. "That's right, it's very close by. But before that, there's something I want to check—"

"Heh, heh! I'm really curious about it!" Eiri added in an awkwardly loud voice. "You put so much work into it, so why don't we go there now?!" She continued pressing Ayaka for a response. "Come to mention it, we haven't seen it yet… Oh, I want to see it. I want you to show it to us!" Eiri was utterly transparent, her voice flat and clumsy.

Ayaka let out a heavy sigh. "…All right, I get it. I can take a hint—I won't ask you any more now. But—" Midway through turning around, Ayaka stopped to glare at Kyousuke. She thrust her pointer finger at the tip of his nose just as he was about to relax. "Big brother. I won't forgive you for two-timing, okay?"

X   X   X

The clear, bright music of a children's chorus filled the classroom at the end of A wing's fourth floor. As they laid eyes on Ayaka's special exhibition for the first time, a single word filled their thoughts: *incredible*.

Walls, floor, ceiling, windows, doors—every surface was covered in photographs.

Kyousuke sitting in class, diligently copying down notes from the blackboard. Kyousuke dripping with sweat as he threw himself into manual labor. Kyousuke gulping down a Garbage Rice Bowl at lunch. Kyousuke sitting in a toilet stall. Kyousuke washing his body in the bath. Kyousuke sleeping soundly in bed. Kyousuke—every photo was of Kyousuke.

The multitude of photographs, each one apparently taken since he had enrolled at the academy, overlapped like the scales of a fish, packed together to completely fill the inside of the classroom. The exhibit was all but deserted—perhaps Ayaka's artistic vision was just too strange.

Turning around to face Kyousuke and Eiri, who had come to a stop near the entrance, Ayaka spread her arms out wide.

"Ta-daaa, it's Ayaka's 'Little Worlllld'! Amazing, right? I arranged everything myself!"

＊　　＊　　＊

"............"

"I asked the teachers and staff, and got them to take pictures for me! Tee-hee! It was really hard work. I wanted it to be a surprise, so I prepared almost everything myself... Ah, of course it's not only pictures but this, too! I also collected these!"

Ayaka gleefully pointed to a long table placed near the wall, upon which was a series of neatly arranged glass cases, each containing a different item: tangles of hair, used tissues, bloody bandages, half-eaten bread, a dirty handkerchief, uniform buttons, indoor slippers, worn socks, a jersey, a recorder, underwear...et cetera, et cetera. The table was adorned with things that had long since gone missing.

"...So you were the culprit, huh."

"Yep. Sorry, big brother..." Ayaka hung her head bashfully and looked up at Kyousuke with teary eyes.

"—*Huh?! You lost something again, Kyousuke Kamiya...? You better start shaping up, moron! What an unbelievable idiot you are. At this rate, you'll lose your life!! No, I'll take it myself!*" He recalled being thus scolded many times by Kurumiya, and other bitter memories of undeserved punishment, but all the anger welling up inside him evaporated as soon as he looked into his sister's tear-soaked eyes.

There was a lot more that he wanted to say to Ayaka, but...

"...All right already... I get it, Ayaka... I understand veeery well that you have a serious brother complex... There are too many things to poke fun at, and I can't possibly handle them all on my own."

"You also have a serious sister complex, though..." Taking a jab at the dejected young man, Eiri sauntered over to a window.

Maina was there, staring enthralled at the photos stuck all over the glass, blocking the light from outside. "Amazing," she mumbled. "Everything in here was designed, prepared, and arranged by Ayaka alone... I can feel her affection for Kyousuke, as well as her tenacity. Oh myyy..."

"Y-yeah..." Nodding, Eiri lined up next to Maina. The two of them marveled at the strange display.

Ayaka had emphatically turned away their offers of help during the festival preparations. It was obvious that she hadn't wanted anyone to interfere. "Little World"—apparently, Ayaka's world was packed with large quantities of Kyousuke. However, among the many pictures on display were a few images of other people: Renko, Eiri, and even Maina had been surreptitiously photographed.

Appearing most frequently—after Kyousuke—was Renko. As they looked around the room, the figure of a female student in a black gas mask and headphones leaped out at them from about one in every twenty photos.

Renko having a friendly conversation with Kyousuke and the others during a break. Renko drinking a jelly pack next to Kyousuke during lunch. Renko helping Kyousuke with his studies. Renko clinging to Kyousuke and fawning over him. Renko pressing her boobs into Kyousuke's back. Renko rinsing Kyousuke's back for him. Renko getting into bed with Kyousuke—

"Bah?!"

"…What is it, big brother?"

Ayaka tilted her head in confusion at her brother, whose expression suddenly changed as he rushed toward the wall. Eiri and Maina also looked up from the photos on the opposite side of the room to stare at Kyousuke questioningly.

"What's he surprised by? That there are gross things in here, too?"

"Oh dear, oh my. There are bathroom and toilet and changing pictures—I think it's all gross things… Are there photos even dodgier than those?"

"Ha, ha-ha…o-oh…th, th-th-th-th, th-there's those kinds of pictures…"

Hiding two photos that he had rushed to pull down behind his back, Kyousuke smiled back at them with a twitch.

—How did she get some of these photos? Has she been peeping on me?!
A waterfall of sweat cascaded down Kyousuke's back, and he glared at his little sister in protest, but Ayaka just giggled.

Putting the photos in question into his pocket, Kyousuke started walking over to question Ayaka.

"……Huh? Wh-what's that…?" Eiri mumbled, voice trembling.

"Hm?"

Eiri's quivering finger was pointing at—a photo of Renko, in the boys' dormitory baths, using her boobs like sponges, washing *every inch* of Kyousuke's body.

"Uaaaaaagh?!"

A death wail poured from Kyousuke's mouth when he saw the photograph. Though he tried to pull it down in a panic, the photo was stuck fast on the ceiling. And it was not the only one.

Two, three, four, five…in total there were six photographs that captured the same scene, all stuck up together. The particularly indecent parts had been obscured by little hearts, but still…

"Y-you… I had my suspicions, but I had no idea that you were this raw. This is beyond redemption, you disgusting, unforgivable creep!!"

"W-wait! It's a misunderstanding, a misunderstanding! That was all Renko's doing—"

"And what about the pictures over there? I don't see anyone *forcing you* to grope Renko's chest…"

"Guaaaaaagh?!"

"Tee-hee. Rub-a-dub-dub, huh, big brother? Tee-hee…"

Kyousuke withered under Eiri's and Maina's cold glares and Ayaka's wicked laughter. Holding his head, hands covering his ears, he spoke in a pitiful voice. "…Th-there was no helping it, all right? She came on so strong in my dorm room, or in the bath…so I gave in to temptation, just a little bit—"

"'Just a little'? 'Just a little bit,' hmm… Looks like there are photos of you giving in to temptation in other situations, though?"

"Aah?! There are ones like this, too, Eiri—waah?! Th-this is much more…s-stimulating… Oh my…"

"Tee-hee. Well, I had even more amazing ones, you know? But I thought they might be out of bounds, so I put those in storage. I'll get them out when I need them, big brother!"

"…He should just die already."

"Oh goodness. Kyousuke really is a perv after all! He's a major player!"

"…………"

—Several minutes later:

Sitting gym-class-style in the corner of the room, Kyousuke was barraged by the three girls' conversation.

"Geez, he's really the worst. What is with him? …I can't believe it!"

"Oh goodness gracious…we're not even supposed to go into the boys' dorms… Miss Reiko must be working with them, right? She's been favorable toward Kyousuke since the athletic festival ended and all."

"Yep, yep. Even she finally realized the appeal of my big brother! From now on I definitely want us to act like a real family—"

"...Huh? But your parents are normal people, aren't they? There's no way they would permit a relationship with a psycho killer like Renko..."

"Yeah. Of course it's impossible, right?"

"N-normally I think it would be impossible... Why would he think it would be all right?"

"Well, I guess you could say that Mama and Papa are sort of free spirits... Anything goes, really, and they don't have strong opinions about raising children. Plus they're always away on business trips overseas and are almost never at home..."

"...Is that so?"

"It is, it is. Right, big brother?"

"...Ah, that's right." Kyousuke raised his face from where it was buried in his knees to answer Ayaka. "Although Mom took care of us until Ayaka and I got bigger... When I was in middle school, Dad was seriously injured in an accident. He was drunk and fell off the train platform and was hit by an express train—"

"He must have died?"

"—and then apparently he was hit in midair by a second train coming from the other direction."

"Huh?! It was instant death, then?!"

"No, no. He's as healthy as ever. Though he nearly died at the time... that's when Mom also started working, and now the two of them are flying all around the world together."

"U-unbelievable..."

"He's completely superhuman..."

The astonishment of the two girls was only natural. Compared to his father, Kyousuke was apparently an entirely normal human being. Although—

"No matter how free and laissez-faire they might be, I can't believe your stupid parents aren't doing anything to help their own children in a situation like this..."

"Right? After you were arrested, big brother, I tried to contact them, but they didn't answer at all... I think there's a chance that Mama and Papa might not even know what happened..."

"Oh my goodness. N-no matter how you were raised, that's—"

"I wonder." Eiri made a bitter face. She sounded like she was worried about Kyousuke and Ayaka. "The academy must have some way of dealing with the families and relatives of students who are sent here. Even if you couldn't get in touch with your parents, maybe…"

"It's all right," Kyousuke said as Eiri trailed off. Heaving himself to his feet, he dusted off his pants as he continued. "That old bastard's not that soft…and Mom's the same. About now they're probably realizing that we've gone missing, and I'm sure they're upset. If time and circumstances permit, they might come here to negotiate directly."

"Tee-hee. It's likely, isn't it. They're monstrous in a number of ways, Papa and Mama."

Faced with this carefree back-and-forth between brother and sister, Eiri and Maina looked at each other.

"H-hmm…well, if that's what you think, I guess it's all right."

"M-monsters…they must be, the parents who raised you two. Somehow I get the feeling that they're really strong!"

"—No." Shaking his head at Maina, Kyousuke smiled bitterly, recalling the image of his parents. "Mom and Dad—especially Dad—well, strong doesn't begin to describe them… If our dad really lost his temper, I think even Kurumiya would wet herself."

$$\times \qquad \times \qquad \times$$

VIEW THE EXHIBIT AS YOU PLEASE.

※HOWEVER, IF YOU STEAL ANY OF THE ITEMS ON DISPLAY, YOU WILL BE SENTENCED TO CAPITAL PUNISHMENT.

—Putting up a sign, the four of them left Ayaka's classroom, went out of the new school building where many people were coming and going, and headed straight for the gymnasium.

Folding chairs were lined up in rows in the graffiti-covered gymnasium, and onstage, following the program, various performances were being put on by the murderous students.

"One pretty lady…two pretty ladies…skipping that one…three pretty ladies… Eh-heh-heh!"

"Wha?! Why did you look right at me?"

"…Ah. I'm having jabs thrust at me in this comic act, but I'd rather thrust in private."

"Don't say that while looking at your crotch!"

"Hey, girl! Do you wanna do some comedy with me? On the stage called a bed—?"

"Partner, don't cheat on me!"

"Bweh?!"

When Kyousuke and the girls arrived at the gymnasium, Shinji and Tomomi were in the middle of a couple's comedy act. Shinji, who had taken a full swing with a metal bat to the cheek, was sprawled out on the stage, spewing bloody vomit.

"Hang on, Tomomi… Y-you really hit him—"

"So what're ya gonna do about it?!"

"Gyah?! To-Tomomi?! Wait! This isn't in the script—"

"So what?! So what?! So what?!"

"What the heeeeeelllll?!"

The curtain slowly fell on Tomomi beating Shinji to death with the metal bat. Kyousuke and the others, seated toward the back, opened their Purgatory Festival programs.

"Umm, next is 'Blood Veil Brides,' so…"

"Renko's performance is the one after this, big brother. Perfect timing!"

"Oh gosh, oh no. Do you think Shinji is all right? He fainted and was going into convulsions…"

"…*Fwah.*"

According to the timetable, starting at eleven thirty, Renko and the rest of the GMK48 members, with a lineup that included other first-year Class B students, would put on a musical performance.

GMK48 was, according to Renko—

"*A forty-eight person band that performs chaotic death electro-core, with me as the front woman. It's centered around the members of Murderers' Murderers, who play in the band between assassinations. Mama discovered how I can transcribe the murderous melody that plays in my head, and she suggested that since we went to the trouble and all… We used the number of Murderers' Murderers and my trademark gas mask as our band name and made our spectacular debut!*"

…Or something like that. In any case, he had thought Renko was joking, but it seemed that the band really did exist. However—

"Wow, there's a ton of people... It was relatively empty when we got here."

Even though the members of GMK48 were criminals, it looked like the band boasted quite a fan base, and the gymnasium was packed. The front two-thirds of the folding chairs had been cleared away to allow for a standing audience area, and throngs of attendees were gathered in front of the stage. Many of them were wearing band T-shirts or had towels wrapped around their necks bearing the GMK48 logo.

"Huh? Is Renko famous?"

"Well, um...I think she's famous within the academy."

As Kyousuke and the others watched, an iron railing was installed between the open area and the remaining seats. The crowd near the railing included several academy students, who must have woven their way through the masses during the same shift break that Kyousuke and the others were on.

Through her actions at the athletic festival, Renko instantly became the woman of the hour, and her popularity had spread throughout the whole school, so it was now possible she had even surpassed Shamaya in number of fans...

Kyousuke felt an indescribable mixture of pride and unease when he thought about Renko's feelings for him. His mood gradually lifted, until he found himself getting quite restless.

"Hey, Ayaka, about how many minutes until it starts?"

"Three minutes, big brother. You can see the clock—why did you ask?"

"Oh dear, oh my. I'm looking forward to this, but somehow I feel nervous... I'm not really used to this kind of atmosphere at live shows and such...oh gosssh."

"...Fwah."

Kyousuke and the others filled the short wait with idle chatter. Their seats, which were right in the middle—

Suddenly all the lights were dimmed.

The tumult in the makeshift theater was instantly drowned out by an explosive death-metal roar that had everyone clutching at their ears. The background music stopped, and the stage was lit up in bright red. The drop curtain, tinted the color of fresh blood, slowly began to rise. And then—

"Oooooooooooooooooooooooooooooooooooooooooooooooooo oooohhhhhhhhhhhhhhhh!"

The moment that a figure was visible standing onstage, the audience burst into cheers. Kyousuke and the others also stood up out of their folding chairs, eyes fixed on the stage.

Up on the stage, lit up by dazzling lights, were the band members who had been on standby—Chihiro hoisting up a deep crimson guitar; Michirou holding a jet-black guitar and striking a pose; a half-naked, tattoo-covered boy with a bass guitar at the ready; Bob on the turntables; Renji at the drums, wearing his ivory-white gas mask; and two others. The seven uniformed students stood there imposingly.

The curtain finished rising, and when Renko appeared in her gas mask from stage left, the atmosphere in the gymnasium seemed ready to boil over. The moment that Renko took the mic in hand, the crowd went silent. The audience waited to hear the words that would come from Renko's mouth—

"Boobs!"

The people clamoring in front of the stage went wild.

"Kksshh. It's a mic test! Ahh, boobs, boobs!"

"Boooooooooooooooooooooooooooooooooooooooooooooooooooooo oooooooooooooobs!"

"Loud, huh."

Laughing at the excited spectators, Renko came far forward. Putting one foot up on a speaker, she looked out over the venue and spoke in a bright tone of voice. *"Everyone, thank you for coming to our live show! The only members of GMK48 here today are me and Renji, but...today, with my classmates mixed in, the eight of us plan to play GMK48 songs! Our band name iiiiiiiiiiiiiiiiiiis..."*

Her voice suddenly grew strained and distorted. Holding the mic with both hands, Renko bent over and screamed.

"MURRRRRRRRRRRRRRRRRRRRDERRRRRRRRRRRRRRRRRRRR FAAAAAAAAAAAAAAAAAAAAAAAAAAAITH!"

Immediately, the seven other students onstage, who had until now been standing completely still, all simultaneously came alive, and a tempest of heavy bass swept out across the room like an explosion:

the drums pounding out percussion so hard the skins were about to break, deep and rhythmic bass, brutal guitar riffs that threatened to tear apart eardrums as they undulated, mechanical electronoise piling up—all in an intricate boisterous dance. Shrieks of young girls leaked out of the sampler, along with the scratching of the turntables, and then, in the next moment, with an animalistic growl that swallowed up all the backing music, Renko sang fiercely.

"_____!"

"Hyaah?!" "Eeeeee?!"

Ayaka and Maina jumped and covered their ears at her volume, which shook the air.

It was a tremendous death-metal voice. The voice of Murder Maid, who had a superhuman throat, was amplified many times over by the microphone.

The fantastically cruel melody, with vocals so warped and distorted that the lyrics were impossible to understand, sprayed out from the gigantic speakers on either side of the stage, blowing fiercely like a typhoon.

There were richly colored stage lights, and laser beams cut through the air. The people in the audience, standing out in silhouette thanks to the shining lights, stretched their arms out toward the stage and jumped up and down in ecstasy.

All the audience members filling the spacious gymnasium to capacity were focused on the eight people in lively motion on the stage, listening to the music they were playing and trying to take in all the ferocious energy they were emitting.

Standing right at the front of the stage, raging, singing, working up the audience with her every movement, was none other than the front woman, Renko. Leaping around to the violent music, she flung her hair and flailed her arms, which were decorated with tattoos. With her dancing and singing, she whipped the audience into a frenzy.

"……Amazing." Kyousuke, overwhelmed by Renko's live performance, unconsciously muttered to himself. "Ah—"

Kyousuke's gaze met Renko's onstage. Since she was wearing her gas mask, he couldn't make out her ice-blue eyes. Between the distance and the darkness, it didn't seem likely that she could actually see him—but he definitely had the feeling that their eyes had met.

He almost thought he could hear Renko's excited breathing.
"—Kksshh..."

The next moment, Renko's violent death-metal voice completely changed, becoming bright and clear. The bestial howl transformed into a beautiful, graceful, feminine refrain.

"Renko..."

She was singing in another language now, so the meaning of the lyrics was not entirely clear, but all the words that Kyousuke could understand were things like *love* and *heart* and *kiss* and *smile*, and from the sentiment in her voice, he understood exactly what Renko was singing about—*her love for Kyousuke.*

Not concerned with the multitudes of people stretching their arms out toward her, she looked straight at Kyousuke—and as she continued singing, looking only at Kyousuke, he found himself completely unable to look away from her.

Her radiant voice, her playful capriciousness, her naïveté, her passion, her existence—he was enthralled, intoxicated. In this state...

—It's fine if I die.

For an instant, that thought floated up in Kyousuke's chest.

Renko roared like a beast again. She started raging around like she was crazy. Kyousuke, who had been drawn in by Renko's feelings, came to his senses and slapped his own cheek.

No, no, wait, wait! I'm sure that I really do like her, I'm in love with her, and I think I'm ready to be killed for a purpose! But sacrificing my life of my own free will, that would be—

...Totally impossible.

Renko loved Kyousuke, and Kyousuke loved Renko, too. Even though he hadn't confessed his feelings face-to-face, the fact that the two of them were in mutual love was already obvious.

Despite that fact, Renko had not killed him yet. It was proof of her tender feelings.

Before summer vacation, when Ayaka had gone crazy and tried to kill Kyousuke, Renko had said, "I can't bear the thought of making Kyousuke sad...and if you can't kill your own feelings for the sake of the person you love, that shows how far your feelings really go."

And for that reason, Renko was waiting. She was waiting for the moment when Kyousuke wanted to be killed by her. Until he felt that deeply for her...

But Kyousuke had not yet been able to respond to her feelings 100 percent. Even though he accepted her fun and cheerful side, it was difficult for him to accept the violent, crazy mass murderer Murder Maid, and it would take more time. More time to establish an emotional bond with Renko.

And yet...

A thought skittered across his mind.

Renko's screaming stopped, and the tempo of the music changed. The guitar riffs jumped around, the synthesizer ran riot like the mechanism was broken, and the white strobe lights pulsed in time with it all.

On the flickering stage, the dark shadows of the eight musicians stuttered about like frame-by-frame playback. It was the height of an especially captivating performance.

Renko's figure was bathed in white light as she danced around violently, and then she collapsed in slow motion.

At first, Kyousuke thought it was part of the performance. But he was wrong. Even when the strobe lights died down and the band returned to the normal tempo of the song, Renko did not get back up. She stayed where she had dropped the mic and fallen, entirely unmoving.

The spectators, who had gotten excited and out of control, noticed the strangeness and started to grow confused.

The rest of the band stopped the show and rushed over to where Renko lay.

"Renko?! H-hang on... Are you okay, Renko?!"

Bob propped Renko's body up as she spoke, but there was no response. Limp and powerless, Renko did not so much as twitch.

"...Ren...ko......?"

There was a terrible ringing in Kyousuke's ears. Reiko's words of warning flashed through his mind.

"Sometime in the near future, probably sometime very soon, Renko is going to die."

*   *   *

No way.

"Oh no! Wh-wwwwh-what could have happened, Renko?!"

"...Is it heatstroke?"

"Isn't it a little early for that? It's still the first song...and it's not even that hot."

".......Renko."

"Big brother? Your face is scary—is something wro—?"

"Renkooooo!"

"Hyah?!"

"Kyousuke?!" "Kyousuke?!"

Pushing Ayaka aside as she peered into his face and leaving the surprised Eiri and Maina behind, Kyousuke dashed forward. Climbing over the iron barrier, pushing through the crowded floor with all his might, he charged for the stage. Ignoring any and all harsh words and angry protests that fell on him, Kyousuke made a straight line for Renko. Intense dread and uneasiness filled his mind. Madly, he called out her name.

"Renko! Renko! Renkooo!"

X   X   X

".......Are you okay?" Ayaka asked.

Outside the gymnasium, Kyousuke sat down hard on the ground. His whole body was covered in sweat. "Y-yeah...sort of?" he weakly replied and held a hand to his swollen cheek.

Behind the worried-looking Ayaka, Eiri sighed. "Really, what were you doing? ...I told you, didn't I? Wasn't it heatstroke? Geez."

"Ha-ha-ha...that's right. I wasn't really thinking about what I was doing..."

—By the time Kyousuke had managed to arrive at the front of the crowd, Renko had already regained consciousness, picked up the mic, and explained the situation.

This time, it was just ordinary heatstroke. She had simply been jumping around too much when the show started. Renko had sucked up some mineral water through her straw, and after she had pulled herself together, laughing with a masochistic tinge, she restarted the live show, raging around in a way that wouldn't lead anyone to believe her body was in bad shape. After that, the performers had finished their set list without incident, performing six songs in total.

Kyousuke, who had rushed to the stage, fearful for Renko's safety, couldn't manage to return to his original spot and had been subjected to frenzied jostling by the excited crowd.

Especially grueling was the part called "the breakdown." In the middle of the song, the beat would suddenly drop and a mosh pit would open up on the floor. In the mosh pit, audience members, intoxicated by the music, would collide, pushing and jostling, flailing their limbs about recklessly.

Kyousuke had gotten caught up in the fray multiple times. He had been punched in the face and kicked in the side, and sometimes a person would even dive down into the crowd. The area in front of the stage, where Kyousuke had spent the remainder of the show, had resembled a battlefield in a Buddhist hell.

By the time the concert ended, his whole body was covered in wounds. He had fled the gymnasium for dear life... That's how bad it had been.

"Oh no." Maina's teeth were chattering. "Th-that was terrible... When we left the gym, a number of guests were being carried out on stretchers. Th-there were even some covered in blood..."

"Ohh...I feel bad for saying, but I really just can't get into that kind of violent music. I'm a pacifist, you know. I only listen to charming pop songs!"

"...That's right. I don't think it matters whether you're a pacifist or not—I can't get into it, either. I can't understand the lyrics, and it's so loud..."

Ayaka had her face puckered up, and Eiri agreed with her, holding her hands over her ears.

The four of them were completely exhausted after listening to the live show by Renko's group Murder Faith; it would be some time before they could even move again. They all sat down by a flower bed and gave their bodies some much-needed rest.

Kyousuke, who had doubts about Renko's explanation of heatstroke, wanted to speak with her immediately and confirm that she was all right, but after the concert had ended, a mass of fans had surged forward toward the stage, and he hadn't been able to get close. And it would have been much more difficult to speak with her while Eiri and the others were around, since they didn't yet know about the secret of Renko's Over Drive. Kyousuke looked up at the sky, still feeling gloomy.

"What's up, first-year kiddos? You look tired."

Someone was approaching them.

With a body covered in blood-colored fur and animal ears sticking up straight from the hood, the bizarre girl wearing an animal *kigurumi* costume was the Costumed Killer—Beast of the Gale Haruyo Gevaudan Tanaka.

Well suited to her *kigurumi*-clad figure, she was gripping a bunch of multicolored balloons in her left hand.

"......Ah. M-Miss Tanyakya..."

"No. I'm sure I told you to call me Haruyo, Maina? Aren't we friends?"

"Ah, ah-ha-ha...th-that's wight...Miss Haruyo?"

"Mm. You utterly defeated me. You should be proud of yourself— you're very strong." Haruyo nodded in apparent satisfaction and softly batted at Maina's head with a fluffy hand.

Maina, on the other hand, made a nervous face, and her small body instinctively stiffened.

...It was understandable.

In the Thousand-Meter Slaughter Footrace event during the previous month's athletic festival, Maina had managed to knock the head off of the *kigurumi* suit that Haruyo was always wearing, winning an impressive victory—but Haruyo, who was apparently extremely bashful, had gone insane when the whole student body saw her bare face. Just as she was about to murder all eyewitnesses, she had fainted from shock and had lost all memories of the incident.

It seemed that Haruyo somehow recognized that Maina was a strong person who had defeated her, and now she acknowledged the younger girl as a stronger rival. But if Haruyo were to get her memories back, there was no doubt that she would obliterate Maina on the spot, so Maina was always fearful around her. Kyousuke and the others looking on from the side were highly nervous as well. Not only was Haruyo herself rather frightening, but they were also worried that she might set Maina off...

"Oh goodness. Miss Haruyo, ummm…a-are you handing out those balloons?"

"Mm. I'll give you one, too. Here."

"…Th-thank you."

Maina cautiously took the yellow balloon.

Haruyo gently handed over one balloon to each of them. "Heh-heh. They're supposed to be ten dollars each, you know? But as a special gift from your upperclassman, I'll give them to you for free."

"That seems too expensive…"

"It's a rip-off!"

"Oh-ho-ho," Haruyo laughed strangely. "Of course, these are no ordinary balloons. They're filled with vaporized *drugs*. If you pop one and inhale the contents, you can instantly *trip* up to heaven!"

—You can't sell things like that!

"You looked tired for some reason, so…all you have to do is inhale, and you can fly away. But once the effects wear off, you'll feel really low. You won't be able to help wanting to breathe it in again. The second balloon costs twenty dollars, and the third one is forty. It's a scheme where the price doubles each time!"

"That's an underhanded way to sell them!"

Since they didn't want to get addicted to the drugs, Kyousuke and the others all returned their balloons.

Haruyo groaned disappointedly, "…Mm," and turned around and left.

As she was leaving, a child accompanied by a young woman ran up to Haruyo and said, "Mama, I want one of those balloons!" and they all suddenly felt very conflicted.

"…Wanna go back?"

"Yeah. My shift is coming up."

"Oh goodness gracious. S-she really is scary…"

"Drug-filled balloons, huh. I wonder if we should have taken them just in case."

They stood up together and headed back to the new school building.

They walked through the premises, filled with visitors coming and going, and passed through the plaza that was lined with refreshment booths such as Death Sauce Yakisoba, Human Meat Meatballs, Brazen Bull Bowls, and Entrails Crepes. When they turned toward the entrance—

*   *   *

"Huh? This is, this is—"

"Well, if it isn't Kyousuke Kamiya and his nasty little group. Heh-heh."

When they had reached the exact middle of the courtyard, they heard a pair of familiar voices and looked over to see two male students approaching them from a booth that read "Death by a Thousand Cuts Kebabs," their mouths hidden behind skull scarves.

"The Yatsuzakis…"

"Yo, freshies."

"Are you enjoying yourselves, first-years?"

The two of them stood in the way, blocking the path, and spoke in friendly tones. The short, lean one was the third brother, Takakage Yatsuzaki, and the tall, big-framed one was the second brother, Motoharu Yatsuzaki. Motoharu's face was mostly wrapped up in bandages.

"Waahh." Ayaka put her hand over her mouth. "What terrible injuries, upperclassman…! Whoever could have done that to you?"

"It was you." Murderous rage filled Motoharu's eyes.

Ayaka did not flinch. Instead, she stuck out her tongue. "Oh, is that so? Tee-hee. Sooo sorry! I don't remember each and every trivial piece of garbage I've cleaned up. Sooorryyy, What's-your-face!"

"……Do you want to be sliced to bits?" Motoharu's forehead twitched in agitation.

"Eh?! A-Ayaka…" Maina pulled on her sleeve, and Eiri pressed on her forehead and sighed.

Cold sweat welled up on Kyousuke's back. "Come on, I told you not to provoke them!"

"What? I'm not provoking anybody. I just spoke the truth! Who are these guys?"

"Heh-heh. As interesting as always, aren't you?" At that point, a new voice joined in. The oldest brother, Takamoto, of average height and size, who had been watching the exchange from inside the food stall, leisurely sauntered over to them.

In his right hand he carried a *shamshir* with a thirty-inch blade. Idly fiddling with the weapon, Takamoto stood right in front of Ayaka. "Don't get too cocky, first-year. If you do, I'll give you a spin over there."

He pointed to the hunk of beef turning on a spit in the food stall. The well-cooked surface had been shaved off with a blade many times.

Glancing at that sight, Ayaka grimaced. "…B-big brother. I just got hungry! We can buy the things being sold at the stalls with our food tickets, right? Since we came all the way over here, let's go buy something while we're here. Ah, but I'll definitely pass on the Death by a Thousand Cuts Kebabs over there! I mean, they look really gross."

The three brothers looked at each other as Ayaka brazenly mocked them.

"Should we kill her?"

"Let's kill her."

"Get it done."

"Huh?! Hang on—"

"Tee-hee. If you think you can, go ahead. Even if you small fries come at me all at once, I won't be the least bit scared! Beat them up, big brother!"

"Me?!"

Hiding behind Kyousuke's back, Ayaka pulled down on the skin below her eye and stuck her tongue out. Motoharu and Takakage also pulled out *shamshirs*, and the brothers surrounded Kyousuke and the others from three directions.

The visitors coming and going through the plaza looked on with interest. "What's this?" "Oh, an exhibition?"

Kyousuke frantically tried to calm the Ripper Jack brothers, who were full of murderous impulses. "Wait, please! I'll apologize for everything Ayaka said, so—"

But of course they would not accept his apology.

"Dieeeeee!"

Kyousuke moved to protect Ayaka from the weapons being brandished by the three brothers, then the next moment—

"Pardon the intrusion."

"……?!"

The deep crimson figure that had slipped in between them hit the three brothers' wrists very hard in turn, causing them to drop their weapons, before thrusting a silver-colored iron-ribbed fan under Motoharu's nose.

"…Excuse me. I acted rather violently. If you don't wish for a repeat performance, you will keep quiet, all right?" Threatening the Yatsuzaki brothers in a cold tone of voice, the girl was clad in a bright red kimono.

Kyousuke and Ayaka—and especially Eiri—stared in wonder at this reunion with an unexpected person.

"Kagura—"

"Hello, big sister, it's been a while. What is with that look? It suits you too well. My heart practically stopped! Though I feel that the skirt is a little too short... As always, you're amazing. In comparison—"

Still thrusting the iron-ribbed fan at Motoharu, Kagura took her gaze off of Eiri's maid outfit. She narrowed her rust-red eyes at the surprised Ayaka, who was still standing behind Kyousuke. "...And as always, you're an imbecile, aren't you, Offal Ayaka? Can your idiocy not be cured except through death? It probably would have been better for everyone if I had let you die just now." She spit the words out with a jeer.

Ayaka smiled sweetly. "And you're irritating as always, Crappy Kagura. I don't think sister complexes can be cured even through death, but it would have been better for the world and all the people in it for you to die of infatuation just now, don't you think?" She shot back at Kagura word for word.

For a long moment, they glared silently at one another.

"...Tch. I went out of my way to save your life, but you're a hateful little girl, aren't you? Do you not understand your situation?"

"I understand perfectly! I wasn't rescued by you—my big brother saved me! I won't be killed by guys like them!"

"......A hopeless sibling obsession, huh?"

"Shut up, sister complex!"

"You shut up, brother complex!"

"Now, Kagura."

Ayaka and Kagura's quarreling was interrupted by a graceful voice.

"L-Lady Fuyou..."

Fuyou Akabane. The current head of House Akabane, a notable family of assassins, and Eiri and Kagura's mother. Fuyou, accompanied by a man and a woman in *Noh* masks who followed behind her like attendants, smiled wryly in half-hearted exasperation. "Kagura, really...I know that you're very happy to be reunited with Eiri and Ayaka, but you're a bit too spirited. Control yourself."

"Ah!"

Ayaka and Kagura, hearing Fuyou's words, were both startled.

"I-I knew that Crappy Kagura was the hot-and-cold type, but... huh? Does she actually like me? Gross!"

"Wha...a-absolutely not! Please stop telling lies, Lady Fuyou! Who could like Offal Ayaka? Really..."

Grumbling, Kagura closed the iron-ribbed fan.

"I'm sorry for my childrens' violent behavior." Fuyou apologized to the three brothers, who were flustered, being unable to follow recent developments. "I trust you are not injured?"

"Ha, haa..."

Fuyou questioned them gently, then picked up the *shamshirs* that had fallen on the ground. As she handed one to the bewildered Takamoto, she brought her mouth close to his ear—

"The next time you try to raise your hand against these people, it will cost you your head."

"......?!"

Takamoto trembled with a start and went pale.

"Ho-ho." Fuyou smiled and slowly pulled her face away. And with that, as if she had lost interest in them, she turned her gaze away from the three brothers.

Facing Kyousuke and the others, she bowed deeply. "It's been a while, Kyousuke, Ayaka...and Eiri. And who could this be beside you, a friend? Lovely to meet you—I am Eiri's mother."

"Ehh?! Ei-Eiri's mother?! N-nnnn-nice to meetchu! I-I'm Mainya Igarachi! I'm classhmates with Eiri...oh goodness..." Maina, meeting Eiri's family for the first time, gave a self-introduction full of nervous mistakes.

"My, my." Fuyou gave a broad smile. "Oh-ho, here we have another one of your sweet friends."

"So you came, Mother... I thought you might." Giving a sidelong glance at the Yatsuzaki brothers making their retreat, Eiri approached Fuyou.

"Yes. This is my beloved daughter's school event—it's only natural that I should participate. And since it seemed that other relatives were also welcome, I brought along Kagura and Basara as well."

"That womanizer, he's off picking up girls."

"As always..."

"...Seriously. Though he's no match for you, Kyousuke."

"In what sense?"

"Never mind."

"My, my, oh-ho-ho. Aren't you getting along well?"

Fuyou pleasantly laughed at Eiri and Kyousuke, who were glaring at each other.

In the background, the man and woman in reddish-brown monks' clothes and *Noh* masks waited obediently.

...Could it be my imagination? Kyousuke was sure he could feel an intense gaze coming from behind the masks. It made him somehow incredibly uneasy.

"Wh-wha—?"

"Eiri..." He had been just about to ask about the servants, when Fuyou opened a red Japanese-style parasol and tilted her head slightly to the side. "Could you make a bit of time for me? It's been so long since we were able to meet like this, after all. Walk around with us. Kyousuke and Ayaka are certainly welcome to join..."

X   X   X

"...Mother. Did Muramasa, Ryou, and Ran not come with you?"

"That's right. This time they are watching the estate for me in my absence. It would be difficult to move around if I brought too many family members...just in case, you know."

"Just in case...?"

"Ho-ho." Smiling, Fuyou turned her parasol.

After that, Kyousuke and the others, who had been planning to go back to Maid Café Hades, ended up going around the Purgatory Festival with the whole Akabane family. However, it was not as if they could neglect their jobs without a word.

"Don't worry about your shifts! I'll tell everyone. Kyousuke, Eiri, and Ayaka are running late because of some business, I'll say..."

—Maina had made this offer herself, so the five of them (seven if the ever-silent servants were included) started to walk around the school building without her.

"Hey, Mom. Don't you want to go in anywhere?"

"...I thought I told you to stop calling her that, Offal Ayaka."

Ayaka asked a question to Fuyou's back as she led them, and Kagura rebuked her in annoyance.

Fuyou looked back over her shoulder, seemingly unfazed. "Yes, Ayaka. There is a place that I personally would certainly like to go... but I don't mind making stopovers on the way, so please don't hesitate when there's someplace you'd like to visit."

"Okaaay! Roger that, Mom!"

"......Tch."

Kagura clicked her tongue at Ayaka, who had answered cheerfully. The young assassin took a bite of the Entrails Crepe that she had purchased in the plaza and handed it to Eiri, who was walking next to her.

As he watched the harmonious exchange between sisters as they passed the crepe back and forth, taking bites, Kyousuke couldn't help but wonder to himself—*the place that Fuyou wants to go, where on earth could it be?*

Fuyou had gone into the school building through the main entrance, then toured around each floor of each building, but the whole time, she had walked on looking detached, not showing interest in anything from start to finish...

"...Mother? There is nothing beyond this point."

"Oh-ho-ho. Well now, come along."

As the group passed the staff rooms on the silent fourth floor of the B wing, Fuyou continued onward, not concerned with the puzzled Eiri, and opened an iron door painted with "No Entry" in red letters.

This was a different roof than the one that Kyousuke and Eiri had visited several hours prior. Easily picking the lock just like Eiri, Fuyou said, "Go ahead. There are things I want to tell you."

"H-huh..."

Inviting the confused group onto the roof, she closed the iron door and relocked it. They stood facing one another in the center of the roof, which was enclosed by iron bars and barbed wire.

Without any warning or notice, Kyousuke was—*suddenly hit in the face.*

"Kyousuke?!" "Big brother?!"

He was unable to even let out a scream, so sudden was the attack. Kyousuke was sent sprawling helplessly, and blood sprayed from his nose as he rolled across the floor and slammed into the iron fence. His breathing was ragged, and his stomach churned.

His right cheek, where he had been hit, burned as if it had burst into flames.

"Guh?! Wh-what—?"

As Kyousuke started to get up, still confused, the man in the *Noh* mask—*the servant who just a moment ago had hit Kyousuke with a right straight punch*—cracked the knuckles in his fist as he approached.

—*I'm going to be killed.* He had the premonition clear as day.

"Mother?! What the hell is this? Stop it! Mother!"

"B-big broth— Kya?! What are you doing? Let me go! Let go, I said! Let gooooooooo!"

Eiri clung to Fuyou, and Ayaka, who had been about to rush over to Kyousuke, was caught by the other servant—the woman in the *Noh* mask—and struggled, flailing her limbs against the restraint.

"...*Fwah*," Kagura yawned slightly.

"Sh-shit—"

Scowling as he wiped away the blood from his nose, Kyousuke looked up at the expressionless *Noh* mask. Anger emanating from his whole body, the masked man spat—

"You're the little shit here, ya stupid brat!"

He grabbed Kyousuke by the collar with both hands as he yelled, forcibly lifting him to his feet.

"...Eh?" It was a voice Kyousuke had heard somewhere before. He couldn't believe his ears.

"No way...it, it can't be—"

Just then, Ayaka's hysterical screams filled the air. "Eeeeeeeeehhh?! Ma, Mamamama, Mamaaaaaa?!"

Before Ayaka's surprised eyes, the woman removed her *Noh* mask and wig and stood there with a bare face—a particular type of extremely thin mask. The woman ran her fingers through her wavy brown hair and narrowed her eyes, which looked a lot like Ayaka's, smiling mischievously. "Yes. It's been a long time, Ayaka, dear."

"......Huh? H-hey...why are you in a place like this, Mom?"

"Ah, hello to you, too, Kyousuke. I've missed you!"

"Why—?"

"That's our line, isn't iiiit?!"

While Kyousuke stared in amazement at the woman waving her hand, the man pulled him closer by his collar. Bringing the expressionless *Noh* mask in close, he growled, "What're you doing in a place like this, you little shit? Sanae and I left you in charge of the house, didn't we? We entrusted Ayaka to you, didn't we?! So how the hell did you end up here, huuuuuhhh?!"

"Gaaa?!"

"Big brotheeer?!"

"Naoki, calm down. You're choking Kyousuke."

Stopped by Ayaka and the woman who had rushed over, the man took his hands off of Kyousuke, who crumpled to the ground, greedily sucking down oxygen. His throat had nearly been crushed.

"B-big brother...are you all right?"

Looking down at the young man, and Ayaka tending to him, the man laughed through his nose. "Hah! Yer weak as always, brat! That's why no matter how much time goes by, you'll always be 'normal.' Yet you call yourself my son, Kyousuke? Try again after a century of training."

"Y-you—"

Kyousuke glared at the sneering *Noh* mask, gritting his teeth.

......There was no mistaking it. The haughty and arrogant attitude, vulgar and violent words, and above all striking and strangling his own son, this person who had no qualms about cruelty was—

"Shut up, old man! Where have you been, and what've you been doing until now?!"

—Naoki Kamiya, Kyousuke and Ayaka's father, who had not contacted them since leaving on an overseas business trip.

Reach Beyond the Calamity

MONSTER PARENTS

TRACK TWO

SCHOOL OF THE DAZE

01. Bitch Burns Red

02. Mental Health
    May Fire

03. I Killed the
    Bitch Sow

04. Bullet for My Big Brother

05. Abandon All Garbage

06. Small World
    ~YANDERE Remix~

AYAKA
KAMIYA
1st EP

"......Kyousuke and Ayaka's...parents?" Eiri muttered.

"Yes," Fuyou noted as she finished carefully folding her parasol. "Naoki and Sanae Kamiya—their parents, in the flesh."

Naoki, who had also removed his mask like Sanae, gripped Kyousuke by the collar again. "—Huh? Where've I been, and what've I been doing? You stupid brat...I was almost killed on your account, wasn't I?!"

With his close-cropped black hair, which featured elaborate designs shaved into the sides, and the many scars covering his face, Naoki had a brutish, intimidating appearance. One look at him was enough to make a lesser man faint.

Kyousuke, fixed by his father's furious gaze, looked around in surprise. "Eh...a-almost killed? You? By whom?"

"By the bunch running this school yer at now, stupid!"

"......?!"

Kyousuke's and Ayaka's eyes opened wide in surprise.

"Actually, they're not from the academy," Sanae added. "Apparently they're assassins sent out by the *Organization* that's been running things in the background. After we'd finished our job and were making preparations to return to Japan, they attacked us at our hotel... and from there it's been an endless game of tag. They've really been tenacious! And we didn't really know why we were being hunted, so it was all we could do just to keep running."

"…Right. It's been a real mess. We've been flyin' around like crazy…"

"Yes, we've narrowly avoided the long trip to heaven, you know… Ah, but, but—!" Sanae's voice grew excited, and she embraced her husband from behind. "It was so much fun getting to travel the world together with my Naoki! It reminded me of our honeymoon. I really enjoyed spending so much time together!"

"S-Sanae—" Suddenly, Naoki's aggression slackened, and he released Kyousuke from his grip. "I was happy too, Sanae, sweetie! We got to spend more than six months alone together, and I was so happy! I love you more than the whole world—nothing has changed since before we got married, Sanae, baaaby!"

"Waaaaaah?! Me too, Naoki, honeeey. I love you!"

Everyone around them drew back as the two showered each other in hugs and kisses. Kyousuke and Ayaka, Eiri and Kagura—and even Fuyou, who lost her smile in a frown.

"……Hey." Kyousuke tried to interrupt.

"Huh? What is it, brat? Stay out of this!"

"Yes, maybe try to read the room a little, dear?"

"Like you guys are ones to talk!"

"Hey, where d'ya get off talkin' to your own parents that way?! I'll kill ya, you damn brat!!"

"And where do you get off saying you'll kill your own son?! I'll kill you, damn old man!!"

"And where the hell d'you get off sayin' you'll kill your dad—"

"Okay-okay-okay, that's enough already!" Fuyou interrupted, trying to rein in the argument. "Stop it, both of you." Clapping her hands, she sighed heavily as Kyousuke and Naoki continued glaring at each other with their foreheads pressed together. "Your…conversation isn't going anywhere at all. Shall we put an end to the emotional reunion for now so that I might explain the particulars of your situation?"

"—Yes, it's just as Fuyou says," Sanae added. "Pull it together, Naoki, dear, and you too, Kyousuke. How long do you two intend to derail the conversation?"

"Waa, that's our mama! Ignoring her own shortcomings and quickly

jumping on the newest bandwagon, thereby completely avoiding any blame or responsibility. What amazing rhetorical evasion!"

"Heh-heh. Thank you, Ayaka, dear."

"...I don't think she was really praising her, though."

"What is with this family...?"

Eiri and Kagura commented on the exchange from the sidelines.

Getting some distance from his father, Kyousuke pulled himself together. "Um, excuse me... I'd like to know what my parents are doing with the Akabane family?" he asked Fuyou, who seemed to know the most about the situation.

Fuyou and the other members of House Akabane were a noted family of assassins, major players in the criminal underworld. So why would they be acting together with Kyousuke and Ayaka's parents?

"Ho-ho. You see, Kyousuke—it's because we Akabane are protecting and hiding the two of them as they travel, running from the assassins of the *Organization*."

"...House Akabane is hiding my parents?"

"Yeah. Fuyou really saved our skins." Naoki leaned against the iron railing, casually nodding toward the woman. "Even if we'd kept running away, things definitely would have kept getting worse... Worst of all, I don't really understand why. Who are these bastards who keep coming after us? Who's sending them? And why're we being targeted in the first place? We tried to find out, but it's still not any clearer. And while we were in that position, it was the Akabane family that reached out to us."

"......I see." Kyousuke nodded in understanding.

"Ah, but...don't you think that's strange?" Ayaka tilted her head. "Why did the Akabane know that you were being pursued, Papa? That's awfully convenient knowledge to have. I don't think it could possibly be the case, but did the Akabane family and my papa and mama...have some kind of connection? Like if you used to be acquaintances or something?"

"Huh? No way—"

"Yes. That's right." Interrupting Naoki's denial, Fuyou confirmed the girl's suspicions. Glancing at Naoki, who had his eyes open wide, Fuyou shrugged her shoulders, not the least bit timid. "It would be difficult to keep hiding it at this point. Why don't you tell them the honest truth? Tell them what you and your wife have been keeping secret until now."

"......"

Naoki was silent. He looked at Kyousuke and Ayaka, who stared back, looking confused.

"—Secret?" Kyousuke asked.

After silently checking with his nodding wife, Naoki sighed. Scratching the back of his head, he finally spoke. "...All right. Uh, Kyousuke. Ayaka. There's something we haven't told you two about, but—"

"What is it?"

"What, Papa?"

"It's about the job that Sanae and I do. We told you lie after lie, convincing you that I was a salaryman working for a foreign trading company and that I was always away on overseas business trips, but...Sanae and I...our occupation... Well, to tell you the truth, we're bodyguards."

"...Bodyguards? You mean like SP?" Ayaka tilted her head quizzically.

"No. Not like SP," Naoki continued. "SP are Security Police forces, so they work for the government, right? The job that Sanae and I do ain't quite so cut-and-dried. The people we guard are mostly *big shot criminals*, and the people coming after them are mostly *assassins*."

"Assassiiiiiinnns?!"

"Yes. Assassins have targets, right? So we protect those targets and keep them safe from harm. It's also our job as bodyguards to turn the tables on any would-be killers!"

"S-seriously...?"

"So cool!"

Kyousuke looked shocked. Next to him, Ayaka's eyes sparkled innocently.

To be sure, Naoki's aberrant physical abilities, muscle-bound body, and scores of scars and bruises screamed, 'There's no way this man works in a respectable occupation,' but Kyousuke had never believed that it could really be the truth... It was no wonder he was unusual in so many ways.

"Uh, umm...well then, uh...could it be that...the story about you getting hit by a train and almost dying was—?"

"Yeah, it was a lie. The truth is that *I was attacked by a vicious assassin and almost killed.* And the reason that Sanae returned to this job is because she was worried about me..."

"It's only natural, Naoki!" The woman in question clung to Naoki's arm, looking up at him with teary eyes. "...I thought you might die, after all. If something like that should happen again... If my Naoki should die while I'm doing innocent housework... When I started thinking about that, I couldn't possibly sit still! I wanted to stand guard alongside you. I wanted to protect the Naoki who protects the clients, with all my body and soul!"

"S-Sanae, honey..."

"Naoki, dear..."

"I told you, stop ignoring the situation and flirting!"

"But it's thanks to Mama rushing out of the house and abandoning us that we ended up here... Well, I ended up being together with big brother, so I don't mind, though!"

"......Tch."

There was a sharp click of a tongue. They turned to see that Fuyou was standing there with a smile on her face. "Ho-ho-ho. You're lovey-dovey as always, I see. Naoki, Sanae...I'm jealous, ho-ho. Truly...as someone who has already lost her husband, I almost feel like I want to shred one of you to pieces right now and let the other one feel what I feel, oh-ho-ho-ho-ho-ho-ho."

"_____"

Naoki and Sanae froze, still embracing.

Several seconds later, they split apart, as if jumping out of the way of something dreadful, and quickly tried to pacify Fuyou.

"Hold on now, don't get crazy on us! We were stupid to carry on like that..."

"Sorry! Sorry, Fuyou, dear!! Look, love makes you blind, so... ah-ha-ha-ha-ha...we should have been more thoughtful of Masato... right?"

"We're sorry!"

Naoki and Sanae bowed in unison.

Fuyou was taken aback—"Oh, this is rare"—and any indication of her displeasure quickly faded. "To say nothing of Sanae, here we even see Naoki apologizing so honestly. I wonder if it's going to rain today? Good thing I brought an umbrella."

"Oh, shaddup..." Naoki looked up at Fuyou, then straightened up. He kept his gaze deliberately averted as he continued. "I also have regrets about his death, ya know... Even now I sometimes can't believe he's gone. Masato was my good friend, after all."

"............Eh?" Eiri, who had been watching with Kagura, opened her sleepy eyes wide. "F-Father's...friend?"

"Yes." Fuyou closed her eyes, as if picturing her husband, who had passed away six years ago. "You are aware that before joining House Akabane, Masato worked as a bodyguard, right? He and Naoki were coworkers, of sorts."

"Wha—?" Eiri stared at Kyousuke's father, who was now wearing an indescribably complex expression.

"Y-you...must be the oldest daughter, the one Masato was always doting on, eh? Little Eiri, was it? We met six years ago at his funeral service, but I guess you don't remember me."

"...I don't...remember," Eiri agreed, bewildered.

"Ha-ha...that's what I thought. You were still so little back then." Naoki smiled, though he seemed somewhat nervous to face her.

Eiri, being Eiri, stared intently at the man, scrutinizing him. "My father and Kyousuke's father were...huh? I-is that so...hmm...," she mumbled, glancing repeatedly at Kyousuke, whose mouth was still hanging open. "In that case, it might be a little easier for him to understand my family...?"

As Eiri muttered to herself, Fuyou looked pleased. "Oh-ho, allow me to introduce you to my daughters again later. In any case, as I said before, we have a long history together, and it was we Akabane who arranged this meeting with the two of you."

"I-I see..." Come to think of it, Kyousuke's summons to House Akabane two months earlier during summer vacation had probably had an ulterior motive. *There really is no end with these people...*

"Thus, after securing the safety of your parents without issue, we moved on to the next matter," Fuyou continued in her refined manner. "Namely, planning how to take back their children, Kyousuke and Ayaka, who had been caught in a wicked trap and locked away."

"Ah—"

...Of course, that was it. Neither Naoki nor Sanae were the type to sit quietly by, knowing that their own children had been tossed into an academy like this. The brief, joking comment that "they might come here to negotiate directly" had miraculously become reality through collaboration with House Akabane.

"Knowing that the Purgatory Festival allows outsiders to enter the school, I had them conceal themselves as my attendants. As a notable family of assassins, we Akabane excel at the art of deception... No one would think that two bodyguards whose job is to antagonize professional killers would have friendly relations with House Akabane, after all. And since we paid scrupulous attention to how we made our approach, we've managed to make it this far undiscovered. All that remains is to—"

"To bash 'em with all our strength!" Chiming in to finish Fuyou's sentence, Naoki cracked his knuckles. "Layin' their hands on someone else's kids... It's no different from a direct attack. This ain't over 'til they're groveling on the ground, hear? I'll smash 'em up one by one and take all the money they have on hand. About ten billion should do for reparations. We'll crush everyone!"

"...Yes, well, as we most certainly won't be doing anything of *that* sort, I plan to have a discussion with the responsible parties. Forcing our way through ought to be a last resort—honestly, I'd expect that such an attempt would accomplish nothing besides earning us a great deal of ill will, so it's really quite absurd to even consider. It's the poorest of plans, the height of folly, truly an apish approach."

"Huh?! What're ya saying? Are you tryin' t' start a fight?!"

"Oh, now, now. Calm down, Naoki, dear." Sanae pinned his arms behind his back and pacified him before he could turn on Fuyou. "It's like she says, darling. I mean, we all decided to do it that way before we came, right? I love that you're so passionate, but put your brain to work sometimes."

"......S-sorry."

"My, my. As I expected, it looks like your wife still holds your reins, doesn't it?"

"Shaddup, you damned fickle hag. It's ten thousand times better than being pulled around by yer puppet strings!"

"Not to worry. I don't especially want to control you."

"Um, Mother...?" Eiri timidly asked once the woman had nonchalantly shut down Naoki's abuse. "By taking Kyousuke and Ayaka back, do you mean...?"

"Yes." Fuyou smiled widely. "We're going to get them to allow Kyou-suke and Ayaka to drop out of school here."

X   X   X

"To go about requesting permission for these two nice kids to drop out, I'll need to have a face-to-face talk with the person in charge of the academy—the board chairman—but unfortunately, I am unaware of his whereabouts."

"Can't you meet him by going to the board chairman's room?"

"In theory, yes. Except that such a place is nowhere to be found. Despite my best attempts to search for it when we came to the academy for the athletic festival…"

"Why don't you ask the teachers? There's no way that they won't know."

"That's a good idea. All right, why don't we head for the staff rooms?"

After a brief discussion, Kyousuke and the others made their way back down into the school building and headed to the staff rooms on the fourth floor. At Purgatorium Remedial Academy, each teacher was given their own private office. Choosing among the doors lined up down the hall, Fuyou tried knocking on the one labeled "Hijiri Kurumiya."

"…It seems she is not in."

There was no response. All the other rooms were the same.

Since the festival was in full swing, the teachers were probably all out. It was a bother, but they would have to go search them out—so Kyousuke and the others headed for the stairs.

"Wooow, that was really a great live performance, Renji. You and Renko were incredible, of course, but your classmates did well, too. I'm so worked up, I'm already soaking wet! I want to hurry up and shower and change—uaah?!"

A woman appeared around the corner and nearly bumped into Naoki. Jumping back in surprise, the woman caught a glimpse of Nao-ki's face and screamed. "Eee?! A k-k-k-k-k-killeeeeeeeeeeeer!"

"Huh?! Who's the killer here, bitch?!"

"Eeeeeeeeeeee?!"

Startled by his shout, the woman hid herself behind the person closest to her—a large man in a school uniform, wearing an ivory-white gas mask.

"............"

The moment that he noticed all that, it was Naoki's turn to flinch. "Gah?!"

"Oh no—" Sanae also looked startled but quickly stepped in front of Kyousuke and Ayaka as if to protect them.

"Y-you...," Naoki growled. *"You're the bastard who came after us, aren't ya? Been a while, asshole."*

"............"

The huge man did not respond.

Kyousuke stared in surprise. "Eh?! Came after you...? Renji did?"

"—Renji? What the hell, brat, you know this bastard?"

"K-kind of..." Kyousuke, who had nearly been killed by Renji at the athletic festival one month prior, had to answer with mixed feelings.

The woman peeking her face out from behind Renji shouted, "Ah!" and waved her hand at Kyousuke. "Kyousuke! Isn't that Kyousuke over there?!"

"......A friend of yours?" Sanae asked, eyeing him suspiciously.

"K-kind of...," Kyousuke replied again. He bowed his head to the person still cowering halfway behind Renji, a woman with silver-white hair and ice-blue eyes who was wearing fashion glasses. "Hello, Miss Reiko."

"...'Miss'? This bitch is a teacher?"

"Yes, she is. Only a temporary one, though."

Put at ease to some extent by Kyousuke's presence, Reiko leaned most of the way around Renji. She was a teacher in name only—in reality she didn't actually teach much of anything at all and was mostly here because of Renko—though she didn't seem as if she was going to go out of her way to mention that fact.

Reiko looked around at everyone standing in the hall, and when she spoke it sounded as if she had finally come to some sort of realization. "...Huh? I was wondering where on earth you assassins were from, but you're targets—or rather, you're Kyousuke's parents, aren't you! And behind you is, umm...House Akabane? Eh, what's with this combination? I mean, what are you doing in a place like this?! I don't really get what's going on—"

"If you don't get it, let me make it clear!"

"Hyaaaaaa?!"

Naoki advanced on the bewildered woman and grabbed her by the nape of the neck. He dragged her out from behind Renji and took her by the collar with both hands, lifting her up off the floor.

"—Miss, we came to get our kids back after you lot snatched 'em away…so shut up and take us to the board chairman's room. Now be a good girl and do as yer told"—he emphasized the point by bringing his face close to hers—"or you're gonna have a real bad time, get it?"

Reiko was taken aback. First she went pale, but then her face, twitching in fear, quickly flushed bright red, and her glossy lips trembled. "A b-b-b-b-b-bad time… You mean… N-n-n-n-n-no way…?!"

"Yeah, that's right," Naoki replied. "I'll make ya surrender, make ya listen, and force ya to do what you're told—hm?"

Suddenly, he raised his eyebrows and stared quizzically at his own hands, then at the chest of the woman he was grappling with.

"……?!"

Naoki's eyes went wide. Stretching the fabric of her short-sleeved blue T-shirt printed with the GMK48 logo were two J-cup-sized bulges. Naoki's arms were pressing into the two soft mounds. He gulped.

"Eee?! I'll be v-v-v-v-v-violated?! You'll hold me down until I surrender, and force me to do whatever I'm told no matter what, and make me have a bad tiiiiiiiiiiiime!"

"Huh?! No, that's not what I—"

"Renjiiiiiiiii!" Reiko screamed. "Destroy this rapiiiiiiiiiiiist!"

"Dad, watch out! Get awaaaaaaaaay!"

"Papaaaaaaaaaa!"

The unyielding monster moved, swinging his right arm at Naoki. The arm, wrapped in thick, sinewy muscle, lashed out past Renji's mistress, aiming to crush Naoki's skull—

"Ballsy."

…It couldn't. Renji's mighty blow *had been casually blocked* by Naoki's left arm.

"What was that, a mosquito or somethin'? Are you some kind of amateur, ya numbnuts? A'course ya can't go up against me without taking yer mask off! Though I'll put you down even without it… I'm gonna give you all the payback I owe you for following us around—buh?!"

As he threatened Renji lowly, Naoki was suddenly struck on the cheek. "Wha—?" Another strike, a left straight, smashed into the bridge of his nose.

"Naoki, deeeeeeaaaaaar?" Sanae, who had punched Naoki, was wearing a wide smile. She drew her right fist back again. "Just now… you got excited, didn't you?"

"……Huh? I didn't—"

"Lies!"

"—Ubuh?!"

Naoki was knocked flying by Sanae's right straight and fell to the floor of the corridor. Sanae straddled him without a moment's delay and attacked him with a flurry of double slaps to the face.

"Stupid, stupid, stupid, stupid, stupid, stupid, stupid, stupid Naoki, you idiooooot! You definitely got excited! You got excited by that big-titted teacher's boobs! That's adultery! That's undeniably adultery, Naoki!!"

"Huuuh?! Why're you so jealous of her huge rack—?"

"I'm not! Don't change the subject, you cheateeeeeeeeeeeer!"

"Wha, that's a false chaaaaaaaaarge—geh?!"

"…………Kksshh." Renji, whose target had been snatched away from him, looked at his mistress, unsure what to do.

Reiko, readjusting the white lab coat she wore over her T-shirt, mumbled, "…Ah, it's okay then. Renji, stop."

Eiri and Kagura were dumbfounded, and Fuyou was likewise stunned.

"Mama is too jealous…," Ayaka muttered, seemingly unaware of the irony of such a statement.

"Good grief. What is with that over-the-top couple…?"

You're pretty over the top yourself, playing up the virgin act. Swallowing his words, Kyousuke decided to ask about something that was really bothering him. "Miss Reiko, is it true that Renji was hunting down my parents?"

"…Yeah, it's true. Sorry? It was the job. It was also meant to test

Renji's abilities—he was instructed to obliterate two targets. Other assassins had been sent after them before Renji, but they were unable to complete the kill... The higher-ups got tired of waiting and mobilized Murderers' Murderers. I've never met your folks face-to-face before, but Renji's done battle with them several times."

"...What about his limiter?"

"He doesn't wear it, no. Even so, he wasn't able to finish the mission, and honestly it was a lot of trouble."

"Seriously..."

That was just like his father. Even Kyousuke, who was feared in public as "Metallica" and "Megadeth," among other names, was mocked for being "puny" and "weak" when he returned home...

The fact that Kyousuke went out of his way to be humble and call himself normal was mainly due to the influence of this bizarre family background.

"—And so? I want to ask something, too—why are they here?"

"Because I led them here." Fuyou answered Reiko's question. She smiled. "House Akabane is providing them with our full cooperation and assistance. Kyousuke and Ayaka—the children of these dear friends of mine—we've come to take them back from you."

"......Oh? I see—so it's like that, is it?" Reiko's eyes narrowed.

Fuyou's eyes also narrowed, and the tension in the air was palpable. "It is indeed. Surely you have no desire to make enemies of the Akabane? As Naoki said before, take us to the board chairman. If you do not obey, what will happen... Well, 'a bad time' will not begin to describe it, understand?"

Fuyou, who had leaned in close to Reiko, whispered and then blew a puff of air into her ear.

"Hyeee?! G-got it..."

"Oh-ho-ho. Good girl." Fuyou laughed and backed away. The "virgin" Reiko covered her ear and blushed bright red.

"Well then, Sanae."

"...Hm? What is it, Fuyou?"

Sanae, who had been making Naoki grovel in the hallway and kneel down on the ground, trampling over and over again on his head with her foot, turned back to the rest of the group.

"It seems that this kind lady is willing to take us to meet the board chairman. Shall we leave your rotten, chest-obsessed husband and be on our way?"

X   X   X

"...We're here. This is the chairman's room."

Reiko had brought them to the basement of the new school building. They had descended a secret set of stairs hidden in a storeroom near the regular stairs on the first floor of B wing. And now, after passing through a series of four iron-clad doors, the group stood in front of a door adorned with a plate that read "Board Chairman's Room." Unusually, the word "Cocytus" was written in English letters below that.

Rubbing the handprints left on his cheeks from Sanae's slaps, Naoki grumbled, "He's awfully well hidden, this damn guy..."

"It's no wonder we couldn't locate him. Is he a particularly cautious person?"

"Well, *cautious* is not the right word, exactly...," Reiko answered as she pushed the intercom button. "The chairman's, umm, a pretty serious hermit, I guess."

Since it would've been rude to bring too many complainants to a small office unannounced, Eiri and Kagura had taken their leave. The sisters should have been arriving back at the public festivities about now.

"...Not coming out, huh." Reiko pushed the button again. The swing-style door, reminiscent of a bank vault, was solid and looked as if it could be opened only from the inside. There was a surveillance camera installed above the door.

However, no matter how much time passed, there was no response. Reiko struck the device repeatedly. "Hey, hermit! You've got guests—answer us. Don't tell me you're asleep in there... I said hey, hey! Hurry up and answer—"

"You're loud, shut up; shut up, you're too loud."

From the interphone speaker came a sluggish voice. It was a husky voice, low for a woman, high for a man, and ultimately of unspecified gender.

"*I can hear you just fine—you don't need to keep hitting the button over and over. I can hear you, so lay off! Auugh, so annoying, such a bother. I'm seriously miffed—this is why I don't like you, Tits McGee!*"

"Quit complaining, and open up already, brat!"

"*No waaay, you're super scaaary, lady. LOL.*"

"Don't you 'LOL' me. Open up, you damn brat!"

"*Okay, okay.*"

After this brief back-and-forth, the lock on the door clicked open. Renji stood in the middle of the open doorway while Reiko barged in; Kyousuke and the others followed close behind.

"Whoa?! Wh-what the hell...?"

"Hyah?! What is this? It's so filthy..."

Piles of trash, clothes, comics, DVDs, and stuffed animals filled their vision—along with all kinds of other things they didn't recognize—scattered around on the floor in a spacious and stupendously messy room.

"Welcome. Don't make yourselves at home!"

In the center of the chaos, on a bed that was floating like a solitary island in the sea of maladaptation, there appeared to be a girl clad in pajamas.

Her age was not really clear. She looked as if she might be about the same age as Kyousuke and the other students, or possibly in her early twenties, and she had handsome facial features. However, her purple-black, medium-length hair was sticking out in all directions, as if she had just awoken, and her eyes, the same color as her hair, were heavy with sleep.

The girl did not even look at her new visitors but kept her gaze fixed on a nearby portable game console.

Reiko kicked aside the garbage on the floor and approached the bed. "Hey, Makina! This isn't the time to be playing games all carefree. These people are—"

"I knooow already. On the cameras, I can see everything. I can see it all on the cameras!" she shouted. The girl, who was apparently supposed to be the board chairman, jerked her chin toward a bank of monitors mounted along an arch above her bed.

The girl was sprawled out, playing video games, the upper half of her

body supported by the bed's reclining mechanism. A variety of things were placed within her reach—system components, an electronic book reader, tissues, ear spoons, lip balm, a beautiful face roller, a coffee maker, snacks, a mini fridge… On a desktop that extended over the bed near her hips, there were even a laptop and a digital tablet.

"What an unbelievable living space…"

"…Hm? Ohh, it's Kyousuke! First time seeing you in the flesh." The girl waved at him while he stared at her in shock. Casually tossing aside a handheld game console, she looked at them with a sparkle in her sleepy eyes. "Whoa, you're a better guy than you looked like through the screen, aren't you? Hey, hey, come closer."

"—Makina."

"Huh? Not you, you can stay where you are, Tits McGee! Stay there and sag to death!" The girl blew her nose loudly and threw the balled-up tissue at Reiko. It hit Reiko's left breast and fell to the floor, adding to the mountain of garbage. "Right in the nipple, one hundred points. Da-naa. ♪"

There was some kind of popping noise from the region of Reiko's temple. "Heeey, Renji? Sorry for the trouble, but could you snap this damn brat's neck—"

"Excuse me. Are you the board chairman of this academy?" Fuyou pushed aside Reiko, who was fuming with rage, and moved forward to stand in front of the girl.

"Huuh?" As soon as the girl raised her eyebrows and looked up at Fuyou, an amiable smile spread across her face. "…Yes, hello. Welcome, thank you for coming! Indeed, I am the board chairman of Purgatorium Remedial Academy, Makina Origa."

A bright, professional smile accompanied her self-introduction, though her eyes, piercing through Fuyou, were not smiling at all.

Fuyou wore a similar expression. "Is that so? Oh-ho, I am grateful for the care you have shown my daughter. I am Fuyou Akabane, the nineteenth head of House Akabane. And these two people are—"

"Naoki Kamiya. Victim A. You sons of bitches stole my kids an' tried to take my life, and…"

"Victim B, Sanae Kamiya. The three of us together are monster parents, you know? We came to ask you to allow both Kyousuke and Ayaka to drop out of school."

Surrounded on three sides by the parents of students, the board chairman's—Origa's—expression stiffened. "I see, I see, I understand," she said, rustling her own disheveled hair. "Wait just a minute, please. I'm preparing the documents now." She began rummaging around in the shelves standing near her bed.

"—Eh? Don't you think this is a little too easy?"

"Y-yeah...I thought it would be more complicated. The little board chairman is nicer than I thought—"

Thwap!

A gelatinous, green, sticky mass arced through the air and hit Sanae in the face. Origa had thrown some kind of slime. She pulled down the skin below one eye and stuck out her tongue, all the while digging around in one ear with her little finger.

"Let students drop out? I absolutely will not! You parents haven't even paid their tuition yet, and you still come to me with such selfish requests? Is this what you meant by 'monster parents'? Nooot a chance! Why are you trying to steal the talent I've gone to so much trouble to recruit? It's unbelieeevable—seriously, where do you get off even trying, tiny titties?!" She angrily flicked some earwax away.

Sanae silently moved away from the bed. She picked up a heavy, nonportable game console from the floor nearby and prepared to slam it down on Origa's head, even as the girl was leafing through a disagreeable (big breast) gravure magazine—

"Control yourself, Sanae." Fuyou placed a hand on the console to stop her.

"Let go, Fuyou. This one's mine..."

"Let's calm down. Allowing your opponent to goad you like this is—"

Origa reached out and grabbed her. "Hmm, maaaybe about a C cup? They're getting there, wifey."

".......Let's kill her, shall we?"

"Quit it, calm down!" Naoki held Fuyou back. She was ready to spill blood after being felt up.

"...Yeeeah, it's not like anything less than an F cup even really counts," Origa muttered.

Naoki snatched the gravure magazine from her. "Miss Board Chairman, listen... Can we be serious here? First you snatched away our family, then you tried to kill us, many times. An' now you're treating us like shit, so..."

"Owww?! Hey, don't grab my hair, baldy—"

"Shaddup. We're tearin' this place down, you little bitch!"

Origa seized up at Naoki's threats. As she stared into his bloodshot eyes at point-blank range, her own dark purple ones opened wide, and a brazen smile spread across her lips. "—Can you do it?"

"I can. At the very least, I'm gonna crush your head in my hands right here and now, get it?" His grip tightened on her head.

Tapping his arm, Origa shouted, "I give, I give, sorry! I get it!" With tears welling up in her eyes, she glared up at him. "U-unbelievable... I oppose such violence! Let's be peaceful, peaceful!"

"Yes. Certainly, let's do that," Fuyou agreed without a moment's delay and put a hand on her cheek. "I would also prefer to avoid violence if at all possible. If we can conclude this without spilling any blood, I would most certainly like to do so."

"...Tch." Origa clicked her tongue. "Ah, ah, shut up... You're really tiresome, you know that? But there's no way around it, is there? If only you two were independent bodyguards, I could kill you just like that, and boom, done! However...since you have the backing of House Akabane, it's not going to be that easy, is it?"

"Yes. Since it is apparent that this institution also has the backing of a large and powerful organization, I would like to avoid open conflict. I'd like us to leave with no grudges and retain our honor... We should talk this out together and find some common ground."

"...Then we agree. Hey, big boobs!"

"Hm? You mean me?"

"There's no one else but you. Everyone else is either a man or has a chest too small to count."

"......You're awfully flat yourself, Miss Chairman."

Ignoring Sanae's jab, Origa motioned for Reiko. Reiko, who had been standing by, bored, next to the bolt-upright Renji, approached the side of the bed, kicking garbage as she went.

"What do you want?"

"Leave the three parents here, and go somewhere else."

"You call me over just to tell me to go somewhere else...? You really are an irritating brat."

"Same to you. Swinging around whenever you walk—those chesticles really are unpleasant to look at."

"Sh-shut up—"

"—At least, that's what they think of them, you know?"

"............"

Sanae's and Fuyou's eyes were full of murderous rage, but Origa showed no concern at all. She seemed to be the kind of person who provoked others as easily as she breathed.

Reiko looked as if she had heard enough. "Good grief. Well if I'm such a nuisance I'll leave, but...don't stir them up too much and get yourself killed."

"Yeah, yeah. If I do, take over for me as chairman, okay, boobies?"

"Oh no, I'm much too busy." Turning her back on Origa's good-bye wave, Reiko approached Kyousuke, who had been watching the situation attentively from a position a little separated from the adults. She placed her hand on his shoulder. "—Well then, I guess we should leave the room. Let's leave the rest up to your parents."

"S-sure..."

"Don't worry, ya damn brat," Naoki said, seeing Kyousuke hesitating to exit the room. He spoke with his usual disrespectful attitude and bold expression. "We'll do something or other. We'll definitely get out of here. Leave it to us."

"D-Dad..."

He dropped his guard for an instant and felt as if he might tear up.

At home they had fought constantly, and when the old man was away from home he had not made a single attempt at communication—frankly, Kyousuke did not like his father much, but even so, in these kinds of situations he was so reliable it made Kyousuke want to cry. Sanae also struck a cheerful, brave pose.

"......Sorry. I'm counting on you, Dad, Mom...and Ms. Fuyou."

"Oh-ho. I don't mind if you call me 'Mother.'" She smiled.

"Ha-ha-ha..." Looking toward the exit, Kyousuke gave a strained laugh. "Hey, Ayaka! We're going!"

Ayaka, who was staring at an imposing set of ornate purple-black armor standing in a clear case in the corner of the room, answered, "Okaaay!"

Several minutes earlier, she had picked up an electric bass from among the various refuse scattered around the room and given the strings a test strum. As always, she did things her own way.

As they left, Reiko stopped as if she'd just had a sudden recollection. "…Ah, that's right."

She turned to look back at Naoki and Sanae, who were looking around restlessly trying to find something they could sit on.

"I didn't get the chance to mention it, but Makina is more or less a boy, you know?"

$$\times \qquad \times \qquad \times$$

"Kyousuke."

They had passed through three doors on the way back, when Reiko called his name, still facing forward, with her hand suspended on the final iron door leading up to ground level.

"Suppose that the negotiations go well… Will you drop out of school?"

"Eh? What kind of—?"

He started to reply immediately and then held his tongue.

Leaving Purgatorium Remedial Academy. That had been the goal, ever since he had been falsely accused as the Warehouse Butcher and forced to enroll at this school against his will.

And ever since Kurumiya had told him, "If you're able to make it to graduation without killing anyone and without being killed by anyone—at that time, I will allow you to return to normal life," he had kept his eye on that goal.

Now the path to that goal, which had been far off in the distance, was opening before his eyes thanks to the unexpected shortcut of parental intervention.

So despite that, why…?

"…Ayaka's not sure that she wants to."

She spoke up as her brother struggled to find his voice.

"I mean, we have fun every day. The murderers here are scary, and the teachers are even scarier, and manual labor is tough, and the food is awful, and the beds aren't comfortable, and we can't go shopping, and we can't watch TV, and we can't eat sweets... If I tried to list all my complaints, I'd probably never finish, right? But I—"

Her small fists clenched.

"I have fun every day! Before I came here, I thought that people were all garbage and school was like a garbage dump...but I've changed a little since then! I met some people who I think are not garbage, and I'm starting to appreciate spending every day with those people here at this school!"

"Ayaka......"

"—How about you, big brother?" The girl gazed at him, her clear eyes shining with tears. "Tell me straight. Aren't you having fun? Don't you think that spending every day with Eiri and Crafty Cat and Renko is fun?"

"Nn—" He gulped. The question could not have been any more direct. Averting his eyes from her gaze, which was just as confrontational as her question, Kyousuke struggled to answer. "Th-that's, uh... What can I say, um..."

"............"

"............"

"Big broth—"

"We're going out." Reiko pushed the door open. She looked back at Kyousuke and Ayaka with a smile. "Should we go back to the Purgatory Festival? I've got to catch sweet Hijiri and the other teachers and explain a few things to them, but...ah, make sure not to say anything to the others students! The two of you dropping out is not set in stone yet, after all. Let's just relax and see what happens."

X   X   X

"Welcome to the other side, our condolences. ♪"

A girl in a maid outfit greeted Kyousuke and Ayaka, who had returned to Café Hades after separating from Reiko. But the next moment, she clicked her tongue—"...Tch"—and brushed back her hair, which was tied up with a frilly ribbon. "I thought you were customers, but it's just you two. Come in through the back, please, seriously... Don't do anything else confusing. Just die."

"Uh, umm......"

"......What are you doing, Crappy Kagura?"

For some reason, the maid who had come to greet them was Eiri's younger sister—Kagura Akabane.

Kagura folded slim white arms that extended out of short sleeves, and she sneered, "Ha! Isn't it obvious, Offal Ayaka? I'm greeting customers in your place, after you skipped out on your shift. Since it was a request from none other than my big sister, there was no way out of it... It's not like after I saw her in her cute maid outfit that I also wanted to wear one and asked her myself, after all. Even now I'm reluctantly—"

"Kagura, sweetie! Come take pictures with us!"

"Okaaay. ♪ Wait just a momeeent. ♪" Kagura answered her customer's summons in a singsong tone and burst into a smile. However, when she looked back at Kyousuke and Ayaka, she returned to her original sour pout. "—Reluctantly doing this."

"Aren't you in high spirits!"

"Gross!"

"Wha...? I-it's not gross!"

So she doesn't deny that she's in high spirits...

Kagura glared indignantly at Ayaka, who recoiled under her angry gaze, though an embarrassed blush was even now spreading over Kagura's face. Her bare legs, which were always covered by the hem of her kimono, were now exposed to the thigh.

...I see. As expected from Eiri's little sister, she has amazingly beautiful legs—

"You're in the way. Get out of here."

"Owwwwww?!"

Eiri suddenly seized Kyousuke by the ear, dragging him to the kitchen area, which was separated from the rest of the café by a partition.

Maina, who came out of the kitchen in a maid outfit, holding drinks, nearly bumped into them. "Oh gosh?!"

"That hurts!" Kyousuke whined. "Can't you be a little gentler?!"

"...Hmph. That's what you get for ogling my little sister with your filthy eyes, idiot."

"Uh—"

As Kyousuke struggled to respond and Eiri turned away from him with puffed-up cheeks, Ayaka entered the kitchen. Peeking her head out from behind the partition, she saw Kitou and Kousaka, who were visiting customers' tables and making comments like "She's cute, huh, little Kagura..." and "Too bad she's got tiny boobs like her big sister."

"Do your jobs," Ayaka ordered before turning to Eiri. "Did you tell them that Crappura is your little sister?"

Eiri, who had changed back into her school uniform in order to lend Kagura her costume, nodded as she prepared juice and sweets. "...I kept our family name a secret, though. And those bothersome bastards aren't around now, either."

"Those bothersome bastards" definitely referred to Oonogi, Usami, and Shinji. Certainly, if those boys knew about Kagura's existence, they would make a total scene.

"...So. What happened to you guys?" Eiri pulled Kyousuke and Ayaka into a corner and asked in a whisper, "You came back after meeting with the board chairman, right? Is he going to let you drop out of school?"

"Um—" Kyousuke faltered for a moment. After hearing the words *drop out* stated so clearly, it took him a moment to pull himself together. "Th-that's right... Just like we expected, the chairman of the academy seems like a troublesome person, but thanks to Lady Fuyou's help, it looks like we managed to avoid a direct conflict... The adults are talking it over in the chairman's room at the moment."

"...I see. That's a relief." Eiri smiled as the tension left her shoulders.

Reiko had told them not to talk to anyone, but since Eiri was already aware of the situation, there was no need to keep it a secret from her.

Thinking about it, Eiri was always helping him. Ever since he'd been thrown into this academy where he was surrounded by deviants, how many times had she—

"How do I say, um...thanks, Eiri." Words of gratitude spontaneously rushed from Kyousuke's mouth.

Startled, Eiri took one step away from him. "Wh-what are you saying all of a sudden? ...It's weird. Did something happen...?"

"No. Nothing in particular, but—" Kyousuke scratched his cheek, trying to hide his embarrassment. He looked into Eiri's eyes as he continued. "When I started thinking about how I might be dropping out of school very soon, it suddenly occurred to me that I've always gotten help from you...and I realized. Even this time, if you weren't here, I wouldn't have any connection to House Akabane, and I probably wouldn't have known that my parents were being targeted by the academy... Hell, when you think about it, I probably would have been beaten to death within a week of starting school here. And so, thank you. I'm really glad that you were here."

"〰〰〰〰〰〰〰〰〰〰?!"

Eiri froze, her eyes open wide. She turned her reddening face away and darted her gaze around, getting flustered like Maina, and stammered out an incoherent reply.

"Wh-wh-wh-wh-wh-what are you saying? ...I-it's fine! I did it because I liked to... You, um... I l-l-l-l-l-like—"

Rattle, rattle, rattle...

...Said the door.

"Aaaaaaaaahhh, there you are! I finally found yooou! I missed you, Kyousukeeeeeeeee! I love love love love love yooouuu!"

"Whoaaa?!"

Opening a staff-only door in the front of the classroom, Renko barged into the makeshift kitchen, dressed in her school uniform. She ran up to Kyousuke and leaped at him with all her might.

Kyousuke toppled over, struck the back of his head, and nearly fainted. "Gah?! C-calm down—"

"Really! Where on earth have you been?! I ran all over the school, looking for you! Even though just one millisecond earlier I had kicked all my fans out of the way because I wanted to meet you! But everything's forgiven now that I've finally found you safe and sound! Eh-he-he-he-he-he-he! Kyousuke, you, um, came to see my live performance, right? And in the middle of the set, you ran to the front of the stage and got all excited! I was so happy and almost exploded with joy. I got the audience all worked up so they would smoosh you in the mosh pit! *Kksshh.* As payback, you can smoosh up on me—"

"Renko!" Kyousuke shouted at Renko, who was sitting astride him as she yammered on and on. "Calm down, I said! First of all, get off!"

"Oh? What's the matter? You're not getting into it... Are we in a rut?" Renko grumbled as she stood up.

Eiri shot her a frightful glare.

"Bloodlust?!" Renko jumped back, shaking. "...Um, ah, what is it, Eiri...? What happened? Why are you looking at me with those eyes like you're staring at your sworn enemy? If you keep making faces like that, you'll get wrinkles. Smoosh, smoooosh!" Renko pointed at Eiri's forehead.

"You should just die." Swiping away Renko's finger, Eiri clicked her tongue in her typical tone.

Renko pretended to panic. "Waah, scary...brrr. But look, you also came to see my concert, didn't you! How was it?"

"...Tch."

"Oh no...I guess you didn't like it. Do you not like that kind of sound?"

"...Tch."

"I-is that so...? Well, people like different things! What kind of music do you like, Eiri? Image-wise I would guess sweet love songs, but your accessories and stuff are a little punkish."

"...Tch."

"Don't 'tch' me. And cut it out with the pointless glaring, would you?"

"...Tch."

"I'd also like you to stop clicking your tongue."

"...Tch."

"Hey, Ayaka...what should I do? I can't get a conversation going with Eiri."

Ayaka, who had been watching the scene from the sidelines, shrugged her shoulders and shook her head. "...It's because you're being a nuisance, Renko. You interrupted something major. And she had finally just mustered up her courage, too! You burst in at the worst possible time, flaunting your sex appeal like you always do—it's no wonder that Eiri would click her tongue and turn into a robot."

"*Kksshh...*," Renko sighed. "...I-is that so? I don't really understand why, but it seems like I did something bad... Sorry, Eiri?"

"Just die."

"Aw, I said sorry..."

"Just die."

"Ah, this time she became a 'just die' bot!"

Renko gave up on Eiri and turned back to Kyousuke and Ayaka.

* * *

"By the way, Kyousuke, Ayaka, I just ran into Basara and heard the whole story... Is it really true that you two are leaving the academy?"

X   X   X

"...*Kksshh*. I see, so you're really going to leave..."

On Ayaka's good judgment, they had left the classroom, and the siblings plus Renko were now walking around the school grounds. The main venue for the Purgatory Festival was the new school building and its surroundings, so all the other areas were nearly deserted.

As they walked in the direction of the old school building, Kyousuke scratched the back of his head. "Well, it's not decided yet whether we're leaving. The school won't necessarily approve of us dropping out. So hey...lighten up!" As he spoke, he stroked Renko's head reassuringly.

However, Renko coldly brushed his hand away. "I won't," she grumbled. "After all—"

Renko hesitated for a moment before continuing peevishly, "If they do let you drop out just like that, you'll be really happy to get out of here, right? That's only natural. Of course you will. It's not like you wanted to come here —you live in a different world, and the twelve people you were supposed to have killed was all my doing, me, the genuine, mass-murdering psycho killer... And I don't know how much longer I have to live—I'm about to break down. *Kksshh...*"

"Renko—"

"...I wonder if this is what they call fatigue. Recently, my body has been feeling really heavy, you know? My heart throbs, and I'm out of breath... I have a headache, and I'm nauseous, and I'm dizzy—it's really awful. More and more, I find myself happy that my face is covered by a mask."

"S-seriously...?"

...I should have known, but until this very moment, I hadn't realized. I was even glad that she had more energy than before.

But Kyousuke had been wrong. Renko had just been hiding it. Trying to keep him from worrying, since he knew about her situation, and trying not to arouse the suspicions of anyone who didn't know the truth...

But why hadn't he noticed?

"I'm sorry. Renko, I—"

"Just kidding!"

"—Huh?"

"I'm lying, it's all lies, I'm lying about being in bad shape. It was all a big lie to get you to sympathize with me! I'm the one who should be apologizing, Kyousuke. For putting on a dumb act like that. The truth is, I'm the very picture of health! The reason I fell over at the live show was simply heatstroke. *Kkksshh.*"

Kyousuke was silent as Renko explained herself in a cheerful voice. Before he could open his mouth to object, Renko continued on. "However—"

"It's true that I'm on the verge of a breakdown. According to what Mama said, if I unleash my Over Drive just one more time... Well, the next time could be the *end* of me! Even if I don't use it, we're not sure if I'll live longer than half a year..."

Suddenly Renko tore at her hair with both hands, clawing at her head around the gas mask. "Aaaaaaaaahhh, geez! Again! I was trying to win your sympathy again! I'm sorry, Kyousuke, really sorry... I'm fine, I'm fine! Unleashing my Over Drive that time was one hundred percent my intention, so I'm completely prepared for whatever might happen. I even would have been fine if I had died right there! So, Kyousuke, there's no need for you to worry—"

"That's impossible, dummy."

"—Eh?"

He quickly embraced Renko, and she quieted. For what reason he did this, Kyousuke couldn't say. But he did know that he was extremely angry. The rage gathered in his belly couldn't be completely calmed, and instead it welled up, giving passion to the words that spewed forth:

"Of course that's impossible, you dummy... I'm happy that you tried to save my life, even if it might have cost you your own, and I'm incredibly happy that you feel so strongly for me. I'm grateful from the bottom of my heart. But—"

His arms grew tense around her, and his voice grew serious as he said:

*　　*　　*

"I love you!"

"*Kksshh?!*"

Renko's body trembled with a start.

Embracing her warmth, Kyousuke continued, "I love you. Isn't it heartbreaking and worrying…? It doesn't matter whether you understood what you were doing or were prepared for the consequences. To see the person I love in this state now and know that I'm the cause… I'm such a shameless person—I'm really just a fool, aren't I? I don't deserve any sympathy. None at all."

"Kyousuke—" Renko relaxed and wrapped both of her arms around his back. She caressed him and laughed. "*Kksshh…!* I see. Thank you, Kyousuke… I'm happy, too. I'm so happy that you return my feelings that my heart has stopped throbbing. Right now, in this moment, I'm so happy and at ease… I'm so glad that it all turned out like this…"

Renko stopped mumbling, and silence settled in. They could have spent forever together like that.

Then suddenly, Renko pulled her body away.

"Kyousuke, if you drop out of school…if you disappear on me, I'll definitely kill you!"

"……Is that so?"

"Yep. It would be terribly cruel to Ayaka, though. I'd have to apologize afterward… I thought about all kinds of things, and in the end there's only one future that I can imagine: killing you, the one I love, with these hands and making you mine—that's the only way. No matter how much I try to quiet my murderous impulses, no matter how much I try to ignore my whole reason for existing…I just can't kill my desire to kill you. And I don't want to. But if possible, I did want to wait until this became *true mutual love*—until you feel that you want to be killed by me, get it? It looks like we might not have enough time to reach that point, so…even though you say that you love me, it can't be true that you want me to kill you, right?"

"……Sorry. I—"

"It's fine—you don't have to apologize. It's enough just that you're worried about me. Besides—" Renko removed her headphones and pulled his body close to hers. She embraced him tightly, pressing her uncovered right ear to his chest. "…Thanks to my limiter, my murderous melody can't play right now. So I don't feel like killing you. I don't feel like I want to kill you. What I'm imagining right now is peaceful—it's strange to me, but—becoming happy lovers with you, getting married and getting a house and having kids, cultivating a happy life together… That kind of future."

"Renko—"

"Even if it's a future that can never come true, a transient feeling, a dream that I would wake up from the moment I took my mask off… At least for me, right now, that's what I wish for, from the bottom of my heart. Especially if you're going to disappear, I want to treasure moments like this."

"…Of course."

He hugged Renko's body back and let his eyes close. The feel of her, her heat, her smell, her breathing, her heartbeat, her emotions… No matter what, he loved all these things about Renko and did not want to be separated from her. He knew, deeply, that he always wanted it to be like this. As if watching a joyful lucid dream, he was wrapped in a fleeting, heartrending feeling of satisfaction.

That's why—I don't want to drop out, Kyousuke thought. Now, more than ever, he couldn't get that thought out of his head.

All That Remains

WE PART TODAY TO MEET, PERCHANCE TO KILL AGAIN

TRACK THREE

KiLLER QUEEN's PEtticoat MaSSaCRE

01. Hatchet Attack!!

02. Anti-Organism

03. Virgin Dissection Hardcore

04. The Princess Burns for an Anomaly

05. Censored Love Song

06. Mon Dieu

SAKI SHAMAYA 1st EP

"As for the negotiations with the academy...I'm sorry, but it seems things will still take some time."

4:00 PM. Most of the visitors had cleared out, and the Purgatory Festival was almost finished. Kyousuke and Ayaka had been summoned over the school intercom to the reception room, where Fuyou Akabane had informed them of the state of the negotiations.

Apparently Origa, to no one's surprise, refused to leave the chairman's room and was not present. Looking exhausted from more than three hours of debate and discussion, Naoki, who was reclining on the sofa, let out a forceful sigh. "Neither of us will give an inch... I didn't think it would be so damn hard for a couple of students to drop out."

Beside him, Sanae also sighed. Her face was lined with worry. "It seems like the academy, or rather, the 'organization' backing it, hates the idea... It's all 'honor' this and 'reputation' that. Anyway, it looks like they don't want to hand you over without resistance."

They had heard that, at the moment, Kurumiya and the other teachers were gathered in a special staff meeting. Reiko was also attending the conference, and the only five people in the reception room were Kyousuke, his family, and Fuyou.

Outside, the other students were busy cleaning up after the festival, and the hustle and bustle of their work was faintly audible.

"Hyeah-haaaaaaaaa! Where are ya?! Where'd ya go, Kurumiya, sweetieeeeeeeeee?!"

Mohawk, who had been restrained and confined during the Purgatory Festival so as not to bother the visitors, had somehow gotten free, and his raucous voice echoed through the school, accompanied by the sounds of things breaking and the screams of other students. However, no one in the reception room reacted.

Fuyou met that display with a "...Well" and then turned to the Kamiya siblings, who were standing next to the sofa. "There is no need to be concerned. We are fighting a hard fight, but we are not deadlocked. Some kind of conclusion will be reached by tomorrow at the earliest."

"I wish we'd hurry up and get there already. I really don't wanna stay too long in a place like this—they might try an' kill me in my sleep or something. Damn, why can't we just get this over with...?"

"Hm? Does that mean you and Mom are staying the night?" Kyousuke asked.

"Yeah. We're planning to stay in the guesthouse."

"Well, we don't want to sleep outdoors, you know. Plus, thanks to Fuyou, we get the VIP treatment, the VIP treatment! A luxury suite!"

"Th-they have those...?"

Kyousuke had thought that his parents would be staying in the same iron-barred rooms as the students, but apparently they'd been given more pleasant accommodations.

"Ehh?!" Ayaka exclaimed, cheeks puffing out angrily. "What's with that?! That's so unfair! It's not fair at all that it's just for you two! Kyousuke and I are locked up day after day in prison-style rooms and spend our nights on hard mattresses, with thin blankets and smelly water and dirty toilets—it's noooooot faaaaaair! Waaah!"

"It's all right, Ayaka," Sanae answered quickly. "We're going to have you stay with us, too."

"—Huh?"

Ayaka's scornful eyes became small dots. "U-umm...you really mean it?"

"Yes. And not just you, but Kyousuke, too. We asked to have you stay in the suite with us while we're here."

"Yeah. That way it'll be easier to keep an eye on ya...but most of all, I couldn't stand the thought of our precious daughter spendin' one more night in a prison like this!"

"…But your son would be fine, huh, you old bastard?"

"Uh? Shut up. Go to yer cell and think about what you've done, brat."

"What did you say?!"

"You wanna go?!"

"Now, now. Calm down, both of you." Sanae quickly subdued both father and son, who looked as if they were about to break into a fight at any second. Kyousuke and Naoki continued glaring at each other after being pulled apart.

"My, my. Aren't you obedient, Naoki," Fuyou chimed in with a wry smile. "And Kyousuke, too…oh-ho. You remind me of Masato. He was truly the hot-and-cold type and would almost never say what he really thought."

"…No, not almost. He never, ever said what he was really thinking. He always just repeated whatever you wanted to hear…," Naoki spat, voice filled with grief. Then, looking sobered by the grim exchange, he scratched the back of his head briskly as he turned back to them. "…Well, anyway, that's how it is. You two're going to stay with us tonight, all right? You'll be able to eat real food and finally get a good bit of rest."

"No."

"Great! Let's get movin'— Wait, 'NO'?!" Naoki croaked, hysterical.

Ayaka, who had brushed aside her father's proposal, repeated herself: "Yep, I said no!" Her reply was calm and confident. "I mean, Kyousuke and I have the closing party for the Purgatory Festival tonight!"

"…Huh? Just forget that—you don't hafta go. You're droppin' out anyway, so—"

"Noooooo!" Ayaka cried and ducked behind Kyousuke's back. She stuck her face out halfway. "I want to go! I want to celebrate with everyone! I told you, no! I'm going to have fun until late at night, go back to the dirty dorms with everyone, get in the dirty bath, and sleep in my dirty bed! I'll do that until we drop out."

"Wha—?" For a moment, Naoki was speechless. Then—"What the hell're you sayinnnnnng, Ayakaaaaaaaa?!"

The man flipped out. Scowling at his daughter, who drew back with a shout, the veins in his forehead popped out as he yelled. "Don't you understand what kinda place this is?! You understand, don't you, hey?! I heard what you did to get in here! But I know you were having a hard time—you were troubled and in pain... You were at your breaking point, so you did that ridiculous thing. That's what I thought, so your mother and I had a talk, and we decided not to scold you until things had calmed down! But now...who the hell do you think you're talkin' to?! What the hell is with that attitude?! Huh?!"

Naoki rose from the sofa and closed in on Ayaka, who was still hiding behind her brother. "It looks like this place suits you just fine, doesn't it?! It looks like you're getting along with this pack of murderers, doesn't it?! It looks like you don't want to drop out after all, doesn't it?!"

"......Don't want...," Ayaka mumbled and gripped Kyousuke's clothes even tighter.

"—What?"

Glaring back at her father, Ayaka raised her shrill voice.

"Ayaka doesn't want to drop out!"

"......?!"

The anger disappeared from Naoki's face, replaced by utter confusion. Kyousuke must have been wearing a similar expression as he stared at Ayaka.

"...I don't...want...to drop out!" Ayaka sobbed. Fat tears fell from her big eyes, and still glaring at Naoki, she pressed her lips together so tightly that they turned pale.

"_____"

Ayaka stared up at her father, who looked down at her with a stern face. Moments passed. The tension was palpable.

"...Hey. What about you, Kyousuke?"

"Eh?"

"Do you want to drop out or not? Which is it?"

"......I—"

Kyousuke did not answer immediately. Then he looked up, meeting Naoki's sharp eyes.

*　*　*

"I…think I want to drop out."

"B-big brother—" Ayaka began to interrupt, but Kyousuke quickly cut her off as he continued.

"Honestly, there are times I also feel like I don't want to drop out, okay? To be sure, this is a terrible place, filled with truly terrible people, but there are some good people among them, too. Some interesting people. Some not-so-hateful people. Even some people I can respect… So if I'm being completely honest, I've had fun here. I even feel like spending the next two and a half years of my youth here might not be as bad as I expected."

However—

"…This is not the place where we belong. No matter how pleasant it is, no matter how much fun we have, in the end it's wrong. We're not murderers. We're just ordinary people. Even if we don't drop out of school now, eventually we'll have to come to terms with the fact that we live in a different world… Sooner or later, we'll have to leave. Normal society versus the criminal underworld… If you and I were to graduate, which do we belong in? Normal society, right?"

"Ooooooooh. Th-that's true, but…" Ayaka stuck her lip out sullenly. "But it would be all right if we didn't drop out right away, right? As long as we abide by the conditions set by Miss Kurumiya, we'll be allowed to graduate like we should!"

"Impossible."

"…Why? If we don't kill anyone and don't get killed by anyone—"

"It's not that." Kyousuke stared into his sister's eyes as he explained. "Think about it. Our parents were being hunted by the academy, right? Forget about graduation—they've already tried to *take away everything we have to go back to*. Can you really trust people like that? Can you trust them enough to keep going to this academy for two and a half more years?"

"…………"

Ayaka was silent. Even after waiting a short while, she did not respond.

"Hmm…you understand well, don't you, brat," Naoki mumbled and returned to the sofa.

Next to him, Sanae let out a small sigh. Smiling, she spoke gently. "It's already been half a year since you started school here, right? They say that wherever you live is home… There's no helping the fact that you feel some attachment. Like Kyousuke said, not all the kids are bad, after all!"

"C'mon, they're killers, aren't they?"

"They may be killers, but a person is a person. You understand that?"

"…………"

Naoki turned away and did not reply.

"So? What will you do, Kyousuke? Ayaka said she's going to attend the closing party and stay in her dorm room until you drop out. What about you?"

"Um—" He hesitated for a moment. "I'm sorry, Mom…but I'm going to do that, too. I feel bad because you went to the trouble to get permission for us to stay with you, but…until we drop out, I want to keep living like we have been. I know it's selfish, but would that be okay?"

"…Well then. What do you think, Naoki?"

"Let 'em do what they want," he spat, glaring at his son. "…But I'll say this much. The reason why Sanae and I hid our jobs from you kids, why we tried to only work overseas, why we tried to stay away from home… Well, think about it, all right? You too, Ayaka."

X   X   X

The closing ceremony had been held in the large auditorium—onstage there had been splatter theater and splatter comedy, a murder rap by Renko and the rest of Fuckin' Park, public execution of the students who had skipped out on their festival duties, and so on. Now that it was over, all the students of Purgatorium Remedial Academy were gathered in the cafeteria of the new school building, which held more than twice as many people as the one in the old school building, enjoying the after-party.

There was an all-you-can-eat buffet, an all-you-can-drink bar, and even all-you-can-smoke suspicious drugs. It had been two hours since the party started, and more than half of the students were completely *smashed*.

"Kyousuke, deeeaaaaaar!"

"Uah?! Just a… Miss Shamaya…wh-what are you—?"

"Oh noooooooooo! You can't—don't say, 'I love you'!"

"I didn't say that!"

"You didn't? Well then, allow me, oh-ho-ho-ho-ho-ho…"

"You're already dead."

"Gyaaaaaaaaaaaaaaaaaaaaaa, *mon Dieuuuuuuuuuuuuu*?!"

Renko dragged Shamaya off of Kyousuke, threw her to the floor, and pounced on her.

With a sidelong glance at Shamaya, who was being beaten with a beer mug, Kyousuke went to the bar counter, received a replacement for his wasted drink, and returned to his table.

"Ah, another round, big brother!"

"Don't you mean 'welcome back'...? No? Well, you're not wrong..."

He sat down beside Ayaka, who was raising her glass in a carefree salute. Picking up mouthfuls of synthetic cannabi● herb chicken, intestine sausage, brain *bagna càuda* (leftovers from the Purgatory Festival), and more, he cheerfully tipped back his glass.

His slanted view fell on Kagura, who for some reason was still wearing her maid costume.

"Hey, hey, hey, hey, Kagura, how old are you?" interjected Oonogi.

"......I'm thirteen."

"Seriously?! You don't look it! You're all grown up, little Kagura!" chimed in Usami.

"Hee, hee-hee...well, except her boobs...hee, hee-hee-hee—gyah?!"

"Just die already."

Eiri was using her chopsticks to fend off the pair, who were persistently harassing her little sister.

Usami writhed in pain as he took a chopstick to the eye. Shinji, who had been making passes at Kagura up until thirty minutes prior, had been laid out on the floor nearby, covered in blood.

"Gaaaaaah?! Stop iiit! Stop that, Chihiro! I-if you keep going, he'll... Azrael, who lies dormant in my left arm, will—" "Nom." "Gyaaaaaah?! I'm gonna die! I'm gonna be eaten to deaaath?!" "Ah, hey...what are you doing, Chihiro, really?!"

Nearby, Bob, who had gotten up from her seat, was trying to tear Chihiro off of Michirou, whom she was biting.

Watching the action, Ayaka cackled, while Kyousuke recoiled a bit.

"Yo! I'm back from beating that pervert girl who tried to rape you, Kyousuke! *Kksshh.*" Tossing aside a mug covered in fresh blood, Renko sat down across from him.

Shamaya was sprawled in a bloody heap on the floor, twitching weakly. Another student, an upperclassman with "invincible" written on her cheek in permanent marker, loomed over her. "Fwa-ha-ha-ha, are you okay, Saki? Now, let me disinfect your wounds…fwa-ha-ha!"

The girl showered Shamaya with the contents of her glass, immediately rousing her back to consciousness.

"Gosou?! Do you want to die that badly?!"

"Aaah?! N-nnnn-no, Saki! Th-this is for first aid purposes only— fgyaaaaaahhh?!"

"Calm down, Committee Chair. Gosou's showing the whites of her eyes, isn't she?!"

"……Indeed."

Kiriu and Kuroki jumped in to hold her back.

There was also a stark-naked clown singing and dancing ("Luu luu laa ♪"); someone in a *kigurumi* costume showing off martial arts moves ("A-cha-cha-cha-cha-cha!"); three boys expertly twirling *shamshirs*; and—"Die, normies, explode!"—an upperclassman grumbling with a glass in one hand.

While Kyousuke was gazing absently at them, Renko prepared her straw. "What is it, Kyousuke? You look down."

"Ah, I was just…thinking about something."

"…About dropping out?" Renko whispered.

"Yeah, that's it," he admitted and then drained his glass.

It had been about six hours since he had separated from his parents, who had headed for their own accommodations. Beside him, Ayaka seemed to have gotten all her energy back and was engaged in a heroic war of words with Kagura.

Calling each other "garbage," "shit," "idiot," and "fool," splashing juice on one another, and grappling, the two of them continued to bicker. Pulling at each other's cheeks, they were having a pleasant fight.

On the other hand, Kyousuke's mind became strangely clear the more time passed, and thoughts floated up one after another without end. Thoughts about the academy, about his parents, about dropping out, and about…

Feeling strangely serious, Kyousuke looked away from Renko and stood up from his seat. "…Sorry. I'm gonna hit up the john."

"Eh? Ah, okay…then, me too—" Renko looked confused and started to say something. Eiri also glanced over, but—

"Yaaaaaay, everyooone! Are we havin' fun or what? Kya-ha-ha-hah!"
"Uaah?!" "Kyah?!"

Tomomi, who had returned from another table, wrapped her arms around both of their shoulders, practically falling all over them. As she did, she trampled all over Shinji, who was still sprawled out on the floor—and probably on purpose, for her part.

When he had slipped out of the noisy cafeteria, Kyousuke headed leisurely for the restroom.

"Ah...Kyousuke."

On his way back, he ran into Maina. She was wiping her hands on a polka-dot hand towel—the one she had received as a gift from Shamaya after the Summer Death Camp.

"Good work today. Everyone's really worked up, aren't they?" Coming to a stop, she smiled tiredly.

"Yeah..." Kyousuke smiled bitterly and then decided to stop beside her. "The first-years are still all right, but the upperclassmen are a little too enthusiastic... Arisugawa and the others overdid everything, and Miss Mizuchi had to put them down."

"Ehh?! Miss Arisugawa was given the electric chair at the closing ceremony, wasn't she? So she's already revived, huh... She's like Mohawk."

"Both of them are problem children, huh? Mohawk is... Wait. Speaking of Mohawk, where did he go? He didn't show up at the after-party."

"Oh no... Miss Kurumiya isn't here, either, so he's probably been locked up and is being tortured."

"...Ah. First time in two weeks, huh? She's probably giving it to him good."

After chatting for a while like this, Kyousuke was about to finally head off to the bathroom, when—

"Kyousuke, um...you're probably going to drop out, aren't you?" As if she had chosen the perfect timing, Maina broached the subject.

Swallowing the parting words that were in his mouth, Kyousuke sighed. "......You knew."

"Yes, sorry...I found out from Eiri—um!"

Maina looked up at him dramatically.

*　　*　　*

"Please don't worry about me!"

The girl drew close to Kyousuke, who had no idea what was going on, and then looked around to make sure that they were alone. "...Because even if you and Ayaka drop out now, I'm going to be fine."

When she said this, he became aware of something for the first time: If he and his sister dropped out, they'd be done with it all, but what about the people they left behind?

Eiri, who had the support of her family and possessed the overwhelming strength of an assassin, would be fine. Renko, who was actively working as a professional killer and was a genuine psychopath, would have absolutely no problem.

However, Maina was an ordinary girl. She had a normal fear of killers, a normal dislike of murder, a normal awareness of crime... She was a completely normal girl.

When he thought about whether it would be possible for Maina to lead a peaceful school life for two and a half more years and graduate safely, he was honestly very concerned.

"...Really? Do you think you can make it in a place like this?"

"Yes, probably!"

"P-probably... Well, even if Ayaka and I leave, I'm sure Renko and Eiri will help you, but—"

"Ah, no. I think Eiri is going to drop out along with you. She can do that, right? Her family has power."

"...Huh? Why—?"

"I told her she should."

"Eh..."

Kyousuke understood her even less than before, but before he could voice his confusion, Maina continued.

"After all, *she hasn't killed anyone*, has she?"

A bitter smile surfaced on Maina's face. "Neither you nor Ayaka nor Eiri, none of you have killed, so...you shouldn't be in a place like this. It's fine for you to leave. But I—"

At that point, Maina held her tongue for a moment and cast her eyes downward. Her bitter smile softened, and she continued. "I have killed. So even if you and Ayaka and Eiri leave, I've got no choice but to go on. I have to go on."

Maina's eyes were not tinged with grief as she looked at Kyousuke. She said it as though it was a matter of course, as if she was resigned to her fate. It seemed that she had steeled her resolve a long time ago. Once again, Kyousuke became aware of the secret strength that was hiding inside the ever-timid Maina.

"......Is that so? I understand, thank you."

For that reason, he quietly accepted her decision. He admired Maina's tenderness and consideration and, above all, her earnest strength, and he cheered her on from the bottom of his heart.

"I'm sorry for worrying too much... You'll be all right, Maina. If possible, I'd like to do something to help, but..."

"Okay, thank you very much. But I'll be all right! I've already gotten plenty of help from you up until now, Kyousuke. Besides—"

"My, if it isn't Maina and Kyousuke?"

Just then, a voice called out to them. When Kyousuke turned around, there was a female student wearing a flour sack on her head before him—in other words, Bob was standing there, holding Chihiro.

"...Slurp, slurp."

Chihiro was licking the area around her mouth constantly, and her face was stained bright red. Only the area that her tongue could reach was clean.

Maina opened her eyes wide. "Oh my gosh?! Wh-wh-wh-wh-wh-what did you do, Chihiro?!"

"...It's Michiro's blood. Slurrp, slurp."

"Ehh?! D-don't tell me you ate Michiro—"

"I stopped her before it got to that point. She just gnawed on him a little."

"J-just gnawed... B-but that's a lot of blood. Oh no."

"Oh-ho-ho. It's fine, it was only his arm. It's not life threatening."

"Ah. I-I guess not..."

Maina looked relieved. Chihiro gazed at her with creepy, bloodshot eyes.

"Could I try one bite…of Maina, too?"

"Nooo!"

"You may not!"

Bob and Maina karate chopped her at the same time.

Holding her head where they had gently hit her, Chihiro pouted. "…Tch. Stingy."

Somehow, it was all very friendly.

"Really…Chihiro's cannibalism is such a hassle. Whenever I take my eyes off her, this sort of thing is sure to happen… And now I've got to go wash this girl's face in the restroom."

"O-oh…what a handful…"

"Bob, you seem kind of like Chihiro's mom, you know?"

"Oh my, no. I'm not old enough to be anyone's mom yet. Really! Well, see you later."

"Okay. Bob, Chihiro, see you later!"

"Bye-bye!"

After seeing off Bob and Chihiro as they headed for the restroom, Kyousuke turned back to his classmate. "…Maina, I didn't know you were such good friends with them."

"Yes, we became close during the summer break. When you and the others were summoned to Eiri's family's house and left…"

"Ah—"

That time. She had been left behind all alone, so while he was standing here worrying about whether she would be all right going forward, it seemed she had had a fun time socializing on her own well before this.

"I actually have quite a few friends, you know? Bob, Chihiro, Michirou, Mari, Irizumi…"

Kyousuke didn't even recognize all the names. Perhaps they were first-year Class B students…

"Since the athletic festival ended, I've been on good terms with Tomomi, too. And among the upperclassmen, Miss Shamaya and Miss Haruyo and even Miss Gosou!"

Those three girl gangster seniors, huh? They probably got along well in a group with Maina the Clumsy Girl. Through her efforts at the athletic festival, Maina had changed her relationships with her classmates, apparently much more than Kyousuke had imagined. It seemed as if she had found her place at the academy.

And so—

Maina smiled broadly. "You don't need to worry at all! Because I'll be fine even if you and Ayaka and Eiri leave. I'll do my best on my own and make up for my own crimes and do whatever it takes to earn my release, and then—"

She took a deep breath, staring straight into Kyousuke's eyes. "I'll meet everyone again. I'll meet you all after graduation, and we can talk just like this and have fun laughing together. That is my goal."

"Maina..."

"The truth is, there is also something I would like to discuss with you, Kyousuke, but..." She turned away, fidgeting bashfully. However, she quickly shook her head and put on a sunny smile. "I think I'll keep quiet until that time. Now of course there are still a few things I feel guilty about, so...Kyousuke. I hope you can drop out without any trouble!"

X   X   X

"......*Fwah.* I'm sleepy." Eiri yawned and rubbed her half-lidded eyes as she folded up the maid costumes.

It was the day after the Purgatory Festival. The students, who had enjoyed the after-party into the early hours, were now tasked with packing away the festival decorations and cleaning up the classrooms.

It was past one o'clock in the afternoon. As he carried a huge bundle of garbage to the incinerator, Kyousuke was preparing to take a short break and talk with Eiri.

"Big brother!" Ayaka, who had cleaned up her own installation, appeared, dashing toward him.

Perfect timing; it'll save me having to go call her, Kyousuke thought, a smile appearing on his face.

"Papa and the others are calling you!"

"...The old man?" Kyousuke's smile instantly disappeared, and his heart leaped in his chest.

Ayaka drew her face near so that any roving classmates wouldn't overhear, and then she lowered her voice.

"Yep. They're going to tell us what they decided."

"......Seriously?"

"Hey. Do you want to go to lunch soon?" Eiri asked. She had finished folding the maid outfits and stood, stretching. Her eyebrows knit together when she noticed the strange atmosphere surrounding Kyousuke and Ayaka.

Maina, who was moving small furniture back into place with Tomomi, also stopped what she was doing and looked at them worriedly.

Eiri came closer and asked, "...Did something...happen?"

Ayaka elucidated the situation to Eiri, too.

"It sounds like they're going to tell us the results of the negotiations. I was told to come and get you two, since we're going to the board chairman's room now, where they'll tell us all the details..."

"...All right, understood. Let's hope it's a good result, hm?"

"Yeah. Ayaka, have you heard it already?"

"Nope. Not yet, but—" Ayaka's expression clouded over. "From the way everyone looked, I wouldn't get your hopes up..."

X   X   X

"Purgatorium Remedial Academy will not allow students to drop out!"

As soon as Kyousuke and the others had joined up with Naoki, Sanae, Fuyou, and Reiko in the spacious but cluttered board chairman's room—the first thing out of Origa's mouth was this blunt assertion. As always, the head of the school was lying sprawled on the bed, flipping through a comic book and picking at assorted snacks.

"...Huh?" Eiri grimaced. "Is this really the board chairman? Doesn't seem particularly imposing..."

Origa's face lifted up from the thick comic book. "...Huh. Is this really a sixteen-year-old? Doesn't seem particularly mature, though..." Looking at Eiri's slim chest while sighing, the chairman quickly returned to the comic at hand.

"Well then—" Eiri quietly backed away from the bed, searching around nearby for something that could be used as a weapon.

"Stop it." Fuyou gently held her back. "Now, I'm afraid we must insist that we take Kyousuke and his sister back, no matter the circumstances." She snatched the comic book from Origa's hands. Narrowing her eyes, the color of fresh blood, she continued, "We attempted to reach some kind of agreement, but in the end neither side would give in. I proposed financial contributions, temporary employee replacements, and various other incentives, but—"

"All are rejected." Origa sullenly cut Fuyou off, fuming over the loss of the comic book. "Things and money and even people can easily be replaced, but faith, trust, and honor are much more difficult to get back. The Organization and House Akabane are in the same business, but at the same time, we are competitors. If we were to be outmaneuvered by such an opponent, our reputation would take a hit... No, it's been damaged enough already, having come to this point. We failed to bring down our targets, and they were snatched up by the Akabane, and we were late realizing that, and then we were infiltrated all the way to the highest levels, so we're already completely wrecked..."

All the more reason why—

Origa scowled up at her. "There's no way you can take them. I'm going to return every insult. I'll rip you all to shreds and do more damage than you did to me."

Next to Fuyou, who stared back at Origa calmly, Naoki cracked his knuckles. "Bring it on! If neither of us is going to give an inch, there's nothing to do but fight it out, eh? If honor is that important to you, let's settle this with our fists."

"H-hey?! Wait a minute, old man! Lady Fuyou!" Kyousuke, who had been nervously watching the conversation progress, interjected by jumping in front of the two of them. "Wasn't violence going to be a last resort?! Like Lady Fuyou said, only when everything else failed—"

"Yes, I did say that. If we act rashly, it could lead to a dispute within the Organization and perhaps even a civil war. There would be no end to the damage... Both the academy and our side agree that we want to avoid such an awful outcome."

"If so—"

"That is why we decided to hold *final exams.*"

"...Final exams?" Kyousuke asked.

Origa grinned widely. "Yes, *truly* final, if you get my meaning. Both parties want to avoid a head-on collision, but neither of us are willing to give any ground, leaving us in something of a stalemate—in that case, why don't we decide victory or defeat with a contest? That's what we agreed. It'll be a bit like your little wager with Reiko at the athletic festival..."

"I-I see..."

"...Only, I'm not sluggish like her." A cruel light sparkled in Origa's eyes. After pointing at Reiko, the chairman drew his thumb across his throat. "The Deadly Exit Exam will be a game of tag, with your very lives on the line. Us chasing and you running away. If Kyousuke and Ayaka can make it off of academy grounds and safely reach the predetermined goal, they will be allowed to leave Purgatorium Remedial. But—"

Origa pointed his thumb at the floor. He smiled haughtily.

"If you don't make it, there will be no dropping out. *And any chance of future release will be rescinded.* Brother and sister will graduate as professional killers, to be used by the Organization until their deaths."

"Wha—?"

"Ehh?!"

Origa shrugged at the shaken siblings. "That is what our side gets, should we win. However, should we lose, we will leave your family alone forever. Regardless of the outcome of the exam, neither the Organization nor House Akabane will hold any grudges, and we will return to our prior working relationship... The point is, if you win, you have nothing to worry about. That's easy to understand, that feels good, right?"

Kyousuke and Ayaka looked at one another.

"U-umm...so in other words, it's all right if we manage to get away, yeah?" Kyousuke timidly inquired. "Who's going to be chasing after us, then? Upperclassmen?"

"And teachers."

"—Huh?"

All the teachers at Purgatorium Remedial Academy were first-rate professional killers. If people like that seriously went after them, Kyousuke and Ayaka, who were nothing but ordinary kids, wouldn't stand a chance...

"Don't worry." A warm hand came to rest on Kyousuke's shoulder as he went visibly pale. Fuyou spoke reassuringly, wearing a gentle smile. "You and Ayaka will not be the only ones participating in the Deadly Exit Exam. Naoki and Sanae and even we Akabane will be allowed to support you two."

"Yeah. Relax, brat. No matter what kinda killers you're up against, me and Sanae'll protect you, all right? You won't have to lift a finger."

"Oh yes! We are expert bodyguards, after all. You'll be just fine!"

Naoki boldly bared his teeth while Sanae looked cool and collected.

"Mother," Eiri spoke up, "...can I also participate in the exam?"

"Yes." Fuyou nodded. "And not just you. Any student who wants to help Kyousuke and Ayaka during their Deadly Exit Exam is able to participate, no matter who."

"Provided," Origa interrupted, opening a package of snacks, chin held out defiantly, "that they are prepared to kill, that is."

The chairman crunched down, chewing noisily.

"However, our side will field *twice as many* combatants as yours. After all, the rules favor the escape team, *aaand* it was your side that requested the contest in the first place. It's only natural that our pursuit team should receive *some* handicap, since we're sooo graciously accommodating your request, don't you think?"

He gave a sarcastic-sounding snort beneath his self-satisfied smirk.

Looking down at Origa lying sprawled across the bed, Naoki laughed through his nose. "Hah! You might have the numbers on yer side, but they're just a buncha students, right? Throw as many amateurs as ya like at us—it won't make a difference! I bet you'll regret it in the end...sendin' out a buncha useless chaff!"

"I'm not sure I see your point... Our students are excellent, you know."

Though Naoki and the others were showing remarkable restraint, Origa sneered back at them with a smile. The now-empty junk food packaging was casually tossed aside.

"—The Deadly Exit Exam will commence four days from now, on Saturday. Until then, take it easy. I'm not going to order any surprise attacks or raids, so you can enjoy as much as possible...what little life you have left."

X   X   X

"Kyousuke, deeeeeeeeeeeeaaaaaar?! Is it true what I hear, that you might drop out of school, Kyousukeeeeeeeeee?!"

Kyousuke and the others had returned to their classroom and resumed their rigorous cleaning, when Shamaya, who had apparently already heard the news, ran in looking flustered.

No sooner had she thrown the door open with a clatter than she ran straight toward Kyousuke and slid headfirst across the ground, embracing one of his legs.

"Please don't go, please don't go, please don't go and leave your dearest Shamaya heeeeeere! Waaaaaah, my word! You can't! I cannot bear to be apaaaaaart! Waaaaaah, *mon Dieuuu!*"

"Wha?! M-Miss Shamaya—"

"I'm disappointed in you, Kyousuke Kamiya!"

While Kyousuke stared in confusion and Shamaya continued bawling, next to appear from the door in the back of the classroom was Kuuga Makyouin—or rather, Michirou—wearing a look of indignation. "Unable to stand the inferno of his own jealousy, one clings to the thread of the spider called forgiveness... Is that right? Don't joke around! What weakness, what cowardice, what guilt—no, shamefulness! Very well, Kyousuke, the spider's thread to which you cling...I'm going to cut it with these hands of mine! Now howl, Azrael! Sing the final movement, the hidden esoteric technique 'Hopes Dies Last'—"

"Kyousuke, Ayaka!"

"Guaaah?!"

Tossing aside Michirou, who was still standing in the doorway powering up, Bob pushed into the room. "I heard that the two of you are going to drop out of school—is that true?!"

"...If it's true, I'm gonna eat you! I won't hold back—I'll eat you... *sluurp.*" Chihiro was clinging to Bob's back, her blood-red eyes glittering.

Furthermore—

"Whaaaaaa?! Dropping out? What the hell?! I don't know if it's family circumstances or whatever, but I've never heard of anything like that! Unbelieeeeeeeeevable!"

"You bribed them, didn't you? You had to resort to bribery? U-unforgivable… I won't fail to punish you, so prepare yourselves!! Justiiiiiiiiice!"

"Fwa-ha-ha-ha-ha! What's this, what's this, am I so scary you're running away? You cowards!"

"……That's right."

"You're returning to polite society, you say? And I thought you and I were two badgers in the same hole, Kyousuke… Seems I was wrong about you. I no longer have any hesitation or compassion for you. Only a thorough smashing!"

"We won't let you run away." "Yep, we won't let you." "We'll slice you both to ribbons."

"Ah…ah…"

The second- and third-year students had apparently heard the news as well, and they barged into the classroom uninvited, forming a chaotic crowd.

"Oh goodness…" Maina gripped her broom. "Th-they must have heard from the teachers…so many people. And our own class hasn't even been notified yet—"

"Fah?! What's this about dropping out?! Kyousuke and Ayaka are dropping out?! Seriously?!"

At the same time that Tomomi raised her voice, the remaining classmates who had been confused as to what exactly was going on stopped their cleaning and swarmed around all at once.

"Hey! What's this all about, Kamiya?! Explain it to us right now!"

"Hee, hee-hee…this is no laughing matter. Never mind the big brother—don't drop out, little sister!"

"Waaaaaah! Dropping out? This is too great! If Mr. Kamiya leaves, I…I…I'll be so happy, oh… Couldn't you just cry?! Ee-hee-hee-hee. At long last I'll have the chance to be popular—"

"No way! Shinji, you're totally unbelievable! Kyousuke really is the best."

"Don't quit, Kyousukeeeeee!" "Ayakaaaaaa!" "Think of poor GMK!" "That's right, that's right!" "This may be purgatory, but isn't it heaven?!"

"You mean that after hooking up with all the girls in here, you're moving on to the outside world?!" "What extravagance—" "Kill him, this womanizer, kill him!" "Okay, I will." "No, me." "No, no, I'll do it." "Well then, I will—" "Go ahead, go ahead, go ahead!" "No way, I'll be killed!"

And so on. Most of his classmates, while they said one thing or another, were surprised, aggrieved, or desperate in the face of Kyousuke and Ayaka's departure and tried to hold them back.

"Y-you guys......"

Meanwhile, their reactions bewildered poor Kyousuke.

When he had first entered the academy, he had thought that all the people around him were weird lunatics and not normal as he was. He hadn't wanted to become acquainted with them, hadn't wanted anything to do with them if he could avoid it. There had been nothing but fear and hate in his mind, and no helping the fact that he wanted to run away.

But now—

"Waah, waaaaaah...*mon Dieu*. Don't quit, Kyousuke, darling...*hic*."

"Guaaaaaahhh?! Calm down! Calm down! Hold back the tears! Calm— Bwaaah!"

"N-no...my flour sack will get wet. When I think about the two of you leaving, I...it's lonesome. I probably won't be able to see you again..."

"...No. I hate it... You can't say bye-bye while I'm still waiting to taste you..."

Shamaya was rubbing her cheek on Kyousuke's leg while Michirou pressed down on his eyes with his left hand. Bob soaked her flour sack, and Chihiro looked at them hungrily and puffed out her cheeks.

In response to the murderous students who were feeling sad about parting, Kyousuke felt a lonely, heartrending pain. He turned to the people whom he would probably never see again after departing.

"...Thank you very much. Thank you, everyone...but, I'm sorry. It's true that we will be dropping out. The truth is, I..."

The secret that he had hidden at all costs until now—the fact that he had been falsely accused as the Warehouse Butcher and that he had never killed even a single person. Now was the time to tell them...

"Kamiya's not going anywhere."

A deep Lolita voice filled the air. The tumultuous classroom fell silent in an instant, and everyone's gaze gathered at the front of the room. The crowd of people parted, revealing a young woman, clad in a brand-name suit, dragging along an iron pipe—the homeroom teacher for Kyousuke's first-year Class A, Hijiri Kurumiya.

Glaring at the students, Kurumiya slowly entered the classroom and stepped up onto the podium. "Okay, listen up, pigtaaaaaards!!"

She slapped her palm down on the lectern in a show of terror. Looking around at the petrified students, Kurumiya snarled out her decision. "Neither Kamiya nor his sister will be dropping out. They cannot. I will not permit it. Four days from now, on Saturday, we here at Purgatorium Remedial Academy will hold a Deadly Exit Exam for the two of them. If they're able to pass, they drop out, and if not, they don't. Also—"

Kurumiya glared at Kyousuke, flashing her crooked fangs.

"You absolutely will not succeed! I'll crush you underfoot... I will run you down completely. I won't go easy on you—I'll go all out, got it?"

—Wham! With both hands, their teacher flexed and snapped the iron pipe in two. Bloodlust radiated from her petite frame, and a feeling of pressure assailed them, strong enough to hurt.

Kurumiya chuckled menacingly at Kyousuke and Ayaka, who were trembling with fear. "The academy that has housed the two of you is a jail ruled by us teachers. Consequently, we have used fear and violence to keep you piggies in line and prevent any pointless fighting. But to leave the academy—if you're going to drop out, it's a different conversation! Prepare yourselves. The Deadly Exit Exam is not playtime like the Summer Death Camp or the athletic festival... It's a genuine *battle to the death*."

"......?!"

From Kurumiya's wide-eyed expression, they could tell that she had gone from teacher to professional killer. Maina squeaked in response, and even Eiri had lost her voice.

The pressure was strong enough to make the Kurumiya they had known up until now, the demonic teacher who had driven Kyousuke and his classmates on, seem gentle by comparison. Many of the students stood trembling in fear—some had even collapsed on the spot.

But Kyousuke understood: No matter how violent or sadistic she had been before, Kurumiya had always conducted herself as a *teacher,* and she had always looked at Kyousuke and the others as *students.*

"Whether you participate in the Kamiyas' Deadly Exit Exam or collaborate with them is up to each of you. But don't forget—I will view those who assist them not as students but as *assassination targets.* This is not a drill. It is life or death. Those who are prepared to throw away their lives, take the Deadly Exit Exam together with Kamiya! I'll slaughter every single one of you and make you into ingredients for garbage lunches. I'll kill you all!"

X   X   X

After Kurumiya's threats, no one wanted to collaborate with Kyousuke and Ayaka. From the start, most students had said, "I don't want you to drop out," so it was no surprise that nobody was willing to risk their life to make it happen. Among the students who refused to help—

"Is that so…a Deadly Exit Exam, hm…? *Kksshh.* Sorry, Kyousuke, sorry, Ayaka… I can't help you, either. I don't want to see the two of you leave… I don't want us to part this way. Instead—

"I thought I might participate in the Deadly Exit Exam on the other team and just try to crush everyone…"

Renko had told them this in a sad-sounding voice and then walked away. They hadn't seen her since.

Kyousuke had made the decision to return to polite society, but Renko belonged to another world. In any case, it would probably be easier for them to separate. Kyousuke also made a point to avoid her thenceforth, hoping to completely sever the bonds that had grown between them.

However—

"…………Dropping out, huh."

He couldn't help thinking of her. He lay on the bed in his cell-like dorm, wearing his tracksuit, which was like a prisoner's jumpsuit. Three hours had passed since lights-out, and yet sleep stubbornly refused to come.

There were thick iron bars over the window, through which he could see the deep blue night sky. Soon he would no longer stare up at this view as he had night after night since entering the academy. The thought made him lonely somehow, and he smiled bitterly at himself for it.

When had it started? When he was alone in his dorm room, it was not thoughts of escape but rather memories of his days in this place that he turned over in his mind.

When had it started? He did not hesitate around the murderous students he had once feared and hated, and moreover, he actually wished them well.

Was it after he had found out about the killings Maina committed and how she suffered over them? Was it after Eiri had confessed that she was not a murderer but an assassin who could not kill? Was it after he had learned of Renko's true character and real nature and seen her frighteningly single-minded feelings? Was it after they survived the Summer Death Camp, despite being nearly killed by Shamaya? Or was it after Ayaka had transferred in? Or possibly after he had been forced to work together with his classmates at the athletic festival for a common cause, and he had felt some camaraderie toward them...?

He really didn't know.

However, there was one thing he did know—thinking back, he was really and truly impressed with himself for being able to survive daily life, which was filled with danger at every turn, and despite it all, it had been fun.

Passing strange days with strange people in a strange place had been entertaining, and half a year had gone by in an instant. He also recalled Ayaka's words: "What do you think, big brother? Isn't this fun? Don't you think that spending every day with Eiri and Crafty Cat and Renko and everyone is fun?"

At that time, he hadn't been able to answer right away, but...

Kyousuke couldn't help agreeing with his sister.

If he could help it, he didn't want to drop out. He still wanted to spend a little longer with the people here and do ridiculous things together. He wanted to go on working together with everyone to overcome brutality and danger and lead an extraordinary school life over-flowing with excitement.

But—

"Well, I guess it's impossible…something like that."

Extraordinary or ordinary? When he had been told to choose one, he had decided to take the second option. He was a normal, ordinary person, after all. He couldn't live in the world together with killers and murderers. This was not the place for him.

But even so, these thoughts—

"…………Renko."

When he thought of her, his chest hurt. Worse than the loneliness he had felt before, the pain welled up inside him, and his heart was thrown into disarray. His resolution, which should have been firm, wavered, and he felt he wanted to remain here…

"Aaaaaahhh, forget her! Give up on Renko, stupid!"

Pulling at his hair in frustration, Kyousuke pressed his face into his pillow. He forced his eyelids closed. He finally drifted off just as the sky was beginning to lighten.

In his short time asleep, Kyousuke dreamt that he was being stran-gled to death by Renko—

The Dangerous Escape Plan

BLOODSTAINED KILLER "TAG"

PANDORA!

01. Korobuyo!!MIRACLE

02. After-School
    Kill Time

03. Oh No Hour

04. Life After Curry (Dead)

05. My Love Is
    a Tempest

06. Hope, Please

**MAINA
IGARASHI
1st EP**

"Hey. Wha'ssat face about, brat? …I told ya to get some rest, didn't I?"

"……Sorry. I could barely sleep."

"What a weak mind you've got, kid…geez."

It was the day of the Deadly Exit Exam, and Kyousuke sported dark circles under his eyes as he dragged his sluggish body forward. His father stood, looking exasperated, clad in a black leather jacket and jeans. He pulled on wine-red leather gloves, spat out the cigarette he had been holding in his mouth, ground the butt into the dirt under a combat boot, and then headed for the school gate.

Ayaka, walking behind Kyousuke and Naoki, shouted and pointed, "Ahh! Papa littered! You can't do that, you can't do that. ♪ I'm telling teacheeer. ♪"

"Ah-ha-ha. It's fine, Ayaka, dear. After all, it's the academy's problem now." Next to Ayaka, Sanae, who was wearing a leather jacket that matched her husband's, giggled. "And the teachers that work here get up to much worse than that, right?"

Kyousuke and Ayaka were still dressed in the uniforms of Purgatorium Remedial Academy. It was possible that this would be their last chance to wear them—no, Kyousuke had sworn to try to make it the last. He shook his heavy, sleep-deprived head, slapped his cheeks, and tried to refocus his wandering mind.

The past three days, the students who were to participate in Kyou-suke and Ayaka's Deadly Exit Exam had been exempted from classes and manual labor, free to spend their time as they chose. After a thorough hazing by his father in preparation for the exit exam, Kyousuke had shaken off all kinds of lingering attachments and had hardened his resolution to drop out of school... At least he thought he had.

He hadn't been able to sleep at night, because he was nervous, not because he still harbored any internal conflict about his decision. Three nights in a row he had dreamt of dying at Renko's hand, and yet this was unexpected...

"Good morning."

As Kyousuke's mind wandered, the Kamiyas arrived at the school gate. Fuyou and the other members of House Akabane were mustered before the firmly closed iron grill and imposing concrete wall that encircled the school grounds.

"Yo." Naoki raised a hand. "You're early—did you sleep well?"

"Yes, of course. Very soundly indeed—"

"...*Fwah*."

Eiri, apparently, had not slept. The only one wearing a school uni-form among the group clad in red kimonos, she rubbed wearily at her half-closed eyes.

"My, my, Eiri looks like she didn't get enough sleep... Could she be nervous?"

"No, Lady Fuyou," Kagura replied with a grin. "She was up late training. I fell asleep before her, and she continued practicing without a moment's rest, saying, 'I will protect Kyousuke and Ayaka'—"

"Don't say such unnecessary things." Eiri bopped her prattling sister on the head with her scabbard. A single Japanese sword was gripped in Eiri's right hand.

"What is that thing?" Ayaka asked.

"The Akabane sword Hien. It means 'Scarlet Luster.' It's a trea-sured family heirloom, very sharp. Mother brought it for me. She was expecting something like this to happen. The Suzaku blades on my nails are only for surprise attacks, so I'm not wearing them now."

"Hmm, it looks amazing! Is Eiri very strong, Fuyou?" Sanae asked.

"Yes, indeed she is," Fuyou answered confidently. "Since she's the daughter of Masato and myself...oh-ho. Even considering her reluctance to take a life, there is no one in House Akabane who can stand as her equal...except for me, of course."

"...Eh?" Naoki looked at Eiri. "I guess if you say so, it must really be true... We're counting on you, okay, Eiri? If Sanae and I get caught up in something, it'll be up to you to take care of the enemy." He gave her a crooked grin.

"Eh..." Eiri stiffened. Her rust-red eyes opened a little wider, and her cheeks were tinged with apparent embarrassment. "...O-okay! Please leave it to me, umm...Mr. Naoki? I will absolutely make sure that Kyousuke and Ayaka can drop out! I-I will try...to make them happy!"

"—Happy? O-oh...thanks?" Naoki, who looked perplexed by the passionate reply, gave Kyousuke a sidelong glance.

"Ohh, Eiri's catching up!" Ayaka clapped.

Sanae nudged her son in the side with her elbow. "Don't underestimate her, Kyousuke, honey."

Kagura wore a complicated expression, and Fuyou carried a look of satisfaction as they watched the situation. Also—

"............"

A little distance away from everyone else, a young man leaned against the concrete wall—Basara, wearing a dark red haori jacket over bright red *hakama* pants, was fiddling with his hair and cell phone.

"Ah!" Ayaka shouted, "I-it's your gay big brotheeeeeer!"

"Yo. I'll pop that cherry of yours, little brat." Looking up from his cell phone, Basara sneered freshly.

Kagura looked at her brother in shock. "B-big brother Basara...are you gay *and* a pedophile?"

"No way. I'm entirely normal. Just now, look...I'm e-mailing with girls I got to know at the culture festival, see? Kirie and Kuchiha and Sayaka—"

"Ah, okay, okay. I understand—you're completely beyond saving. You're depressing me, so please keep e-mailing in silence."

"Whatever," Basara answered and immediately went back to his phone, grinning and engrossed.

Naoki checked his wristwatch. "Eight fifty-seven, huh...the Deadly Exit Exam starts in thirty minutes, and they're not here?"

"They're supposed to come at nine, though… They're probably running late. In that case, they should get some kind of penalty—"

"Sorryyy, were you waiting?"
"Hwaaa…w-we made it…"

Just then, Reiko came racing down the walkway, through the courtyard, and up to the gate. Appearing alongside Reiko, who was wearing a lab coat over a brand-name suit, was—
"…Crafty Cat?"
"Maina? Why are you—?"
After Kurumiya had threatened the class, Kyousuke and the others had approached Maina. "We don't want you to participate in the exam," they had said. Kurumiya was right: It was a death game—a matter of life and death. There was no need for Maina to put her life on the line when it would be enough for her just to pray for their success…they had said. In spite of that—
"Ah, ah-ha-ha…sorry, Kyousuke, Ayaka. But I can't just wait on the sidelines. I can't do it! Please let me help you, too!" She bowed vigorously.
It seemed Maina was planning to give it her best. Kyousuke and the others looked at each other.
"Wh-when you say 'help'…"
"Honestly, isn't she kind of a burden? Won't she just hold us back—?"
"I will not! But if I do, please abandon me!"
"No, no…"
There was no way they could do that. However, Maina was stubborn. Kyousuke scratched at the back of his head, at a loss for what to do.
"Hey…that girl, is she strong?" Naoki whispered to Kyousuke. "She looks like she couldn't kill a bug."
"Hm? Ah, aah…she's not weak. But…"
Naoki, Sanae, Fuyou, Eiri, Kagura, Basara—there was no denying that Maina simply could not compare to the others.
Sanae looked her in the eyes. "Sweetie? We appreciate the thought, but we will be up against professional killers. An amateur like you will die in the blink of an eye."
"I don't care! I'm ready for anything!"

"Um…you might not mind, darling, but it'd leave a bad taste in my mouth if you were to go and get yourself killed. Consider the feelings of the people around you, and you'll see this is for your own good. So be a good girl and—"

"Okay. I'm adding one more participant to your team!"

—Before Naoki could persuade Maina to leave, Origa's voice suddenly came out of nowhere. They looked up to see Reiko holding a tablet computer. The screen showed a pajama-clad Origa pecking away at a keyboard while speaking.

"Adding Maina Igarashi to escape team, and…okay, that means you have nine people. Then the pursuit team will consist of eighteen competitors. Is there anyone else who wants to jump in and participate?"

"Hang on—"

"Wait a minute!" Kyousuke objected, pushing Naoki aside. "What do you think you're doing, approving her just like that?! Maina isn't—"

"Oh, shut up. It's fine—she said herself that she would participate. We here at Purgatorium Remedial Academy respect our students' intentions!" Origa answered seriously, though it was betrayed by a smug sneer.

"Y-you—" Kyousuke started to approach the tablet, but Fuyou laid a hand on his shoulder.

"Now, now, isn't it all right? If our chances of success increase, even if only by a little bit, we should take advantage of her courtesy."

"L-Lady Fuyou…but—"

"There's no need to worry." Smiling, Fuyou walked over to Maina. Her eyes, the color of fresh blood, narrowed thoughtfully. "I witnessed your performance at the athletic festival, dear, and your sweet appearance belies your inner strength… If your opponents are other students, you will not be killed that easily. I don't know how you'll stand up to the teachers, but…you should just leave them to our capable hands. No problem."

"Mrs. E-Eiri's Mother…" Maina marveled, looking starstruck.

"You may call me Lady Fuyou."

At their exchange, Basara, who had been preoccupied with his e-mails, closed his cell phone and nodded his agreement as he approached Maina. "We should take advantage of people's courtesy. Especially if it's such a cute girl, right? You'll be all right, Maina..."

Basara dropped to one knee in front of the youth and took her hand. He looked up at Maina, flashing white teeth in a picture-perfect grin. "I, Basara Akabane, will protect you."

"Ehhh?!"

Maina was entirely flustered. "Oh goodness gracious! Th-thank you vewy much! Uh, umm...M-Mishter Basara? Th-that's vewy reas-suwing! But I...I, I, um...th-thewe's subbody ewse I wike aweady, so, ub...waah."

"...Ha. Just how little integrity does he have...?"

"Seriously...oh well. But it is definitely reassuring, since Maina will be with us... When the need arises, I'll also back him up. No objections to that, right, Kyousuke?" Eiri asked.

Kyousuke was dumbfounded. He looked to Naoki, who waved his hand dismissively.

Sanae whispered something into Ayaka's ear and grinned. "Kyousuke, honeeey?"

...*What's that supposed to mean?*

Kyousuke, who looked at Maina last, saw the unwavering resolve in her eyes and nodded. "......Understood. But make sure you stay alive, okay? Let's all do our best so that nobody, not one person, dies. If we don't, I won't be able to leave here with a smile...Maina, Eiri, Ayaka, Dad, Mom, Lady Fuyou, Kagura, Basara, everyone!"

"Huh? What're you saying, damn brat?" Naoki shot Kyousuke an arrogant sneer. "That's always been the plan. We don't need you to go out of your way to tell us." He clenched his fists, hands covered in leather gloves.

"Yep, yep!" Sanae agreed, thrusting a fist into the air. "We're gonna beat them at their own game! We'll show them the power of monster parents!"

"Tee-hee. That's just like Ayaka and big brother's mama and papa!"

"...Certainly is. That overconfidence is exactly like you, Offal Ayaka."

"The only people allowed to address me so casually are beautiful girls. Kyousuke...do you want to die?"

"Come now, you two. Stop turning on our allies."

"...*Fwah*."

"Oh gosh...I'll do my best!"

On-screen, Origa shrugged at the enthusiastic group. "Well, try your hardest, okay? As was previously discussed, your goal is the harbor on the westernmost tip of the island. The Deadly Exit Exam will last from nine thirty, when first period starts, to four o'clock, when fifth period ends."

In other words, the time limit was six and a half hours.

"In total I will be sending out eighteen pursuers. The first five will start thirty minutes after you leave the school gate, with groups of up to five additional participants being sent in every thirty minutes after that. Incidentally, the pursuit team will be made up of the six home-room teachers for each class, plus twelve specially chosen students... You can enjoy learning the detailed lineup as they catch up to you!"

"......Understood."

Six teachers, each of them an elite assassin. Kyousuke was barely acquainted with any of them besides Kurumiya and Busujima, though he was certain that they were on the same level as those two or maybe even more powerful.

He had some idea as to who the students would be as well. They were probably the ten students who had been on the Red List that Kurumiya had made for the athletic festival, plus Renji, who was still being considered an exchange student.

And—

Renko...you're going to come after me, too, aren't you?

He thought about the state she had been in since four days earlier, when he had talked to her about the whole affair.

—Would Renko come chasing after them? What was she planning to do if she caught up to them? Would she block Kyousuke and Ayaka from dropping out? Would she take them back to the academy? Or would she...?

"*Kyousuke. If by some miracle you are able to drop out...if you disappear right in front of me...I will surely kill you!*"

Just as he had seen in countless dreams, Renko would probably come to kill him. He would probably die at Renko's hand. At that time, he would—

"...Kyousuke?"

Kyousuke snapped back to his senses as someone called his name.

He found himself staring into ice-blue eyes that closely resembled Renko's, looking at him curiously.

Reiko held out something that looked like a pair of handcuffs. "Here you go. It's a GPS tracker. You don't have to wear it on both hands—just put one wrist in. As Makina explained, this will allow the pursuit team to track your current location. Don't take it off during the exam. And—"

Bringing her mouth close to Kyousuke's ear, she whispered:

"Renko is planning to kill you. Now more than ever, I don't think there's any point in trying to persuade her otherwise... Will you accept her feelings or not? Either way, you'd better prepare yourself."

That was all she said, and then she slipped past him. For a moment or two, Kyousuke stood stock-still, holding the GPS handcuffs.

"Well then, okay...with that, we should be finished with all the preparations?" When everyone had finished putting on the handcuffs, Origa looked around at all of them. "There are twenty minutes left until the exam starts. Let's not have any hard feelings on either side, regardless of the outcome! Whether you kill or get killed, hunt or get hunted, win or lose, this is the real deal, isn't it?"

The opening chime rang out at nine thirty—

Biiiiiiiiiiiiiiiiiiing, booooooooong...
Baaaaaaaaaang, boooooooooong...

—and the nine people on the escape team leaped out of the open gate all at once. The first Deadly Exit Exam in the history of the academy had begun.

X   X   X

"Run! Let's gain as much distance as we can!"

The path cut through dense woodland. Feet pounding over packed earth, Kyousuke and the others raced along with determination.

Naoki and Sanae were in the lead, with Fuyou and the rest of the Akabane family serving as anchors in the back, encircling Kyousuke as the whole troop sprinted with all their might. Naoki carried Ayaka, and Basara carried Maina.

The journey from the academy gate to the goal was estimated to take four or five hours at most. However, since they would be traveling over rough terrain and since the pursuit team would be doing their best to interfere, there was not that much leeway in the six-and-a-half-hour time limit.

As Naoki had shouted, they needed to gain as much distance as possible in the thirty minutes before the first group of pursuers was sent out. They hoped for a simple escape, but…there was no way it would be that easy.

Sure enough—

"…Oh? It seems that someone has joined us," muttered Fuyou, who was running in the rear of the group.

It had been less than an hour since they had left the academy.

"Huh?!" Naoki turned to look back, slowing down and preparing to attack. "Already? They're too fast!! What the hell kind of speed—?"

Quickly, Naoki's mouth clamped shut in surprise. In the distance, beyond the rustling leaves, there came a low rumbling sound, like an engine growing rapidly closer.

"…Tch." Naoki clicked his tongue. "They're using some kinda vehicle, aren't they? So that's why… Hey, you guys, hold up! We gotta turn on our pursuers!"

"Yes," Fuyou confirmed, coming to a stop. "There are currently four people in pursuit." She turned around and opened her parasol.

Kagura and Basara (the latter of whom had put Maina down) stepped forward on either side of Fuyou, as if to protect their mother.

"One person every two seconds… This won't take more than ten. I'll cut them down by myself."

"I can kill all of them in half the time. But why don't we kill them together?"

Kagura took out her iron fan, and Basara put his hand into his kimono sleeve.

And then—

* * *

"Ah...ah..."

"Heh-heh, found you! We'll hunt you to our heart's content!"

"We couldn't kill you at the athletic festival or the Purgatory Festival, so..."

"This time for sure, we'll slice you to bits! The teachers won't have to do anything. With our blades, we Ripper Jacks will mutilate and kill!"

Amon Abashiri, Takamoto Yatsuzaki, Motoharu Yatsuzaki, and Takakage Yatsuzaki. The four of them were straddling off-road bikes, chasing after Kyousuke's group.

"Ha!" Kagura laughed through her nose and opened the iron fan gripped in both hands. "I thought I had seen their faces somewhere before. Aren't they the third-rate losers who went bright red when provoked by Offal Ayaka at the culture festival? They're no opponents for me!"

Basara shrugged and jeered. "Ha! You're right. Judging from the look of it, they're far below average. Calling them underdogs would be an understatement!"

The moment he laid eyes on Basara's face, "Faceless" Amon Abashiri, who had been silent, suddenly went insane.

"Ah......ah......aaaaaaaaaaaahhh?!" Abashiri abandoned his bike and leaped to the ground, brandishing an enormous chain saw. There was a low reverberation—*dududududu*—as the spinning blades hummed.

With a shrill voice loud enough to drown out the chain saw, Abashiri charged at Basara. "Faaaaaaaaaaaaaaaaaaaaaaace! Give it to meeeeeeeeeeee. Give me your faaaaaaaaaaaaace!"

At the same time—

".......Ah. Isn't that the little girl that came to get in our way?"

"Yeah. She's just as audacious as the Kamiya girl, isn't she?"

"Looks like she's underestimating us—should we kill her?"

"Let's kill her."

"Let's do it."

The Ripper Jacks seemed to have narrowed their focus to Kagura. They dismounted, and each drew a pair of sharp *shamshir* swords. Three brothers carrying six blades that shone as they advanced.

Kagura's and Basara's smiles disappeared at the same time.

"Flap, Hayabusa."

"Dance, Kujaku."

Slice!

The blades of their specialized weapons, double-edged sword and iron-ribbed fan, swung faster than the eye could see—

Decapitating their prey and sending the heads flying.

Crossing paths, Basara took Abashiri with his double-edged sword, while Kagura took Motoharu and Takakage with her iron-ribbed fan—*killing them all in the blink of an eye.* The only one to escape death was the oldest brother, Takamoto.

"............Ah?"

Takamoto balked while his younger brothers' heads danced before his eyes. And then:

"Please die."

Kagura's iron fan lashed out at the back of his neck.

"AaaaaaaaaaaaaaaaAAAAAAAAA!"

"......?!"

Takamoto raged. Swinging his own blade, he deflected Kagura's attack, stepping back to put some distance between them.

"Motoharu?! Takakageee! Gah...you biiiiiiiiitch!"

Two corpses lay fallen, fountains of blood gushing from their severed necks. Pulling his gaze away from the remains of his siblings, Takamoto glared at Kagura with eyes full of rage. The skull scarf that he always wore had slipped off, and his face was exposed, revealing bared teeth.

Kagura clicked her tongue, seemingly unfazed by the death glare.

"......Tch."

Shaking the blood off her fan, she frowned. "I failed to kill one, huh...? I'm the one who should feel irritated. It's an embarrassment to have my attack deflected by such a pathetic little minnow."

"Ah-ha-ha! That's so true, right? Get it together, Kagura... Are you trying to dishonor the Akabane name? Although I suppose I shouldn't talk. I mean, I only killed one, after all."

Turning off the chain saw, Basara looked at the head held in his hands. Grasping the hair in his left hand, he removed the bandages wrapped around the face.

"Geh?! My my, you're terribly burned. What an awful visage... I guess we know why you were shouting things like 'Give me your face.' My condolences."

Mumbling to himself, Basara casually tossed the head aside. It landed with a wet thud. The blood flowing from the severed heads and bodies, six pieces in all, quickly stained the forest path. In just an instant, only several seconds, the scenery had completely changed.

"Uh—"

Kyousuke, who had watched the scene dumbfounded, from beginning to end, fell to his knees the moment he smelled the scent wafting on the breeze, assailed by nausea. Maina fell flat on her backside, and Eiri anxiously asked, "......Are you all right?"

Ayaka stared, eyes fixed on the corpses, but Sanae covered her face with her hand and said, "Don't look too much, okay, honey?"

Naoki groaned. "I guess they were students, but...no mercy, huh? Nasty..."

"Is it nasty? Oh-ho. That's an awful thing to say." Fuyou swung her kimono sleeve and covered her mouth as she laughed. "Oh-ho-ho! Both Kagura and Basara carried out kills in a single stroke, didn't they? There shouldn't have been enough time to feel pain. It's an extremely humane method of execution. The point is—"

Fuyou paused for a moment and looked pointedly at Takamoto. "You there. Just try to lay a hand on these people, and your head will roll next."

"......?!"

Takamoto jumped with a start, and he took his eyes off Kagura. Fuyou smiled.

"—Is what I should tell you. Moreover, since you tried to lay hands on them, it was self-evident that it would come to this. You should not feel bitter toward House Akabane but rather toward your own immaturity, weakness, indiscretion, cliché, and stunted nature... oh-ho—Kagura?"

"Yes, Lady Fuyou?"

"Put him down."

"Yes, Lady Fuyou."

Kagura nodded and brandished her iron-ribbed fan again. Taka-moto flinched and whined. His fiery rage at the murder of his younger brothers was replaced by cold terror at Fuyou's icy threat.

Basara, meanwhile, yawned. "...*Fwah*. Well, be sure to take him out with the next attack! If you fail to kill him again, I'll make you regret it, okay?"

"Hah! Nonsense. A fluke like that won't happen again. I'd never fall behind the likes of you, big brother. Why don't you hush and go back to your e-mails or something?"

"Okeydokey." Basara put both of his swords away and pulled out his cell phone instead.

"...Hmph," Kagura snorted and turned toward Takamoto. "Well then, shall I take your life? Farewell!" She crouched low, preparing to launch into another assault.

The next moment—

"Yeees, *farewell to you all, too!*"

"......?!"

Two figures leaped into view, attacking Kagura and Basara simulta-neously. Kagura instantly jumped out of the way, and at her feet was something silver—a long shape like a snake wriggled, moving straight past her. As for Basara—

"Uagh?!"

His attention focused on his e-mails, Basara was slow to react. Something struck him from above. Deep crimson fragments scattered from Basara's hands.

Basara, who leaped back in surprise, and Kagura, who was correct-ing her stance, took aim at the newcomers.

"Kuh—" "Whoooa?!"

The shapes suddenly changed. They changed angles, they changed trajectory, they changed speed, and Kagura and Basara moved to escape the attackers that came after them again and again.

Kagura guarded herself with her iron-ribbed fan as one of the mov-ing shapes cut a path through the air just above the ground, then sud-denly flew upward.

"Soar, Yatagarasu."

As he took a step back, Basara pulled a hidden weapon from his sleeve. The black *shuriken* that sliced through the air was quickly obscured by the branches and foliage of the trees overhead.

Ching!

The flying blade was blocked by a streak of silver.

"...Tch." Basara scowled, looking upward, his gaze fixed on—

"My, my. You failed to kill me again...and I thought you were going to get me that time, heh-heh! That's just like you Akabane—can't you do anything the nooorrrmal way?"

A young man wearing a bright red dress shirt and slender white pants, with flashy blond hair and heavy, gaudy makeup. He smiled, his lips glossy with lipstick, and narrowed his eyes, fringed with mascara-covered eyelashes. He stood atop a branch, looking down at Basara. In both hands, he was gripping strange, exotic weapons:

Silver weapons like snakes, or perhaps vine whips. Dangling loosely from the top of the branch on which the man was standing, nearly thirty feet in length and bristling with jagged teeth that sprouted like thorns in thick bunches, *they were not whips but blades.*

The ground and tree bark were mangled and sliced where the man's weapons had passed by, covering them in innumerable gashes. Basara's right arm, which had been grazed by one of the strange blades, was in the same state. Blood dripped from the hem of his tattered sleeve.

Still partly dazed, Takamoto looked up at the man. "M-Mr. Barazono..."

"Takamoto, darling!" The man smiled. "What's that face for? Are you feeling blue because your brothers got killed? Oh-ho-ho, how cute... I don't get to see you make expressions like that very often, Takamoto, honey. But—"

The man's smile disappeared. He looked down at Takamoto with cold, hard eyes. "...I'm disappointed. I thought you three boys were capable of so much more, and yet two died so very quickly. And the only one left is stuck in such a predicament—it's no good, is it? If you're not any use, then get out of the way. I—Dahlia Barazono of the Kaleido Blade—shall attack my dear student's enemies."

"Hah!" Kagura sneered. "Are you planning to take all of us on by yourself? That goes beyond overconfidence. If you want to die that badly, have your wish—"

"Back off."

Basara checked Kagura before she could attack, his voice low.

"—What?" Kagura looked back suspiciously. Basara—

"I'm gonna slaughter this fairy. I'll torture him to death. How dare you... How dare you *destroy my precious address book*, you bastaaaaaard?!"

—Basara was livid, baring gritted teeth, veins bulging on his forehead. In his bloody right hand, he gripped the shattered remains of his cell phone, the upper half of which had been completely cut to pieces along with his arm.

"...Huh?"

"Eh?"

Kagura and Barazono gasped in unison.

However, Basara was apparently quite serious. Wracked by furious bloodlust, he groaned. "Kirie, Kuchiha, Kaoru Sakuya, Shiki, Alyssa, Ritsu, Ryouko Makishimamuza—and those are just the girls who I picked up at the culture festival, not counting Maiko and Maria and Anza and Yuu and Kiki and Sophia and Ingel and Miss Nao, and so many others! Now I can't contact any of theeeeeeeeem?! Aaah...hey, what am I supposed to do? What am I supposed to do about this, seriously?! It would be so tiresome to go to each one of them and ask for their numbers again, but...plus, what about the girls whose addresses I don't know? Hey, what do I do?"

"E-even if you ask me..."

"...I don't know."

Kagura and Barazono were astonished by the young man, who was now shouting in anger.

Basara turned and chucked the broken, unusable cell phone behind him. "Lady Fuyou..." He pulled a *chakram* blade out from his left sleeve. "Please take Kagura and the others and go ahead. *I'll deal with this guy.*"

"My, my...is that all right?"

"Naturally. I plan to torture him to death, so it may take a while—"

Basara answered, then looked at Kyousuke and the others. An embarrassed smile crossed his lips as he looked at Maina, her trembling shoulders being held by Eiri. "Sorry, little Maina…I won't be able to protect you anymore. I have to kill this bastard. But wait for me. I'll definitely catch up after I finish this…so I want you to stay alive until then. Now that my whole girlfriend directory has been destroyed, you're the only one I have left…if I lose you, too, then I…I…!"

Lukewarm gazes poured down on Basara, who ground his molars, looking heartbroken.

Eiri sighed and helped Maina to her feet. "Big brother…"

"Hm? What is it, Eiri? 'You have me, too, big brother'? Even for me, incest is a bit too much…"

"…Just die already."

"She's right," Kagura agreed. "You really ought to do us all a favor and die in the process of killing that teacher. But"—she closed the blades of her iron-ribbed fan and turned on her heel as she spit out the words—"if you get yourself killed, it will harm the Akabane name, so please do whatever it takes to win. May you find fortune in battle, brother."

"—Hah-hah. Leave it to me!"

With that response, Basara let loose the *chakram*. The ring-shaped blade sliced through the air, swooping toward Barazono. However—

"Hah. Hooraaaaaay!"

When Barazono swung his left arm, a snakelike sword flipped up and intercepted the *chakram*. Spinning his own exotic weapon, he easily deflected every one of the bunch of *shurikens* that came flying at him next.

"To have such a good man as this for company! We are going to have plenty of fun. I'll make you forget all about those girls you lost, hmm?"

Leaping off his branch, Barazono fluttered about beautifully. He twisted his body and moved both arms, and his two strange weapons wriggled, pulsed, and squirmed as if they were alive.

As the name Kaleido Blade indicated, Barazono's sword techniques were infinitely unpredictable. With a high-pitched, metallic roar, he commanded the two swinging blades as they came in for an attack.

"Wail, Hototogisu."

Basara unleashed a great variety of concealed weapons from the sleeves of his kimono and from the hem of his *hakama* pants to meet the oncoming assault. Metal and metal, blade and blade collided. As Kyousuke and the others ran off, the musical sounds of swordplay echoed through the forest behind them.

They moved forward without looking back. Back from the way they had come—

"Aaaaaaaaaaaaaaaaaaaaaaaaaaaaaaaaaaaaaaaaaaaaaaaaaaaaaaa hhhhhhhhhhhhhhhhh!"

"......?!"

Takamoto's scream cut through the air. Kyousuke unintentionally looked back, and his eyes were met with the image of Takamoto springing at Basara, *shamshir* raised overhead, and the immediate aftermath.

"Ah—"

Courtesy of Basara's sickle and chain, Takamoto was quickly decapitated.

X   X   X

Splash!

Kyousuke scooped up cold water with both hands and rinsed his face. It was but a slight relief.

After separating from Basara and running for another hour, Kyousuke and the others had decided to take a short rest by the banks of the river that ran through the forest. The river was shallow, about twenty yards wide, and the water flowed fairly quickly, sending large rocks tumbling downstream. In the shade of an especially large boulder at the edge of the water, Kyousuke took a deep breath and closed his eyes, standing on a dry part of the riverbed. Inside his mind, the spectacle he had witnessed not long ago—the merciless slaughter of the other students—replayed itself many times over. Over and over and over and over.

"Hey."

A blunt voice from above interrupted Kyousuke's thoughts. He paused, still kneeling next to the river.

"You okay, brat?"

"......You can see for yourself."

Kyousuke raised his dripping face to see his father standing beside him, puffing on a cigarette. He had removed his sunglasses. He wasn't looking at Kyousuke, staring instead out over the river. For a while, time flowed by in silence.

"First time?" Naoki eventually asked. There was no need to wonder what he was talking about.

"...Yeah." Kyousuke nodded weakly.

Naoki exhaled purple smoke and laughed. "Ha-ha. Even though you spent half a year in an awful school swarming with murderers?"

".........."

"Well, I guess that makes some kinda sense. There wouldn't be much point in recruiting and training a whole bunch of killer students if they just let 'em murder each other left and right, eh? You'd hafta wonder what the point of having teachers in the first place was. But look—"

Naoki turned to Kyousuke. His expression was stern but earnest. "Maybe you hadn't seen it firsthand, but almost everyone at that school got there by *doing that kind of shit*," he explained.

Perhaps Kyousuke had been trying not to see the truth until just now...

"Even the ones that you said were good, that were interesting, that you couldn't hate, that you could respect, every single one of them has committed a murder. Aside from you and Ayaka and Eiri...every one a' the bastards has killed at least one person, some way more than that, right? Is it 'fun' living with people like that? Is it 'all right' to live out the next two and a half years of your youth with them?"

He could neither answer nor refute his father's words.

Thoughts and feelings that until now had remained vague suddenly had substance. The weight of the truth pressed down on him. Terror and disgust—Kyousuke remembered those feelings from his arrival at Purgatorium Remedial Academy, feelings that had been worn away in the course of half a year of school life until they had evaporated. He clenched his fists and ground his teeth.

Naoki puffed on his cigarette. "The reason me an' Sanae hid our jobs from you, Kyousuke...was because we didn't want to pull you kids into this world."

"—Eh?"

"It's also the reason we tried to work mostly overseas and almost never came home. Because our jobs aren't respectable and there's a lot of danger...it's not uncommon to meet killers like those. So you hafta pay special attention to how you conduct yourself. We tried to be careful and not get you kids mixed up in it. But despite it all—"

Naoki chewed on his cigarette, and a vein bulged on his forehead. His leather gloves creaked. "To think things turned out like this, huh...!"

"......Mm."

Kyousuke's body was paralyzed, brimming with anger. He was full of unspeakable feelings. He had been sent to Purgatorium Remedial Academy because of the physical ability he had inherited from his father and because of his own recklessness in using it. His plan to protect his sister had driven him into a corner, and in the end, he had to be rescued by his family. It was truly pathetic...

"S-sorry. If only I had done a better job—"

"—Huh?"

As he started to apologize timidly, Naoki glared at him with narrowed eyes.

I-I'm gonna get hit! Kyousuke thought and stiffened reflexively.

"What're you apologizing for, brat? You didn't do anything wrong... I messed up. I didn't protect you at a crucial time."

"............Huh?"

He couldn't believe his ears. In the fifteen years since he had been born into this world, Naoki had never once apologized to Kyousuke. Even though he had apologized to Ayaka and Sanae, he had always been excessively strict on Kyousuke, and never in his wildest dreams did Kyousuke think he would ever hear his father admit guilt.

Turning to face his bewildered son, Naoki continued.

"That's why this time we came to protect you. I said it before the exit exam began, but I won't let 'em lay a single finger on you or Ayaka... and you're absolutely going to be allowed to drop out of this school. I'm gonna get you out of this shitty place immediately and take you back where you belong. And then, Kyousuke—"

Naoki grinned broadly and laughed. "We'll have a good meal together as a family, okay? Like old times."

"Old man......"

Looking at that powerful smile, the anxiety and fear that had hovered over him quietly dissipated. The father who had always been nothing but an object of fear was more reassuring than anyone else right now.

Embarrassed by his sudden sentimentality, Kyousuke looked away, raising his hands to his face to hide his spontaneous smile.

"O-oh…that's right—let's do that. How should I say, that's really… um… Thank you? You're still the same old man. You've done nothing but talk a big game, but somehow or other I…r-respect you, you damn geezer!"

"—Huh?"

As soon as Kyousuke had spit out the words, Naoki's expression changed. The relaxed atmosphere instantly became tense, filled by a terrific feeling of oppression. Kyousuke went pale.

Naoki was squinting his eyes and furrowing his brow. Had he hit upon something that would make his father lose his temper? He tried to explain himself in a mad rush.

"No, that's…that's not right! Calling you a 'damn geezer' was just me trying to hide my embarrassment. I didn't mean to use abusive language, so, um—"

However, Naoki ignored that. He kicked off the dry riverbed and closed the distance between them in an instant, grabbing Kyousuke by the shoulders and violently pulling him close.

"Waaaaaah?! I'm s-sorry—"

"*There's a sniper on the opposite shore!* Everyone, hide behind the rocks!"

"……?!"

Naoki shouted, and the next moment—

"Ayaka—guh?!" "Mamaaaaaa?!"

A scream and a shriek rang out.

There was a bullet hole gouged in the surface of the rock just where Kyousuke had been standing moments before Naoki had pulled him out of the way.

Taking cover behind a nearby boulder, Naoki spit out the word "Bastard!"

Sanae and Ayaka were taking refuge behind a rock formation some ten yards away, but—

"Sanae!"

Sanae stood grimacing with her back to a boulder. Bright red blood was flowing between her fingers as they held her right shoulder.

Ayaka began to panic. "Aaahhh, Mama's...Mama's gonna die! W-we have to have a moment of silence—"

"Don't. I'm all right, it just grazed me... I'm not dying, I'm not dying." With a bitter smile, Sanae took off her leather jacket. She took medical tools out of her waist pouch and began to perform first aid with practiced movements.

Naoki breathed a sigh of relief. *"Phew...looks like my family is safe for now. But the others—"*

"It seems as if everyone is uninjured."

"Whoa?!"

Startled by a voice suddenly very close to his ear, Naoki stumbled backward. The moment he moved out from behind the boulder—

Bang! Bang! Bang!

"Whoooooooaaa?!"

A hail of bullets cut through the air. Desperately dodging them as he crawled back to safety, Naoki shouted, "Are ya tryin' to kill me?!"

Fuyou was standing with them behind the boulder, appearing as if out of thin air. She put her hand to her mouth. "Oh my, I am sorry. I was not trying to surprise you...oh-ho-ho!"

"There's nothin' to laugh at. Geez...well? Is everyone all right?"

"Yes. You can't see from here, but Eiri and Kagura each quickly took cover behind a rock. Maina, despite the barrage of bullets, is miraculously untouched and escaped to hide in the same place as my Eiri. Furthermore, there are no snipers on this shore."

"...You sure?"

"Yes. For now, that is...though there are five of them. There's a danger that they may surround us in a pincer attack, so we can't afford to take our time. What should we do?"

"Let's see—that depends on their skills, but—"

Naoki picked up a stone near his hand and casually threw it.

—Instantly, the small rock was blasted out of the air.

"Guh..." Naoki was at a loss for words. "D-damn, they're accurate... Are they some kinda freaks? If we just rush out like assholes, they'll shoot us down in seconds."

"Probably. If I were to guess, one of them is the teacher 'Outrange Outrage' Mihiro Mizuchi. A sniper of unparalleled accuracy, said to have once shot a mosquito out of the air from a distance of two kilometers. If we try to escape through the forest, it's likely that we will be picked off through the gaps in the trees."

"Seriously...?"

"However." Fuyou took out a deep crimson cell phone and smiled. "The remaining four people are probably students. Surely they will not be as skilled. I believe my children can break through their ranks without any trouble. Hello, Kagura?"

"Yes, Lady Fuyou?"

"I have a request. Three minutes from now, when it is precisely midday, you and Eiri shall advance on the snipers on the opposite shore. Eliminate them."

"...Acknowledged. I will kill them all."

"It seems there is only one true sharpshooter among them. Please be careful, all right?"

"All right. But I don't expect any trouble. I highly doubt they could follow the movements of two Akabane through a narrow scope. They might try, but I have no intention of letting them succeed."

Kagura's voice was full of confidence, and for a moment Fuyou seemed as if she was about to say something to her, but—

"...Yes. I'll leave it to you, all right?" she said and ended the call, then called Eiri next. Normally, the students at Purgatorium Remedial Academy did not have cell phones, but Fuyou had provided them to enable communication between the members of their party. Kyousuke and Ayaka had also been given one each.

"...Understood. I can't kill them, but I can subdue them..."

"That's fine. I will be there to assist you when the moment comes. We're counting on you."

Fuyou finished issuing instructions to her daughters and closed her cell phone.

"—Kill."

She threw off her long-tailed haori jacket and tossed it out from behind the boulder.

"......?!"

Kagura and Eiri leaped out from behind their cover and began to cross the river. The air was suddenly filled with a frightening cacophony. The clack of Kagura's geta kicking off of a boulder, the ping of bullets grazing rocks, the scrape of Eiri's shoes digging into stone, the unique and peculiar sound of gunfire hitting water... The sisters, crossing the river on a bridge of rocks, did not hesitate.

In moments they had finished crossing the river and arrived on the opposite shore. Now they would annihilate every single one of the snipers lurking in the thicket...

"Eh?"

Kagura sounded confused. The haori jacket that Fuyou had thrown as a decoy fell undamaged to the ground. The clatter of geta stopped.

—*Splash!*

The sound of water, as if someone had lost their balance *and fallen into the river from atop a boulder.* The sound of Eiri's shoes also stopped, and silence descended over the riverbank.

"............Eh?"

Eiri let out a shocked noise. It did not look like whoever had fallen into the river was coming back up. There was also no response from Kagura. All expression vanished from Fuyou's face, and a chill ran up Kyousuke's spine.

—*Impossible.*

"Ka...Kaguraaaaaaaaaa?!"

"Wha?! Hey, idiot, don't be hasty!"

"Tch—"

Kyousuke leaped out from behind the boulder, followed by Naoki, and then Fuyou stepped out from the opposite side. As he was being dragged back by the scruff of his neck by his father, Kyousuke's eyes fell upon—

An unmoving figure lying prostrate on the water's surface and *blood flowing out of its head, dyeing the river bright red.* Also—

"Oh-ho-ho-ho-ho! How do you do, fugitives?"

"......Miss...Shamaya?"

Standing on the opposite shore was a beautiful girl. Her long, honey-colored hair was flecked with red, and her emerald-green eyes sparkled in the sunlight. In her right hand, Saki Shamaya held a gory hatchet.

Blood spatter covered her hair, her face, and her uniform, a ghastly adornment to her natural beauty.

"Th-that blood—"

"…Yes?" Shamaya looked down at her own body. "Oh, this? I got a little messy while disposing of my target. I do apologize for my sullied appearance."

"—Target?"

"Yes, that's right. Those insolent bastards trying to lay hands on my dear ● ● ● ● friends Miss Akabane and Miss Igarashi and interfering with my darling Kyousuke's Deadly Exit Exam!"

…I'm sure I just imagined the word before friends *just now.*

On top of a boulder about five yards away from the opposite shore, Eiri mumbled a quiet "…Just die already." At her feet was—

A female student who apparently had had her head smashed in by Shamaya's hatchet and then been tossed aside, her corpse leaning against the boulder.

—A long black braid. With a yellow armband that read "Public Morals Committee" running around her left arm, the girl in the water was easily recognizable. Facedown, she did not so much as twitch.

Kagura had stopped about halfway across the river and was staring blankly at Shamaya.

"……Huh? Wh-what are you talking about…target? Disposing of? ● ● ● ● friends? My big sister is still a virgin in body and soul, so even assuming that last part is a complete fabrication…it's impossible to understand. That was your ally…wasn't it?"

"Yes, she was an ally."

Past tense.

Shamaya hoisted the bloody hatchet and smiled sweetly. "However, things have changed. Kuroki and Kiriu and Miss Mizuchi—"

—*Swoosh*. A sound from inside the thicket.

Shamaya whipped around to face the noise. "And yooooooooouuu! I'll dispose of every one of you and save my darling Kyousukeeeeeeeee, Miss Gosooooooouuuuuuu!!"

She threw the hatchet. The spinning blade flew through the air and disappeared into the thicket.

"Fgyah?!" A shriek filled the air. "Gyaaaaaaaaaaaaaaaaaaaaaaaaaahhh, ooowwwwwwwwwwwww?! D-dying...I'm dyiiiiiiiiiiiiiiiiiinnngggggg?!"

A female student with a black ponytail rolled out of the bushes. Holding the top of her bleeding right shoulder and crying out in agony, she writhed around on the sandy silt.

Shamaya sighed and approached the girl—Anji Gosou of the Public Morals Committee. She kicked her in the stomach and grinned.

"How do you do, Miss Gosou?"

"Sa-Saki......" Gosou's cheeks twitched as she looked up at Shamaya. The word "ultimate," among other words, was written on them. Her voice was small and pitiful, and her body trembled with fear. "Y-yyyy-you bitch, Saki... D-d-d-d-d-don't tell me everyone's... Miss Mizuchi, you...k-kkkk-killed them...didn't you...?"

"Yes." Shamaya nodded and narrowed her emerald eyes. "I did kill them. I crept up on them while they were focused on sniping, and one by one...oh-ho-ho. Especially Miss Mizuchi, I gathered up all my gratitude for her taking care of me until now and thoroughly... I mangled her face so badly that you wouldn't be able to recognize her anymore! Ha, ha-ha-ha-ha-ha-ha ...it was the greatest! To hack and cleave to my heart's content at the person above me, the one who was always so thorough in her punishments! Ahh, it felt so good. Plus I helped my darling Kyousuke, and afterward—"

Shamaya's eyes glittered sadistically. She pulled a second hatchet out from her skirt. "Afterward, all that's left is to kill you. The useless Miss Gosou!"

Shamaya raised her weapons overhead.

"Eee..." Gosou gulped. "Sa-Saki...don't tell me, from the very beginning—"

"Yes. I was always planning to betray you. That way it would be easier to kill you, you understand. My feelings of longing for Kyousuke are the real thing...and for that reason, I am doing my very best, killing for the sake of the outcome that my darling Kyousuke desires!"

"Miss Shamaya..."

"Saki—"

"Well then, Gosou." Looking down at her astonished classmate, Shamaya prepared to strike. "Adieu."

The hefty, dark gray hatchet swung down at the top of Gosou's head—

"〰〰〰〰〰?!"

—but before the blade reached her, Gosou's eyes rolled back in her head, and bubbles of spittle formed at the corners of her mouth. She had fainted from the terror.

"Hm?" Shamaya raised her eyebrows. She stood, frozen in mid-swing. "......*Sigh*. I suppose that's fine. Sh-she's always been a bit off... and in a different way than Miss Igarashi, mind. Ah, well, my desire to kill her has completely withered away. Whatever shall we do with this poor idiot...?"

Shamaya grumbled in complaint and lowered her hatchet. Closing her eyes, she took a deep breath. Then—

"Kyousukeeeeeeeeeeeeeeeeeeeeeeeeeeeeeeeeeeeeeeeeeeeeeeeeeeeeeeeeee eeeeeee!"

"......?!"

Still gripping the hatchet in her right hand, Shamaya, covered in the blood of her victims, leaped onto a boulder and with ferocious speed crossed the river and thrust herself at Kyousuke. Eiri and Kagura had to jump to avoid her.

"I love yoooooooooooooooooooooooooooooooooooooooooooooouuu uuuuuuuuuuuuuuuu!"

"Shama—"

"Don't be an idiot, Kyousuke! Now that your guard's down, she's gonna try and kill—uaaaaaaaaaahhh?!"

Naoki, recognizing the danger in Shamaya's erratic appearance, had moved to protect his son, but Shamaya threw her hatchet to the side and energetically embraced him. Naoki was pushed to the ground as Shamaya rubbed her hair and clothes and face, sticky with blood, all over him, wriggling vigorously.

"I did it, I killed them! I fulfilled my duty! I did my very best to be useful to my beloved Kyousukeee! And so, and sooo, now I can use all my power to show you my love, right?! We'll do ●●, ●●, ●●●●●, ●●●●...●●●, and ●●●, and even ●●●●... ha-ha-ha-ha!"

"Ahh?! Hey, wait a second! I'm not Kyousuke—waaaaaaahhh?! Why are you trying to take off my belt?! D-don't tell me... Hey, quit it! I told you I'm not Kyousuke—heeeeeey?!"

"Oh-ho-ho-ho! I killed three people, so you can do it to me three times, all right? That's the reward for my efforts! My prize, my prize, oh-ho-ho-ho-ho-ho-ho!"

"U-uhh..."

Naoki was completely flustered, and Shamaya, blinded by her passion, did not seem to realize that he wasn't Kyousuke. If his father hadn't intercepted her, Kyousuke would have been in his place—Kyousuke shuddered at the thought. Beside him—

"Naoki, sweeeeeetie? You knew this would happen, and you let her tackle you on purpose, didn't you? Are you finished preparing to die?"

Having finished treating the bullet wound in her shoulder, Sanae had come out from behind the boulder and now stood cracking her knuckles.

"My, my. In any case, I'm glad everyone is safe... Her betrayal was a happy miscalculation. However, Kyousuke...whatever kind of relationship do you have with this girl? I want to hear all the details. When we have the time...oh-ho-ho..."

Fuyou smiled as she put her long-tailed haori jacket back on.

Eventually, Shamaya realized that Naoki was not Kyousuke, and then she assaulted Kyousuke instead while Sanae laid into her husband. Once the uproar had settled down, Kyousuke and the rest of the nine of them left the riverbed behind.

X　　　　X　　　　X

"—And?" Naoki demanded, holding his swollen cheek as they ran through the forest. "What kinda relationship do you have with that girl, you damn brat?"

Shamaya, being well acquainted with the terrain of the island, had taken the initiative to lead and was helping Kyousuke and the others with their escape.

Kyousuke, who was being pulled along by the girl in question, turned to look back. "W-well...how should I say, she...is an upperclassman who has helped me out sometimes? At the Summer Death Camp she nearly killed—I mean, we got to know each other and then became friends(?). After that—"

"That's when we started dating, isn't it?" Shamaya pulled on Kyousuke's arm, and her cheeks blushed faintly red. "And then after that I spent night after night with my dear Kyousuke, grinding and pounding—"

"Miss Shamaya?!" "What did you say?!"

"In my wildest dreams, I mean. That is what I truly desire! *Mon Dieu!*"

"............."

Kyousuke and Naoki were at a loss for words as a squirming Shamaya shared her unspeakable fantasies. Ayaka, running alongside Naoki, made her opinion clear: "Gross!"

However, Shamaya did not seem the least bit bothered. Even though nobody had asked, she enthusiastically told them things that ought to have been censored, well and clearly showing her carnal desires—or rather, her truest feelings—for her dear boy toy.

"...I've told you about my longing for my darling Kyousuke. And honestly speaking, I don't want us to be separated. I don't want him to drop out. However..."

Squeezing his hand, Shamaya spoke plainly. "I don't want my beloved Kyousuke to be sad any longer. I don't want to force my own feelings if it means that I also trample his desires underfoot. And that is why I have decided to accept the privilege of collaborating with you on his Deadly Exit Examination. After all, the fact that Kyousuke is the Warehouse Butcher—*isn't true, is it?*"

"Eh?! Miss Shamaya, when did you realize—?"

"I didn't. I was informed by Miss Mizuchi before the examination started. It was a false charge that got you enrolled here, and in truth you have never killed a single person, she said. Perhaps she was trying to disenchant me, since she knew how I love you so. Unfortunately for her, it had quite the opposite effect."

"...Opposite effect?"

"Yes. My heart has been touched by you, Kyousuke, fighting without fear and conducting yourself with the utmost courage, even though you're just an ordinary person! I truly wanted to do everything I could to help you. In place of Kyousuke, who cannot kill anyone, I would do the killing, I thought..."

She smiled. The smell of blood still hung on her.

"Miss Shamaya......"

Kyousuke couldn't shake the fear and disgust he felt toward the Killer Queen, but when it came to the young woman Shamaya...he still held on to some feelings of goodwill and friendship—

"...Thank you so much. After all, I can't bring myself to hate you,

Miss Shamaya. I can't understand how you can kill people, and I don't want to, but…I can see that there are a lot of good things about you, too."

Kyousuke had honestly come to feel that way. Since witnessing his first death, his heart had weighed heavy in his chest, but now he felt just the slightest bit lighter.

"…Hmph," Naoki snorted.

"Kyo-Kyousuke, darling…"

Shamaya's eyes were perfect circles.

Looking back into her clear emerald-green eyes, Kyousuke continued, "That's why, to tell you the truth, I think I'll also feel lonely when we part…never being able to see you again once I drop out—"

"Never again? Surely that's not the case?"

"Uh, no, you see…"

Shamaya would be graduating into the criminal underworld, so if Kyousuke managed to drop out and return to polite society, there would be no chance that they would meet again. For an ordinary person and a professional killer to have any involvement would be crazy—

"No need to worry! If there are no chances to meet, then we can just make our own opportunities. Whether underground or in broad daylight, it's the same world… Using any spare moment between assignments, I will take the initiative to come and see my darling Kyousuke! And force my way…oh-ho-ho. Living in the criminal underworld, I won't have anything to do with the laws of polite society. I plan on doing just as I please!"

"—Huh?"

Hang on a second.

"Didn't you just say that you don't want to force your own feelings and trample mine underfoot?! You're brimming over with desire to trample them!"

"That was that, and this is this."

"They're the same!"

"Oh-ho-ho! Your mouth says no, but your heart says yes… It will probably hurt a little bit at first, but before long I'll make it feel really good, okay?"

"Hurt?! Just what are you planning to do to me?!"

It was too frightening. Somehow or other, even after he returned to his former life, it seemed as if Kyousuke would still be looking over his shoulder for the Killer Queen. Something like happiness and something like exasperation... He had quite complicated feelings.

Shamaya, panting and drooling, her tongue half hanging out of her mouth, looked as if she would violate more than just the law.

"Gross!" Ayaka again voiced her objection.

Seeing Shamaya's wicked, disgraceful behavior, Naoki looked up at the sky. "...For a moment there, I almost thought that maybe I was the idiot in the room. But these guys are really hopeless!"

X   X   X

"Uh, um...excuse me. Mr. Naoki?"

They had been running through the forest for a little while. As if she had made up her mind about something, Eiri called out to Naoki.

"Yeah. What's up, Eiri?"

"Ah, umm...it's about my father, well...u-um... What was he like?" Eiri seemed unusually tense.

"Kyousuke, darling, did you know? The name for avocados is derived from the word for b●lls. In other words, it's said that girls who love avocados also love b●lls—"

Nodding along to Shamaya's rambling, Kyousuke strained his ears to hear the conversation between Eiri and Naoki.

"What he was like, huh...? Let's see—" After several seconds' consideration, Naoki said, "Well, he was a good guy. He had a mean look in his eye and he wasn't very civil, but he was kind and very attentive to people close to him. He was the same way on the job, and an excellent bodyguard."

Naoki's tone was gentle as he described his friend. Eiri listened with great interest. "He was, how should I put it...a distant man. He was cold but could be considerate, was reticent but strangely charming, had a fierce look but was surprisingly girly on the inside..."

"Girly?!"

"Oh yeah. Because he loved sweet things, that guy. Parfaits and cakes and ice cream, he even loved avocados!"

"............"

Thanks to Shamaya, for a moment they caught hold of an odd

meaning to Naoki's words. Shamaya was still continuing her fervent speech about something or other, but the contents were too awful, so Kyousuke had decided to ignore her.

"...Hm? That certainly is surprising. But maybe it kind of makes sense? I noticed it once or twice when I saw him caught up in reading my girls' comics."

"Ha-ha-ha! Ah, I crack up just thinkin' about it. That guy always did have a weakness for the sappy stuff—he was such a romantic... Come to think of it, he fell in love with a woman he was guarding once."

"Ah, how romantic! What happened to their love?"

"......The woman was murdered by an assassin named Crimson Cradle. That ended their relationship."

"M-Mother...that's awful. And my father married someone like that..."

"He didn't choose to marry—he was forced to marry. Because she stalked him, night and day, and never let up. But, well...someway or other, in the end, it wasn't all bad, right? He seemed relatively happy at the wedding. Not like he had fallen in love but more like he had been trapped in love."

"O-oh...so that's how things got this way. It seems entirely different from the story I heard from mother. He had some troubles, didn't he, my father...?"

Eiri was extremely interested in hearing new stories about her father from the mouth of his former friend. Naoki, who was telling her about her deceased father, also looked cheerful, and the atmosphere was one of quiet harmony.

Before long, Naoki took on a serious tone. "You know what, though? Talking like this, I can really feel that you must be his daughter, Eiri. You're exactly like Masato."

"......Huh? I-I'm...like my father?"

"Yeah. You look like your mother, but your eyes and your heart are like your father, aren't they? You seem like a nice, kind girl, Eiri."

"Ehh?! Th-th-that's—"

"Well then, Naoki. Go right ahead and accept her as Kyousuke's bride!"

"Whuh?!"

Naoki gaped at Fuyou, who had suddenly intruded into their conversation, and Eiri's voice squeaked as she gasped, "M-Mother?!"

"Ho-ho!" Fuyou laughed and whispered into Naoki's ear. "If I do say so myself, speaking as her mother, Eiri really is a splendid daughter! Her face and figure, her personality, and her pedigree… It's a rare girl who combines all three of these traits in one person, you know? And our side will by all means support their love and help them to build a happy home—"

"FUUUUUUUUUUUUCK!"

Suddenly, a single female student came crashing out of a thicket behind them. Kagura, bringing up the rear of the pack, turned around and took a combat stance with an iron-ribbed fan in each hand.

"Waah?!" Maina drew back, and Sanae moved to protect Ayaka. Naoki and Eiri put their conversation on hold, and Shamaya prepared for battle.

Middle fingers raised to the sky, her multicolored hair bristling, she was Pretty Fucking Sick—the senior student Kurisu Arisugawa.

Kurisu glared at all of them with bloodshot eyes and ranted and raved hysterically. "You're fulla shit! You've gotta be fuckin' kiddin' me, motherfuckers! Why do I hafta…hafta do this kinda life-endangering shit?! Goddamn! Jesus fuck! I'm cursin' the gods here, holy crap! Damn it, damn it, damn it, damn iiiiiiiiiit…I'm gonna slaughter every one a' ya!" She had absolutely zero chill.

"Huh?" Kagura gaped. "Is this girl insane…?"

For some reason Kurisu was all alone, and her only visible weapon was a single survival knife. She was probably concealing something else, but even so, it was hard to believe her recklessness.

In truth, Kurisu, who was stringing together abusive language, seemed completely desperate and quite frightened. The hand holding the knife was trembling, her teeth were chattering, and her skin was pallid. It looked as if she was about to vomit.

After all, she had probably been forced to participate in the Deadly Exit Exam against her will. She was probably trying to hide her fear behind strong language. It was hard to see her looking so pathetic.

"Eh…she looks really scared, so how about letting her go—?"

"Diiiiiiiiiiiiiiiiiiiiiiiiieeeeeeeeeeeeeeeeeeeeeeeeeeeeeeeeeeeeeeeeeeeeeeee eeeeeeeeeeeeee!"

Kyousuke tried to speak up, but Kurisu let out a desperate battle cry and charged straight at them. Frantically swinging her small knife, she attacked the opponent closest to her—Kagura.

"This is too idiotic."

"—Ah."

Kurisu did not manage to so much as graze her. To intercept the blade aimed at her chest, Kagura cut a swath through the air with the iron fan. Kagura slashed diagonally upward with her fan, cutting Kurisu's torso, ripping her open from the middle of her right side to her collarbone on the left side.

"Uh…ugyaaaaaaaaaaaaaaaaaaaaaaaaaaaaaaaaaaaaaaaaaaaaaaaaaa aaaahhhhhhhhh!" Kurisu screamed. Bright red fresh blood spurted from the gash cut through her belly.

"Wha—?"

Along with the blood, an immense number of insects gushed out from within Kurisu's flesh and clothes, spread their red-stained wings and legs, and began swarming Kagura, tearing at her skin with hundreds of claws and stingers and barbs.

Kagura reacted nimbly, dancing wildly with both fans. Even as she retreated to escape—

"Agagagagaga?!"

—more insects came leaping out of Kurisu's mouth and ears and nose and pursued Kagura. A huge quantity of biting lice and caterpillars and hookworms and beetles and grubs and roundworms gushed forth, so many it was a wonder where they had been hiding.

"Guh?!"

A blue flying insect, like a strange wasp, stung Kagura's left hand, and she dropped one iron-ribbed fan.

"Crappura!"

"Ayaka, watch ou—?!"

As she moved to protect Ayaka, who had leaned forward, Sanae was stung on the back of the neck by a red flying insect resembling a weird grasshopper. Like a blizzard, the remaining insects, drawn to nearby prey, attacked.

"Exterminate, Shijuukara."

A narrow light glistened in the corner of Kyousuke's eye.

The next moment, all the insects were shredded by invisible blades, reduced to mincemeat, killed en masse. Not even a single one of the spiders that had begun to swell Kurisu's eyelids and crawl out of her eye sockets survived.

In an instant, the swarm had been reduced to a mountain of chitinous corpses and a lake of sticky goo.

"......?!"

Fuyou paid no mind to Kyousuke and the others, who all stood, frozen in midmotion, wherever they had been trying to get some distance or set up to counterattack. She dashed over to Sanae, who had fallen to one knee.

"Pardon me." Tearing Sanae's hand off of her neck and putting her lips to the sting, Fuyou sucked hard.

"Nngh?!" Sanae let out a noise of surprise and pain. Fuyou briefly pulled her mouth away and spit before kissing Sanae's neck again. After repeating this many times, she peered into Sanae's face.

As she did, Fuyou's expression suddenly clouded over. "This is... probably not good..."

"Ohh—" Sanae's face was flushed red and contorted in agony, covered densely with beads of sweat. Her breathing was labored, and she hung her head.

Ayaka shook her shoulders, yelling, "Mamaaa! Mama, what happened?! Mama—"

"Nnngggh?! Stop it, Ayaka, don't rock me so violentlyyy!"

"Eh? Ah, sorry! S-something happened to your body..."

"It's poison."

"Poison?! Is Mama dying?!"

"...I don't know," Fuyou said hesitantly. "I cannot say for certain—" She turned to Kagura, who, like Sanae, had also been stung.

And although Kagura had managed to suck the poison out of her hand on her own, she was now wobbling precariously on her feet.

"A-apolo...gies...Lady...Fuyou...I...f-failed..."

"—Kagura?"

She looked as if she was about to collapse any moment. Her coppery-red eyes were nearly closed, and her gaze was distant and unfocused. A weak voice trickled from between her partly open lips. "It's getting hard...to stay...conscious...and...I'm getting very... very...sleepy now......"

It seemed that Kagura had been dosed with some kind of sleeping poison. Glaring at her as she fought the drowsiness, Ayaka grumbled, "…What the heck? I wasted my energy worrying about you. That's the perfect poison for an idiot like you."

"Sh-shut up…Offal Ayaka…if you were the one…to get poisoned… you already…would…have lost…consciousness… Damn…just die… already…!"

While rapidly losing consciousness, Kagura glared back at Ayaka.

And then—

"Huh? Too bad, we only got two of them…," said an exhausted voice.

A sullen middle-aged man in a suit as tired as his voice appeared from the same thicket as Kurisu, scratching the back of his head.

It was Kirito Busujima—the homeroom teacher of first-year Class B and a poison expert. Gazing at Kagura, who was fighting sleep, and Sanae, who was flushed and gasping for breath, Busujima said, "That girl got the sleeping toxin, and the lady got the fever toxin…no, the aphrodisiac."

"Eh?"

……*Aphrodisiac?*

Come to think of it, when Fuyou had sucked on her neck and Ayaka had shook her by the shoulders, Sanae's reactions had been awfully intense—

As the group processed this new revelation, an indescribably complicated silence descended upon them.

Fuyou sighed and held her forehead.

"I ought to be happy, since her life does not appear to be in danger, but…do you have any serious interest in murder, sir? If you were going to drug us, certainly you had more respectable poisons to use."

"Yes, well, that is true. I have many poisons that are quite lethal, like neurotoxins and hemotoxins. However, wouldn't that be kind of boring?"

"—Boring?" Fuyou's eyebrows twitched.

But Busujima did not flinch. His gloomy attitude was unchanged. "Yes. I may not look it, but I am an entertainer. I live to please. Stuffing my *friends* into the body of a student and sending them to you was a surprise present!"

Busujima looked at Kurisu, who had fallen to the ground. Her body had been filled with insects and then sliced open. She now lay lifelessly in an ocean of blood, eyes rolled back, surrounded by the scattered corpses of Busujima's "friends."

She seemed to just barely be breathing, but with so much blood loss, there was probably no way to save her. Perhaps knowing that this would happen, Busujima smiled gloomily. "Since I went to the trouble of making that 'bug bag,' I tried to use a nice variety of poisons. From paralysis toxins, sleeping toxins, neuralgia toxins, fever toxins, headache toxins, convulsion toxins, vomiting toxins, diarrhea toxins, and other assorted nonlethal toxins, to fun choices like aphrodisiacs, laughing toxins, crying toxins, farting toxins, hiccuping toxins, toxins that make you speak with a Kansai accent, toxins that make you speak like an aristocrat, toxins that make your boobs grow huge…and even some that might be beneficial, like strength toxins, reinforcement toxins, excitotoxins, analgesics, and energizing toxins, and then—"

His exhausted affect suddenly dropped. Busujima smiled like a venomous snake opening its mouth to swallow its prey. "Fiendish, exotic toxins, like neurotoxins, hemotoxins, putrefaction toxins, corrosive toxins, liquefying toxins, disintegrating toxins, scorching heat toxins, intense cold toxins, swelling toxins, lunacy toxins, death toxins, plague toxins, and so on that would lead to instant death even in small doses. It's a wonderful variety! Though I didn't use nearly all of them in the 'bug bag' opening act…"

Beside the smiling Busujima, two venomous snakes appeared from among the trees. The snake that came out of the thicket on the left had black patterns like tattoos running across its pure white scales. The one that dropped down from a branch on the right side was covered in white patterns like mandalas on its jet-black scales.

Both of them were over thirty feet long, with bodies as thick as logs. Flicking their pink tongues in and out of their enormous, triangle-shaped heads, they fixed their gray eyes on Fuyou, their prey.

Kyousuke and the others stared at the unrealistic spectacle in disbelief.

"H-hey…what are those things…?"

"…They're actual monsters, aren't they?"

"Mr. Busujima, just how big is your c●ck?! Something like that won't go in…"

"B-big one…go in…uah?! Y-your abdomen would—"

"Geez! Be quiet, Miss Bitch! Mama'll have a reaction!"

"Eee—"

"Maina! You can't cry—be quiet!!"

"...Hey, the drowsiness is wearing off...no, wait, shit...!"

Eiri pressed her hand over the panicking Maina's mouth, and Kagura shook her head in irritation.

Busujima, attended by the two huge snakes, twisted his face into a triumphant smile. He spoke in a theatrical tone. "Now then, before we begin the opera, I'd like to introduce today's cast. First, the large white snake over here is White Chapel, my dear Mizuchi, and the large black snake on this side is Black Sabbath, my darling Orochi. Their venoms are a neurotoxin and a black-death toxin, extremely deadly, so strong that even I cannot handle them carelessly. It's their one flaw... If even a drop of either toxin were to stick to my skin, it could kill me quite easily. Do take plenty of care, won't you? And then—"

Like a cobra opening its throat, Busujima raised both arms. "Poisonous toad Ikeda, poisonous slug Tsunade, poisonous lizard KJ, poisonous scorpion Klaus, poisonous spider Arakne, poisonous giant hornet Abu, poisonous grasshopper Aba...and many others."

Yellow, purple, red, brown, peach, orange, green...toxic creatures in ominous, poisonous-looking colors poured forth from thickets, from between trees, from branches above, from beneath the ground, from the treetops, from the blue sky, from inside of Busujima's suit... An uncountable number surged forth, and the lush green forest was awash in brilliant colors.

When they looked overhead, seeking refuge, wasps, grasshoppers, mosquitoes, moths, and so on were fringing the foliage of the trees and were even in the sky... Countless numbers of flying insects had formed flocks and were flitting about, the chorus of their flapping wings reverberating through the forest.

It was mayhem, as if all the innumerable creatures living on the island had gathered together at once. In the center of the toxic cloud that covered everything in all directions—Kyousuke and the others, who had been surrounded, leaned close to one another as they gazed out at the desperate scene. They could do nothing but look on in horror.

"The cast for this performance numbers six hundred sixty-six players, and *every one of them possesses a powerful poison.* It goes without saying that their fangs and claws, their stingers and barbs are all quite dangerous. However, there are some whose very flesh and blood are toxic, so even touching them requires special care! Each and every one of their poisons is fiendishly effective."

All 666 of these creatures were Busujima's special weapons, and each and every one of them was armed with the potential for certain death. Named Kirito "Venom Opera" Busujima, this was his specialty.

"M-Mr. Busujima……"

They had seriously underestimated him. Among the teachers working at Purgatorium Remedial Academy, everyone had looked down on Busujima, seeing him as nothing more than a droll, unappealing, middle-aged pushover. However—

"Despite how things may appear, since I am more or less a teacher, I am making an effort to treat my students gently. I won't force you into submission with brute force or torment you meaninglessly…but unfortunately, not everyone in front of me right now is a student of mine. Mr. Kamiya and Miss Kamiya and Miss Akabane and Miss Igarashi and Miss Shamaya…I am here to participate in the Deadly Exit Exam, but what I really want is—food for my friends. To let them hunt and feed."

As he spoke, Busujima's eyes were undoubtedly those of a predator's. It made them realize that any attempts at persuasion would be futile, in the same way that there could be no reasoning with massive man-eating snakes.

Like a conductor directing his orchestra, Busujima slowly raised his arms. The two huge black and white snakes raised up like deadly sickles, and frogs, slugs, lizards, scorpions, spiders, wasps, grasshoppers, and many other kinds of poisonous creatures crawled toward Kyousuke and the others to attack.

"Well then, let us begin the Venom Opera, in which my friends will feast and devour their prey—"

"Shall we end the performance early?"

Fuyou waved her right arm, sending narrow flashes dancing through the air. Instantly, the toxic creatures closest to Kyousuke and the others simultaneously erupted into showers of blood and ichor as they were mangled and sliced to smithereens. Again, Fuyou continued with a sweep of her left arm.

—*Hyun!*

With the faint sound of blades cutting air, a razor-wire web formed around Kyousuke and the others, protecting them even as it slaughtered their attackers. Scores of toxic creatures were cut to ribbons.

"Waaaaaaaaahhh?!"

Busujima scrambled madly in retreat, and the head of the white snake fell to the ground before his eyes. The snake had been slow to escape, and its raised head and torso had been carved into neat round slices. The remaining two-thirds of its body had been finely minced, and blood sprayed from the many wounds as the snake died.

"—Huh? M-Mizuchi…dear……" Busujima's eyes were open wide, and his face contorted wildly. He wailed. "Mizuchiiiiiiiiiiiiiiiiiiiiiiiiiiiiii iiiiiiiiiiiiiiiiiiiiiiii?!"

Fuyou smiled scornfully. "My, my. I've killed your lead actors, haven't I…? Your wicked play, or whatever it's called, will have to end before the second act."

Extending from Fuyou's sleeve were ten barely visible steel threads, just flashes of light—ultra-superfine Japanese blades, each no thicker than a strand of hair. The network of wires stretching around them was revealed by the bodily fluids of the many dead creatures—it looked just like a *birdcage.*

—*Crimson Cradle.*

"N-nasty……" Naoki shuddered.

"Naoki," Fuyou said gently, turning to face him. "I will cut open a path of retreat. Take Kyousuke and the others and go ahead, please."

"—Is that all right?"

"Yes. Because I don't need any extra burden."

"Huh? What're ya sayin'—?"

"I am not a bodyguard," Fuyou interrupted. "I am not accustomed to protecting others during combat. To do so would prevent me from fighting to my fullest. Now please go. I am entrusting my daughters to you."

"……Understood."

"Oh-ho, thank you very much. Well then, I will join you shortly—"

As Fuyou turned back to face Busujima, a gray shadow silently descended upon her from overhead, lashing out with one arm. The shadow took aim at the back of her neck, its attack carving an elegant arc through the air.

"Lady Fuyou!"

Kagura quickly blocked the attack with the iron-ribbed fan in her left hand. She swung immediately with the right-hand fan as well but struck only air. The human figure that had appeared in the air above her mother had vanished, only to reappear in a crouch beside Busujima.

The man wore a suit the color of cold ashes and a bowler hat tipped low on his head. He was old, with a stooped back and a pure-white mustache. His eyes were cloudy, yellow, and dull, but still he stared intently at Fuyou and Kagura.

"...Hm? Waah?! M-Mr. Greyman...how long have you been there?!"

"Fwoh-fwoh-fwoh..."

No one, not even the other teachers, knew a single thing about the mysterious man except for his alias, the Moon Maniac—not his origin, nor his personal history, nor his true identity or specialized weapon. The longest-serving, oldest instructor—Greyman—answered Busujima with an eerie laugh.

"The virginal young lady or the beautiful mature woman...both of them are such appetizing prey." Greyman suddenly vanished. The next moment, he appeared behind Kagura. "I'll take my time killing you, I think...," he whispered and licked Kagura's ear.

"〰〰〰〰〰〰?!" Kagura's body trembled. "D-die, please!"

But even as she spun, swinging her iron fan, the man was already gone, reappearing once again at Busujima's side. "Fwoh-fwoh-fwoh! Mr. Busujima. Which bit of prey do you prefer, I wonder?"

"......The beautiful mature woman." Busujima's eyes shone with resentment as he glared at Fuyou. It seemed befitting for one who had just had his beloved pets slaughtered. The large black snake, coiled up nearby, also opened its mouth and threatened her.

Greyman laughed, "Fwoh-fwoh-fwoh!"

"Lady Fuyou..." Kagura prepared the blades of her iron-ribbed fans and lined up beside her mother. "Please allow me to kill them with you... I will butcher that disgusting old man..."

"My, my. Are you recovered from the poison?"

"...Yes. Thanks to him I am completely awake... When I recall that licking sensation, any trace of drowsiness vanishes completely— Kyousuke Kamiya! And also, Offal Ayaka?!"

Kagura looked back at Kyousuke and the others and narrowed her rust-red eyes. "...I'm entrusting you to my sister! No matter what, stay safe and stay alive, and pass your Deadly Exit Exam. I will not accept any other result."

"Kagura—"

"Go, please!" Kagura urged them on as she blocked Greyman's next attack with her iron-ribbed fan.

"May you find fortune in battle!" Fuyou cried, her steel threads dancing wildly.

That moment—

"—Run!" Naoki shouted. A swarm of Busujima's creatures flooded toward Fuyou, and Kyousuke and the others sprinted away with all their might, slipping through a sudden shower of gore.

X   X   X

"Whooooooooooaaaaaa?!"

"Naoki, stop!"

Behind Kyousuke, who was dashing down the uneven path behind his father, Maina had managed to trip on something and taken a spectacular dive. Sanae, who was running in the rear of the line, called them to a halt, and Kyousuke and the others stopped running for a moment.

"...Miss Igarashi, are you all right?" Sanae asked, looking worried.

"Ye-yes...I'b sowwy, I'b okay!...hah...hah...," Maina answered, staggering to her feet. After running for dear life for ten-odd minutes, her breathing was ragged, and her hair was plastered to her forehead. She didn't look the least bit all right.

"Geez!" Ayaka rushed back to Maina. "The. Third. Time! This is the third time, Crafty Cat! Get it together already!"

"Ohh...so-sowwy..."

"Don't say 'sowwyyyyyyyyy'! I told you not to hold us back, didn't I? If you don't shape up, we're really going to leave you behind!!"

"Come now. Don't talk like that, Ayaka, dear. Goodness!" Sanae chided. "She's trying her hardest for your and Kyousuke's sake, isn't she? Really..."

"...Waah."

Sanae stroked Maina's hair, keeping an eye on Ayaka, who sullenly had her cheeks puffed out. She sighed, unfastening the second button on her shirt. "Besides, look...this isn't exactly easy for me, either. The poison hasn't completely worn off yet... Can't we slacken the pace a bit?"

Looking to his wife, who was flushed and squirming, Naoki scratched the back of his head. "Ah... Y-yeah, I guess we can let up a bit. We've got some leeway timewise, and there are only five people left after us, to our seven. I mean, we'll probably be all right even if we don't rush, so let's ease up and save our energy."

"...Mmm. I understand," Ayaka replied, acceding to her father. Leaving Maina behind, she turned and started walking again.

Shamaya stepped up next to Maina. "Miss Igarashi. Shall we be off, then?" She gently took Maina's hand. Maina stared in wonder. "Oh-ho-ho... If we do this, I think it will be a little easier. If you seem like you might fall again, I shall assist you. There is no shame in accepting help when offered."

"M-Miss Shamaya..."

Gripping her hand tightly, Maina looked up at her senior's smiling face. Eiri's expression likewise softened, and she followed after Ayaka. Kyousuke also continued on. The group moved forward, slower than before, making their way down the craggy mountain path. After another fifteen minutes, they reached a clearing, where they encountered a nostalgic signboard.

~WELCOME TO LIMBO, FUCKIN' PIGS!!!~

And then—

"So you finally showed up, huh? I got tired of waiting, you traitors. If you manage to get through here, your goal will be close at hand. But don't think you'll pass so easily. Prepare yourselves!"

In front of the campgrounds surrounded by a tall fence and barbed wire, below the signboard that greeted visitors, a blood-colored beast was waiting in an imposing stance. Haruyo Gevaudan Tanaka—the mass murderer and foremost fighter at the academy. Beside her stood—

"............"

—a silent man with his arms crossed, back turned to them. On the back of his sleeveless black martial arts uniform, the word "prison" was written in elegant script. Bloodlust radiated off of his whole body like heat shimmers, surrounding him in a terrifying aura. The man slowly turned around.

"Wah?! He's bald!"

"His belly is huge!"

Ayaka's and Sanae's voices were in chorus.

"Rude, basic bitches!" Haruyo was enraged. "Did you not see the word 'prison'? Who do you take this gentleman for? You are in the presence of the exalted master of the strongest fighting technique in the criminal underworld, the Assassin's Fist! Known as Break Fast, he is the honorable master Shidou Muguruma! Hey, take note! Take note! Take note, you impertinent bastaaards!"

"I don't mind."

"A-apologies, master..."

Silencing Haruyo with but a word, the man—Muguruma—turned toward Kyousuke and the others. Wearing a necklace of thick prayer beads, Muguruma spoke bluntly, though his voice was refined and almost foppish.

"My head may be bald, and my belly may stick out, and the smell of my aging body may be so intense that it forms a nearly visible aura... All of this is true. It is unavoidable!"

The last point was one that no one had mentioned, but... Did that mean that what was drifting off of him was not bloodlust but the stench of middle age? Even if that was true, the odor was giving off tremendous pressure.

Muguruma's round black eyes—it would have been hard to describe them as anything but "dull"—turned toward Kyousuke and the others, who were overwhelmed in several different ways. He continued speaking in an extremely handsome voice that did not match his outward appearance. "Everybody. If you want to pass through this place, you'll have to do so over our dead bodies!"

C-cool...

Moving from his position under the signboard to block Kyousuke and the others' path, Muguruma uncrossed his arms.

Haruyo also lined up next to Muguruma and repeated, "Over our dead bodies!"

Naoki took a step forward, cracking his knuckles. "Fine with us! We'll scatter you like the hair scattered off of your bald head—"

"This would normally be the point where we say such things," Muguruma interrupted. "However..."

"...Huh?"

"I have a proposal. Why don't we hold a true martial arts tournament right here, where both parties can compete fair and square?"

"......What did you say?"

Turning toward the frowning Naoki, Muguruma spoke brightly. "We are two, and you are seven. *Go on ahead, leaving behind the same number of people*, namely two. If you do so, I will not lay a hand on five of you. You may pass through this place without complication."

"Hah!" Naoki laughed off the suggestion. "How convenient for you to go on about what's fair, baldy! We have seven people, and you have two. If we beat your asses like this, it'll be over way faster! Spare us the bad jokes—"

"*Really, how about it?*"

That instant, the stench drifting from Muguruma, or rather, his aura of bloodlust, instantly intensified. The feeling of oppression dominating the place doubled in a flash. Dwelling in his round black eyes was a demonic glint.

"Certainly, you have the superior numbers, while we are at a disadvantage. However, young man...beasts are ferocious when cornered, you know? I don't believe all of you will make it out safely! My fighting style is quite powerful. It can annihilate anything in all of creation, the evil spirits of mountains and rivers—and kill anything alive! If you want to taste it, I'll let you eat your fill...and then die! It will be too late for regrets once you're on the other side, you know? Once more, I ask—"

Muguruma slowly raised both arms. Holding an austere pose, he steadied his breathing. "...Who shall be our opponents?"

*   *   *

"I will stay behind."

A cold voice rang out, strong enough to cut through the powerful pressure emanating from Muguruma. Glaring at Muguruma with fortitude and big eyes, fists and small body trembling, was—

"...Mai...na......?"

"I will take responsibility for this place. I'll show you that I can absolutely hold him back! So everyone, please head for the goal. I don't mind doing it on my own, either!"

"...Huh? Wh-what a stupid—"

—There's no way you stand a chance. It's suicide. Give it up!

With those words on his lips, Kyousuke paused when he saw the look in Maina's eyes. Hardened determination. No matter what was said, or by whom, nothing would shake the unrelenting resolve that glittered in the depths of her clear irises.

He understood. Maina was prepared to die...

With a bitter smile, Maina continued. "This is the least that I can do for all of you, after all... I don't want to be a burden. I don't want to just rely on everyone—I want to help everyone, too! Help everyone and atone...for my sins..."

"Crafty Cat..." Ayaka looked at Maina with tearful eyes.

"I'm sorry," Maina apologized. "I've caused you all a lot of trouble and made you hate me... Well, starting now, I'm going to make up for all that! The trouble that I've caused the people around me, and the disasters I've caused with my clumsiness, and the murders I've committed, by putting my life on the line—"

"...I guess there's no helping it."

With a sigh, Shamaya brushed her hair back and stepped forward next to Maina. Placing a hand on the confused girl's head, she smiled gently. "Whatever the circumstances, leaving you behind on your own would be much too reckless, Miss Igarashi. I shall stay here with you. Really, come now...how could I ever leave a girl like you behind?"

"Miss Chamyaya—"

"Besides..." Shamaya stopped caressing Maina's hair, and her

expression grew severe. "If you die, you won't be able to complete your atonement, will you? It's me saying this, and I have happily killed more than seven times as many people as you, but…if you really feel that way, then keep living. And go back to the academy."

"Ah—" Maina's eyes were open wide. Her expression, which had looked ready to crumble, hardened with new resolve. "Okay! Th-that's right… I'll definitely make it back! I won't lose!" Her fighting spirit burned brightly.

"Oh-ho-ho." Shamaya grinned wickedly. "Yes, that's the spirit! Now, let us take down that overweight baldy and the *kigurumi* girl tout de suite. And then, Kyousuke, darling…please marry me."

"…No way. Please don't add any strange conditions!"

"Ah-ha-ha! Forgive me."

"Have you finished your parting words?" Muguruma asked, striking a pose that seemed to temper the waves of bloodlust rolling off of him. "Well then, you should go. You shall go…and these two shall endure the full might of our ultimate assassination techniques! Soaring Skyyyyyyyyy Fiiiiiiiiist!"

"Demolition Earthquake Strike! Ah-chaaaaaaaaaaaaa!"

"Waaaaaaaaaaaaaaaaaaaaaaaaaaaaaaaaaaaaaahhhhhh!"

"We'll strip off that costume until you're both bald!"

As Kyousuke and the other four made their way around the battlefield, Muguruma and Haruyo, acting in sync, leaped into action, while Shamaya and Maina charged forward with fierce determination.

Life After Me, Death After You

HEARTBREAK DOWN

TRACK FIVE

Heavenly A cup

01. EVERY DAY AT THE
    BUST STOP

02. Lollipop
    Candy ♥ Chest PAD ♥ Girl

03. T・E・D・D・Y
    ~LOVELY DREAMER GIRL~

04. Heavy Starry Nail

05. Eiri Akabane,
    She's Sweet (LOL)

06. Double Suicide

EIRI AKABANE 1st EP

Less than three hours remained until 4:00 PM and the end of the Deadly Exit Exam. However, passing the House of Limbo, Kyousuke's group had crossed about three-quarters of the distance from the academy to the goal. From there, they expected to reach the westernmost edge of the island within the hour if they ran. They were making good time.

There were still three people left on the pursuit team. However, the escape team had five—Kyousuke, Ayaka, Naoki, Sanae, and Eiri—and aside from Sanae, they were all more or less uninjured. If things continued like this, they would have no trouble completing the race and securing their release.

That was what Kyousuke had thought, but...

"Naoki?! Pull yourself together, Naoki! Answer me, Naoki—"

"Papaaaaaa! You can't die, Papaaaaaaaaa!"

Sanae was calling out to her husband, who was lying on the ground, unmoving. Ayaka's shrieks echoed through the air. Eiri had a hand on her blade, frozen in place.

—Dark red.

A river of blood poured from the left side of Naoki's head. Kyousuke didn't understand. He didn't want to understand. He stood stock-still, staring at the scene before him...

*　　*　　*

"…Hmph. That's one little piggy down, eh?"

A sweet, lisping Lolita voice spoke to him. Looking toward the source, Kyousuke's eyes seized upon a petite figure, barely more than four feet tall. Standing five yards away from Naoki, Sanae, and Ayaka, and three yards from Kyousuke and Eiri, that female teacher was—

"……Miss…Kurumiya—"

"Oh, Kamiya. Looks like your testing is going well, huh? Heh-heh-heh…"

Narrowing her big, round, charming eyes and twisting her springy, soft-looking cheeks into a grin, Kurumiya twirled her newest weapon. The blood clinging thickly to the surface spattered around her as she did so.

The air was filled with a heavy metallic tang as a light breeze blew through Kyousuke's hair.

"Did you think you could make it out just like that? Did you think you could break through? Did you think you could get away? Heh-heh-heh…the answer is NO, you pigtards. I will not permit it. Like I told you before this examination started, I'm not going easy on you, and I will kill you. There are about three hours left until the end of the exam, but it won't take five minutes if I just crush the four of you here. Checkmate… Time to die!"

With a sadistic smile, Kurumiya shouldered her new weapon. By now they were quite familiar with her narrow, crooked iron pipe—*but this was not it.*

Instead, she carried an enormous metal truncheon.

The business end of the charcoal-gray, octagonal rod—which was more than six feet long—was densely packed with spikes, as though it had very sharp horns. A stylized red ogre plushie swung from a strap attached to the handle. The club was so heavy that the moment she shouldered it, the soles of Kurumiya's shoes sunk slightly into the ground.

Naoki had taken *a direct hit* from that massive truncheon.

Several minutes earlier, after Kyousuke and the others had passed through the House of Limbo to continue on through the mountain path, Kurumiya had ambushed them from the trees. Naoki had dodged the first swing, which the teacher had aimed at the top of his head, but before he could recover his footing, he had taken the full force of a sweeping follow-up attack and been quickly disabled.

Sanae had immediately returned fire with a pair of pistols, but Kurumiya had used her heavy truncheon as a shield, dodging and rolling across the ground, lowering her guard and then raising it again, toying with her prey. In the blink of an eye, Sanae had used up all her ammunition.

Now Kurumiya moved to attack, but Eiri quickly drew her sword and forced her to momentarily back off.

"...Good grief, it looks like that idiot Reiko ended up causing a lot of trouble. I mean, what could I really expect? Hmph...just about this kind of mess, I suppose. Honestly, this is such a disappointment—it's really boring! Without his limiter on, that Slaughter Maid was a much better challenge than this... Well, I guess still being in one piece even after a nice solid hit from my Ogre Killer is impressive enough. As expected of a bodyguard, aka a human shield...parent and child are both monstrously strong."

"............"

Kurumiya was the real monster here. In all his fifteen years, Kyousuke had always believed that his father was the strongest person in the world. Even after witnessing Renko's and Renji's incredible powers, that perception had not wavered, and it had never even occurred to Kyousuke that his father could lose to anyone. And that made it all the more shocking to see—

"Naoki! Naoki?! Naoki, hey...Naoki!"

"Uua...uaaa...he's gonna die. Papa's gonna die..."

Even as she frantically called her husband's name, Sanae slid fresh magazines into her guns and leveled them at her foe. Ayaka, meanwhile, sobbed and wept. Naoki, for his part, failed to move, his eyes still closed...

To Kyousuke, that terrible scene might as well have been the end of the world.

"—Hm?" Kurumiya suddenly scowled. For a moment, Kyousuke thought that maybe Naoki had regained consciousness, but that was wrong. The woman stared intently at his father's unconscious face. "...Ah. I see, heh-heh-heh..."

She smiled with satisfaction.

"What's so funny?" Sanae glared at her.

"Nothing," Kurumiya replied. "I just remembered something, is all. A job about four years ago, right before I started working at this academy. My methods involved eliminating everyone in the vicinity of my target, but…back then, there was one person I failed to take out."

—*The bodyguard.*

"……?!"

A wave of dread passed over Kyousuke and the others.

If what Kurumiya had described had happened four years ago, Kyousuke would have been in his first year of junior high school. The same year as the incident when his father had been hit by an express train—no, had encountered a vicious assassin and nearly been killed. Kyousuke's world had been turned upside down. And that assassin had been…

"So that was you."

Someone else said it before Kyousuke could find his voice.

"…Oh? You took that hit and are still standing, huh? Looks like you've improved a little, haven't you? I seem to remember sending you to the brink of death with just one blow last time. Heh-heh-heh…"

"Yeah? Shut up, ya damn pip-squeak." Naoki had regained consciousness and was rising to his feet. The side of his head was spattered red with bright blood. Thick veins bulged across his scalp.

The man held Kurumiya's gaze, standing fast, and said, "Don't tell me that my kids had you for a homeroom teacher, Bellows Maria… Four years may've passed, but you're as tiny as ever, ain'tcha? I thought you were an elementary school kid! I guess you looked like a nursery-schooler last time, so at least ya've grown a little, eh? Though I think I can see a few new wrinkles!" Naoki raised his chin, dripping with a mixture of blood and sweat, fearlessly provoking his nemesis.

A vein bulged on Kurumiya's forehead when she heard the word *pip-squeak*—the one name she could never abide. "Haah? What did you say?! Try saying that again, you immortal bastard!"

However, Naoki ignored her fluster. Instead, he grinned broadly at his dumbfounded son. "My bad, Kyousuke, I got careless…but you don't need to worry anymore. Whatever pain an' suffering you and Ayaka owe the little bitch, I'm gonna pay it all back with interest right now! I'm gonna beat the shit outta her...so you go stand over there, and burn the image of yer gallant father into yer memory, brat."

"O-old man..."

Kyousuke's broken hopes were resurrected by his father's arrogant grin.

My old man won't lose. There's no way he'll lose!

Kyousuke's faith in his father pushed aside all the fear and despair that Kurumiya inspired; he suddenly felt perfectly secure.

"Hmph!" Kurumiya snorted. She tightened her grip on the massive metal truncheon. "If you want to settle up, then go ahead and try! It's pointless, of course, but you're welcome to give it a shot...heh-heh-heh! I'll murder you in two seconds! I'll splatter your brains right in front of your family's eyes. Now die!"

The Loli leaped at them, moving with demonic speed and agility despite her unwieldy weapon. She swung the huge truncheon, and once again, the wicked club, bristling with sharp spikes, made to smash into the left side of Naoki's head.

"Gaah?!"

Yet it was Kurumiya who staggered, spewing vomit.

Her truncheon had caught only air. Naoki had ducked under the blow, dived forward, and slammed his right fist into her stomach.

"Gbwuh?!"

In a flash, he smashed his left fist into the bridge of Kurumiya's nose, sending her spinning through the air.

"Not good enough. Not nearly good enough!"

Kurumiya grabbed Naoki by the collar and pulled him close for a head-butt.

"Kuh—gyaah?!"

Naoki showered Kurumiya with blows, sending her staggering backward. He grabbed hold of her hair with both hands and drove his right knee into her face once, twice, three times, four times... After the fifth blow, fresh blood sprayed everywhere, and after the eighth, the truncheon finally fell from Kurumiya's limp hand.

"Orrraaaaaaaaaaa!"

With a bellow, Naoki hurled Kurumiya, sending her body soaring through the air. Her back smashed into the side of a cliff before falling headfirst to the ground.

"Guuuhhh…y-you bastard…you really did it now!!" Kurumiya staggered to her feet, holding her nose. "I won't forgive you…absolutely not! Raising a hand against me is something I'll make you regret in hell—"

"You'll be the one with regrets!"

"……?!"

Kurumiya had been glaring at Naoki, but now her body went rigid and her round eyes opened wide. The man was closing on her, carrying her enormous truncheon over one shoulder and wearing a vicious grimace.

"Earlier you gave me a wallop with this thing, didn'tcha? Well, I make it a point t' always get payback. I'm gonna smash yer head in, too. And not just once. No, I'll do it twice for whatcha did to me four years ago, an' three times for makin' Sanae feel sad, and four times to show ya just how much I appreciate you takin' care of my kids… Altogether I'm gonna have to smash ya at least thirty times!"

"Wait! Your calculations don't add up!" she shot back. Wiping the blood from her nose, she ground her teeth in frustration and pulled two familiar iron pipes out from beneath her clothing. "Don't push your luck, you pigtard! These are more than enough to handle someone like you… I'll discipline you and your big mouth, which is so very like your son's. Time to dieeeeee!"

Kurumiya rushed at Naoki. However—

"Nah—I think *you're the one who's gonna die!*"

Naoki swung the massive truncheon.

His reach with Kurumiya's new weapon was twice that of her iron pipes, and that difference was the difference between life and death. Before Kurumiya could close on him, Naoki slammed the truncheon toward Kurumiya's temple…

Yet a moment before the impact—

"Hyeah-haaaaaaaaaaaaaaaaaaaaaaaaaaaaaaaa! Kurumiya, babyyyyyy yyyyyyyyyyyyyyyy!"

With a battle cry like rolling thunder, a figure leaped down from atop the cliff, throwing itself between the teacher and the truncheon.

"Kuawsedrftgy Hijirilp?!"

"Wha—?"

The truncheon slammed into a head adorned with a bright red Mohawk hairdo. Blood and gore sprayed everywhere. After taking the blow meant for the object of his obsession, the figure went flying, landed hard, and then rolled across the ground.

Spread out on the dirt, the newcomer did not so much as twitch.

"...Mo...hawk......?"

Kurumiya wore an expression as if her soul had fallen out as she stared at the fallen student who had taken the hit from the truncheon in her place—the academy's foremost problem child, the boy with the Mohawk hairdo.

To everyone's amazement, Kurumiya's eyes, which were open as wide as possible, welled up with—

Tears.

"M-M-Mo...Mohaaaaaaaaaaaaaaaaaaaaaaaaaawk?!" Kurumiya screamed and rushed over to him. Holding the upper half of his body, she called out to him hoarsely. His eyes were closed, his expression pained but satisfied. "Hey, are you okay?! Open your eyes! Why won't you open your eyes, morooooooon?!"

"......................."

But Mohawk did not respond. A large hole was cratered into his skull where he had taken the full brunt of the truncheon, spilling dark red gore. It was without a doubt a fatal wound.

However, Kurumiya was—

"Mohaaaaaaaaawk! What is it? Why won't you get up?! No matter how hard I smashed you, you always came back, every time, didn't you?! So why are you dead? Are you gonna let somebody besides me kill you that easily, you bastaaaaaaaaaard?!"

Shaking the young man's blood-soaked shoulders, holding her face close to his ruined visage, Kurumiya continued shouting without pause.

Naoki still gripped the gory truncheon, frozen in place, looking absolutely astonished. Kyousuke and the others were exactly the same. Was it possible that Mohawk, the kid everyone thought was immortal, had died? And that at his death, Kurumiya, who had hated him more than anyone else, was—

"Mohawwwwwk…"

—sobbing? It seemed like the shock of Mohawk's death had hit her harder than any of Naoki's attacks. In a voice that none of them had ever heard before, Kurumiya repeated his name over and over again.

"_____"

Finally, Kurumiya's wailing tapered off. Mohawk still showed no signs of resurrection.

Kurumiya sighed and stood up. She took off her jacket and laid it over her prized pupil's face.

"I'll end you."

As Kurumiya spit the words, the atmosphere completely changed.

Tremendous pressure was radiating from her body, and she glared at Naoki with fiery eyes. Her face and body were dyed bright, bloody red below her nose, and her clenched teeth creaked.

In each hand she gripped a new iron pipe that had suddenly appeared from somewhere. Crossing the familiar weapons over her shoulders, Kurumiya turned to her foe. Compared to the truncheon that Naoki had stolen from her, the pipes were like toys. However—

"Sanae, honey…" Naoki's voice was tense as he called his wife's name. He was visibly shaken. A single droplet of sweat rolled down Naoki's temple. "…Run."

"Naoki—?!"

"Dieeeeee!"

Kurumiya roared and sprang forward. Her fury was like nothing they had seen before.

Naoki was barely able to hold her off, deflecting her fierce blows with the truncheon as her twin weapons struck down at him with the ferocity of an angry god. The high-pitched sound of metal on metal filled the air.

"—No, I can't!"

Several gunshots rang out in rapid succession. "—Kah!" Kurumiya, who had been pressing the attack, pulled her weapons in and jumped back, dodging Sanae's gunfire.

Chasing after her, still blasting shot after shot, Sanae shouted a reply.

"I won't run away! I will stay here, and this time for sure, I will protect my Naoki!"

"Wha—?! This ain't the time to fool around—"

"I'm not fooling around! The reason I returned to this job was to keep you from being hurt that badly ever again! If I run away from here, what use am I?!"

"You idiot!" Naoki threw away the truncheon and pulled a gun out of his breast pocket. His gunfire joined his wife's. "You oughta be more worried about our kids than about me right now! You promised, didn't you, Sanae? You promised to protect the kids! To do a parent's duty... Look, I'll handle this bitch one way or another, so you take the kids and hurry—"

"It's fine!" Kyousuke shouted, loudly interrupting his father's speech.

"Ah?" Naoki scowled at him, while Sanae looked surprised.

Kyousuke stared at the two of them. "It's fine, so go with him, Mother! I can protect myself. And I'll absolutely protect Ayaka, too! I don't want to cause you any more trouble than I already have... It's not your fault that we're forced to fight in a place like this. It's my fault, after all! So—"

Kyousuke recalled their conversation on the riverbed. His voice grew to a roar as he shouted, "Let me conquer the end of this test with my own two hands!"

"Kyousuke..."

Sanae stared on in wonder. Naoki's brow was wrinkled. Both of them had stopped shooting at Kurumiya.

"...Hmph. If you think you can, give it a try." Surprisingly, Kurumiya did not rush to attack them. Instead, she stood where she was and reshouldered the iron pipes. "There are still two pursuers left—"

"...Two?" Naoki gestured toward Mohawk. "Ain't it just one?"

Kurumiya shook her head. "No. He was not supposed to be participating in the exam. He probably just came looking for me. And because of that, he threw his life away. What an amazing idiot, stupid to the very end... But anyway, there are two pursuers left, though I should be the final teacher."

Naoki warily leveled his gun. "...Do ya really think there's anyone stupid enough to believe the words of the enemy?"

"Hmph!" Kurumiya snorted. "I'm not lying. I hate lying! I told you the truth, out of pity for Kyousuke and Ayaka, as their homeroom teacher... I won't lay a hand on them, as a favor to my 'old friend,' Kamiya. So what it all comes down to is—"

Kurumiya's eyes were blazing. She bared her fang-like incisors. "You two remain here, and I'll let them go on ahead...so that there aren't too many obstacles in my way!" She thrust an iron pipe each at Naoki and Sanae.

"This little pip-squeak is really pissed off," Naoki grumbled, lowering his gun and taking off his leather gloves.

"Hey, ya damn brat!" He flung the gloves at Kyousuke. "Get out of here. If we fail, you won't know it." As he spoke, Naoki cracked his bare knuckles.

"Old man..." Kyousuke picked up the leather gloves that had fallen at his feet. "—I understand. You focus on not getting yourself killed, okay, you old geezer?"

"He'll be all right; this time I'm right alongside him!" Sanae smiled at her son.

Ayaka, protected behind her mother's back, puffed out her chest. "We'll be all right, too! Big brother has Ayaka right alongside him!"

"Yes. You take good care of Kyousuke, all right?"

"Okaaay!" Ayaka clenched her fists and ran over to her brother.

Sanae moved closer to her husband. "Eiri, please take care of Kyousuke and Ayaka! And—"

"...Leave it to me." With both Naoki's and Sanae's eyes on her, Eiri answered reassuringly. "I won't let the remaining pursuers lay a single finger on them! Well then, should we go, you two?"

"Y-yeah..."

"Tee-hee. You're really motivated, aren't you, Eiri!"

Eiri talked a big game, her rust-red eyes seething. Kyousuke, who thought he could guess what she was thinking, turned to leave. His mind was occupied by thoughts of one of their remaining pursuers.

Renko Hikawa. The psycho killer love of his life.

As they grew closer to the goal, the lingering affection that he should have shaken off already coiled around him like shackles. It was a complication that he couldn't share with anyone, even as it threatened to strangle him...

Kyousuke surreptitiously fisted his hands, now protected by Naoki's gloves.

X   X   X

"......Hey. Kyousuke—"

They had left Kurumiya, Naoki, and Sanae behind and were dashing through the forest toward the far western edge of the island. Kyousuke braced himself for a question about Renko, but—

"When this is over and you go back to your former life...what do you want to do?"

—Eiri was apparently interested in making small talk.

After leaving the academy? Now that she mentioned it, he hadn't really thought about it. Up until Ayaka had transferred in, he had thought only about reuniting with her once more, but...

"Hm, what do I want to do? First of all, I guess—"

"You want to make out with Ayaka!"

"Right, I want to make out with— Wait, no!"

Ayaka looked disappointed, while Kyousuke looked exasperated.

"You could do stuff like that even without winning your freedom, right...?"

"Ah-ha-ha. You're right! We can flirt and make out anytime, anywhere!"

"......Okay, okay, congratulations on your beautiful love," Eiri grumbled in monotone. Before her, the siblings had entwined theatrically. "So...? What do you want to do, really?"

"Umm..."

Her question wasn't any easier to answer the second time. Nothing came to Kyousuke's mind, to the point that the emptiness surprised him. For the time being—

"I'd like to fill my chest with a big breath of free air, I guess?"

"...Huh?" Eiri looked as if she didn't buy it. "What does that even mean...?"

"What about you, Eiri?" Ayaka asked.

"Is there anything I want to do? I guess I'm not becoming an assassin anymore."

"Mm. Yeah, guess not—"

Eiri put her hand on her chin. Then, after she contemplated for a moment, her eyes sparkled. "The very first thing that comes to mind is to live alone! In the city, if I can. My family home is in the country, and the city seems like it has all kinds of exciting things. After that, I would go shopping and buy lots of cute clothes and accessories, eat lots of delicious food, experience lots of fun activities, and I'd even like to try going to school! High school or college or vocational school, going to a real school…and there are also lots of jobs I want to try in the future! There's confectioner, and florist, and dressmaker, or clothing designer, and I also want to try things like nail stylist and model! And then—"

"My big brother's wife."

"Right, Kyousuke's wife— Wait, no! What did you say?!"

Ayaka had led her right into it. Frantically, Eiri tried to take it back. However, Ayaka looked slightly doubtful.

"It's…not true?"

"N-no, it's…not *not* true, but…th-there's an order to these things, and…I mean, I want to go shopping and to cafés and to amusement parks and everything together, but…it's still too early to say how I really feel—I mean, that's…"

Eiri blushed and mumbled unintelligibly, then bit her lip and looked back at Kyousuke and Ayaka. "I want to stay with you two even after we leave this place. I want to spend time together and laugh together and have fun together and live an everyday life together, where you can think, 'Thank goodness we dropped out—'"

"Too bad, but that's not gonna happen."

Before she could finish her heartfelt wish, Eiri was interrupted. She turned back to look for the culprit, and in that moment—

"—Because I'm gonna kill you aaaaaaaaall!"

A figure came flying in from above.

It was Renko, with her limiter removed. Her arms, adorned with black tattoos, swung toward Eiri's head.

"Renkoooooo!"

Slipping out of the way of the attack, Eiri, in one smooth motion, drew her sword, carved a deadly arc through the air, and returned it to its scabbard.

Renko dodged the elegant attack with a backward somersault. Immediately afterward—

"_____!"

—a huge figure flew out of the thicket to their right and rushed at Eiri. It was Renko's little brother, Renji Hikawa.

He was not wearing his ivory-white gas mask, either; his limiter had also been removed.

A wild animal free from his chains, Renji pressed in on the girl with incredible speed, arms spinning like two pinwheels. With the furious acrobatic fighting style that he had demonstrated at the athletic festival, he sprang at her like a tornado. Wind surged and roared around him as he launched into a supersonic kick. Eiri—

"Annoying."

—dodged his attack with a casual sidestep and, as Renji passed by—

"You're in the way, so..."

—pulled her sword from its sheath as she turned, and—

"Move it!"

—drawing the Akabane sword Hien, she carved a large diagonal slash upward. Again and again she struck at the rampaging Renji—two flashes, three flashes, four flashes, five flashes—each rapid gleam was a slash of her sword. The blade was quickly painted red. And then—

"......?!"

Blood sprayed from Renji's entire body.

The back of his neck, his sides, his upper arms, his lower arms, his legs—in every place touched by the blade of Eiri's sword, Renji's steel-strong muscles had been sliced through.

"............?!"

With a confused grunt, the young man collapsed. The Slaughter Maid, who had been too much even for Kyousuke and Renko together, was...

"............Huh?"

It can't possibly be over already?!

"Wh-what? That guy was Renji...right? Whaaaaaa?"

Kyousuke was at a loss for words, and Ayaka strained her eyes for a better look. Renko, who had witnessed her brother die in an instant, froze in the middle of closing the attack distance.

"...Ah-ha, ah-ha-ha-ha...ah-ha-ha-ha-ha-ha-ha-ha-ha-ha-ha-ha-ha!"

Suddenly, she started laughing hysterically. "What's this, a dream? Ah-ha-ha-ha-ha-ha-ha—ow?!"

She pinched her own cheek and seemed to come to her senses. "It's not a dream?!"

She looked considerably shaken.

"...Hmph." Eiri sheathed her sword. "You're next, Renko. You fool... Don't interfere with their exam. Move it!"

"No way!" Renko spread her arms out to block the way. She wore a tank top and her school-uniform skirt, along with a leather choker. Her ice-blue eyes were glaring feverishly. "You're the one who needs to stay out of the way of my romance!! Kyousuke and I are in love—there's no role for you to play! You're the one who needs to move it, third wheel! Home-wrecker! Tiny tits!"

"⁓⁓⁓⁓⁓⁓!"

As Renko hurled abuse at her, Eiri chewed her lip. "............I get... ...that—" Gripping the hilt of her sword, she cast her gaze downward. "I get that you are in love with Kyousuke...and that Kyousuke likes you, too... I really do understand that right now I'm being an idiot, a third wheel who can't read the room, a greedy home-wrecker...a... tiny tits...? And that there's no way I can beat you—but listen!"

She raised her face and her voice. "Even so, I've decided that I will not give up on my own feelings! I've decided to protect Kyousuke and Ayaka! Against the likes of you—"

Eiri glared at Renko, a violent emotion that resembled bloodlust surging around her. "I won't hand over Kyousuke to the likes of you! I will stand in your way... If you don't like that, just try to move me by brute force, you bombastic-breasted basket case!"

"Eiriiiiiiiiiiiii!"

Renko screamed, baring her canines as she leaped forward to attack. "Shut uuuuuuuuppp!! Shut the hell up, you tiny-tittied temperamental bitch! The murderous melody that plays for you is as one-dimensional as your chest. It's nothing but noise—it's so grating I can't stand it. I just want you to hurry up and dieeeeee!"

"...Hmph." Easily dodging Renko's right punch, Eiri smiled. Taking a crouching stance, she popped the hilt of her sword out of the scabbard and, looking back, drew it smoothly into a sideways slash—

"Fgyah?!"

—Before she finished the attack, Eiri instead launched into an upward kick, catching Renko, who had ducked to avoid the sword, on the bottom of her chin. Renko spun through the air, and Eiri followed up with another kick to her stomach.

However—

"Whatcha doin' there? A sword like that's no use at aaaaaall!"

—Renko easily blocked the second kick, grabbing hold of Eiri's leg. She smiled wickedly. "How about I break your pride, your sleek, sexy legs—"

"Just die already!"

"Uwah?!"

Before Renko could snap Eiri's leg, she was forced to retreat by Eiri's sword.

"...Tch." Eiri clicked her tongue. "D-don't rub on me! Do you want to have your arms lopped off, you perv?!"

"Heh-heh. Oh nooo, sorry, sorry! They had such a dreamy texture, so I just... Even your kneecaps are silky smooth, aren't they? They're a good match against my boobs! Well, in my case, it's more like sexy than sleek, and more squishy than smooth, though—right, Kyousuke?"

"Oh, shut up!"

"Uwah?!"

The moment that Renko's attention was focused on Kyousuke, Eiri closed the distance between them, striking with her sword. Renko, who toppled over to avoid the attack, fell on her backside and held her head in her hands. "Eeeeee〰〰〰?! I-I'll be...k-k-killed, waaaaaah?!"

"...Are you making fun of me?" Eiri glared down at Renko, unamused.

Renko stuck her tongue out playfully. "Not at all! But I'm not nervous at all, either! I mean, Eiri is sooo nice. You're reluctant to even wound me, let alone kill me, right? That's right, isn't it, because we're friends! From the first time we met half a year ago, we've done nothing but fight...though I like you, Eiri. I even love you! And somehow or other you feel the same way about me, don't you?"

Eiri's eyebrows twitched as Renko innocently chattered on. Dropping her hands to her sides, the bigger girl stared at the smaller. Eiri gave an exasperated sigh.

"......Well, I guess so. Honestly, I don't exactly hate you, either. You're irritating and loud, but there have been lots of times that I felt like we were having fun together…and you have lots of qualities that I don't have."

"Like boobs!"

"That kind of spirit is annoying, you know? I really hate it when you don't read the mood of the conversation. And when you just do whatever you want no matter how anyone else feels, and carry the whole thing away—"

"Like my boobs!"

"—Shut up."

"Oh…s-sorry…th-there're two boobs, so I thought I'd say it twice…"

Renko apologized while holding her left and right girls up, and Eiri looked down at her coldly.

Tightening her grip on the *katana*'s scabbard, Eiri forcibly continued, "I don't hate you. But look, Renko, if you're planning to kill Kyousuke… if you've come to selfishly snatch away Kyousuke's life, I won't go easy on you! We may be friends, we may be good friends, but—*I will cut you down.*"

So declaring, Eiri placed her hand on the hilt of her sword again.

However, Renko's attitude did not change: "Ah-ha-ha! Is that so, is that so? That's wonderful! Even though you can't kill no matter what! You say that, but I'm planning to kill you, you know? And not just you… Kyousuke, whom I love, and Ayaka, who idolizes me…I intend to send all of you off together. That way you can have a happy, mass-murder ending, right? Happy death, happy death! Ah-ha-ha-ha-ha-ha-ha!"

"……Renko."

"Right—"

Eiri closed her eyes. Slowly, she turned to the girl, who was still laughing to herself. "I understand your feelings perfectly well…and so, I will make one request."

"Sure, what is it? If you're trying to talk me out of it, it's pointless. I've already decided! I will kill Kyousuke. Kill him and be bound to him forever! So, Eiriiiiii, for mine and Kyousuke's sake—"

"All right then. *Won't you please die?*"

"—Eh?"

Unsheathing Hien, Eiri slashed at Renko with all her might.

X   X   X

"Uu—"

Renko stumbled, her ice-blue eyes open wide.

Then, from a mouth that was open as wide as her eyes, poured a terrible scream.

"Ugyaaaaaaaaahhh?! C-cccc-cuuuuuuuuuuuut?! Uwaaaaaaaaahhh?!"

Renko collapsed, showering the ground in fresh blood as she writhed. A river of crimson poured through her fingers as she clutched at the top of her left shoulder. She had failed to completely avoid Eiri's attack, and the Akabane blade had struck true.

Renko had lost any semblance of her previous composure, and she glared at Eiri through tears. "Hey, Eiriiiiii! What the hellllll?! I'm gonna bleed out! Uuu...th-the blood's not stopping...it huuuuuurts, *sniffle*."

"You're better off dead."

Eiri's cold eyes seemed to pierce straight through Renko as she once again gripped her sword. Letting go of the scabbard and readying the blade with both hands, she asked emotionlessly:

"...But surely it will take more than that to kill you? At the Summer Death Camp, you had your head hacked up by a hatchet, but you still recovered quickly. Even if I make you experience some pain, it shouldn't be any problem for you, right? Well? How many more times do you want me to hit you?"

"Zero times, obviously, you idiiiiiioooooot!" Renko screamed, backing away from Eiri.

She timidly removed the hand pressed against her left shoulder to check the status of the wound.

"Yikes..." Renko grimaced. "Th-this's a serious cut... It goes all the way to the bone, you biiitch!!"

"Naturally. There is nothing that cannot be cut by an Akabane sword. It doesn't matter how tough your body is...like that big bastard I took down first—"

Eiri looked over at Renji, who was lying faceup on the ground. Though the many cuts that scored his body had already begun to heal, he gave no impression of getting back up. The large pool of blood around him was still spreading, even now.

Eiri returned her gaze to Renko. "—*I'll bleed you dry.* Even with your freakish resilience, even if every wound closes back up... Your blood won't go back in once it's been spilled, will it? If I'm careful with how many times I cut you and how deep, I can bleed you out just shy of death—you won't even be able to move...and you won't be able to get in our way, will you?"

"E-Eiri—" For the first time, a shadow of fear crossed Renko's face. However, she snarled.

"Eiriiiiiiiiiiiiiiiiiiiiiiiiiiiiiiiiiiiii!"

Renko screamed in rage, as if to drive away the fear. Dragging along her bloody arm, she sprang. Her strength, speed, and unchecked ferocity were all terrifying; she was like a wild beast.

"...*Fwah.*"

Eiri avoided Renko's furious assault with a yawn—

"Gyah?!"

—and hit her with another stroke of the sword as they passed. She struck Renko's back, splitting the fabric of her tank top and bra as well as the flesh beneath. Renko stumbled and pitched forward, clenching her teeth.

"Don't...you...daaaaaare..."

Fighting through the pain, she turned to look back at Eiri; the pupils of her wide, bloodshot eyes were narrow points of rage. A hiss of deeply held resentment poured from the gaps between her grinding teeth before—

"...get...in...my...WAAAAAAAAAAAAAAAAAAAAAAAAAAY!!"

"......?!"

—with an inhuman, vocal cord–shredding scream, Renko rushed at Eiri again.

Despite the volume and intensity, Eiri calmly avoided the attack. Just by moving her body slightly, she sidestepped Renko's powerful punch, slashing at an unprotected armpit.

"Aaaaaaaaaaaaaaaaaaaaaaaaaaaaaaaaaaa!" Renko screamed again. Desperately, she tore at her hair with both hands. "Come oooooooooooooooon! What the helllllllllllllllllllllll, Eiriiiiiiiiiiiiiiiiiiiiiiiii?!"

With a shrill, distorted shriek, Renko cast aside any concern for her own safety and frantically scrambled after Eiri, all four limbs swing-

ing madly, even as Eiri continued to avoid her reckless charges. Renko looked as if she had gone even more insane, bloodlust and passion overwhelming her senses. She continued to scream:

"I love Kyousuke! I'm in love with him! I want to kill him! Kyousuke also— Kyousuke feels that way, too! Despite that, why are you butting in?! You're getting in the way, Eiriii! I thought you would never doooooo that!"

Screaming and shouting in a frightful display, Renko leaped at the girl again and again, but her hands never got close.

Eiri sighed, still lightly and nimbly avoiding Renko's savagery. She tilted her head, dodging the fist aimed at her face, and shrugged. "...Didn't I tell you before? I won't just give up on my feelings. And so I will crush your feelings. If you don't want that, how about you try to crush me?"

"Uuuuuuuuu..." Renko groaned at the nonchalant dismissal and then suddenly screamed, "—Kyousukeee!"

Kyousuke—who had been watching this all with gritted teeth from the sidelines as he stood protecting Ayaka (albeit as Eiri protected him)—stiffened upon abruptly hearing his name.

"Put a stop to this intruder!!" Renko continued, wildly swinging at Eiri. "I want to get close to you! I want us to love each other! I want us to kill each other! Didn't you say to me, Kyousuke—?"

Her blue eyes wavered even as they pierced through him. She looked as if she was going to cry.

"You said you loved me! S-s-so...sooooooooooooo!"

Sobbing, Renko spun both arms like a windmill gone wild—or a child having a temper tantrum—keeping Eiri at bay as she howled loudly enough to drive herself hoarse.

"If you feel anything for me, then at least...at least face me yourseeeeeelllllllf!! I won't ask you to stand there and let me kill you, and I don't think you'll be open to my feelings—I just want you to acknowledge them! Face me and accept my love, and then with your own words and your own hands you can toss me aside! Kyousukeeeeee!! If you don't, I'll—"

"...You're so noisy."

Eiri ran the edge of her sword up Renko's left leg. Blood sprang from her thigh, and Renko fell over with a shout.

"Gyah?!"

"Renko?!"

Kyousuke nearly broke down and rushed to her side, but Eiri shot him a warning glare. "You chose polite society over her, right? In that case, listen up. There's no need for you to stubbornly stick by her."

"B-but—"

"No buts!" she quickly rebuked.

Renko shoved back to her feet—"Eiriiiii—augh?!"—and Eiri slashed at her again.

"Mr. Naoki, Ms. Sanae, Maina, Shamaya, Mother, Kagura, Basara… every one of them has risked their life for you so that the two of you could get out of here! Do you want that all to be a waste?! If you get killed or if you get hurt and can't make it to the goal, then 'sorry' isn't going to be enough!"

That's why…

Eiri looked down at Renko, who was crouching, bleeding from her right underarm. Likewise, red dripped from the silver of her sword.

"I will simply do my best to get you safely through this exam. I will defeat Renko," she coldly announced. "I won't allow her to lay a finger on you or your little sister, so…let's leave the parting words and final exchanges for after this farce is finished, all right?"

"…………"

"Big brother."

Ayaka gently covered Kyousuke's clenched fists with both of her hands. He said nothing. His gaze shifted away from his almost lover, who was lying on the ground covered in wounds, and he groaned bitterly.

"I feel the same way…I think," Ayaka said to him. "I like Renko a lot, but…of course the most important person is you, big brother. That's why…see? Give it up, big brother, okay?"

"Ayaka……"

The most important person in the world, his beloved little sister. If it was Ayaka asking, Kyousuke could say nothing more. He would give up on Renko and bring this conflict to an end…

Or he should have.

But despite everything, Kyousuke still—

"Uuu…Kyousuke…Kyousukeee……" Renko, painted all over in

her own bright blood, staggered to her feet again. The flood from her wounds had slowed to a trickle, but her face was pallid, her breathing ragged. When she turned her ice-blue eyes toward Kyousuke, he could see that they were somewhat vacant and unfocused.

It was hard to tell whether her unsteady swaying was because she was drunk on bloodlust or whether it was—

"Kyousukeeeeeeeee!"

Mustering her strength, Renko sprang at Eiri.

However, despite Renko's speed and vigor, her right arm, which was already almost entirely numb, was easily dodged. Eiri took a mere half step back and—

Vwooosh.

—Renko's fist swung through empty air. And even though Eiri had left her untouched, Renko collapsed.

"Huh?" Eiri scowled. "Somehow you're suddenly out of energy, huh...? And I thought you were more tenacious than that. Please, now is the time to give it up."

"......Kyou...suke......"

Renko lay on the ground, unmoving. Turning her back to her, Eiri went to pick up the scabbard for her sword. She wiped the shining blade down and tossed away the bloody tissue.

"Well, shall we go? There are no pursuers left... Assuming, that is, that the rest of our team hasn't been killed. Regardless, we should not allow their efforts to be in vain. Let's hurry up and get this exam over with." She sheathed her sword.

Behind her, Renko let out a quiet groan. "......ait...plea......"

The five fingers of her outstretched right hand dug deeply into the dirt. Lifting her face from the ground, she called out to stop the little assassin as she grew more distant. "......Wait, please...Eiriiiiii...... It's not...over yet...is it...? I can still...move, so...I'll kill—"

Eiri paused, turning to look back over her shoulder.

Renko glared at her, baring her teeth. "I'll kill you...kill Kyousuke, be bound to him...and because he'll probably be lonely by himself, I'll kill Ayaka, too...and after that...nothing...will hold me back......!"

"Huh? If you're able to do something, then give it a try...ah, though..."

Amazed by Renko's tenacity, Eiri ran a hand through her deep red hair.

"Tch." She placed a hand on the hilt of her sheathed blade. Turning on her heel, Eiri rushed back to where Renko was lying.

The fallen girl was still baring her fangs, and her lips curved upward in joy. Her right hand, which had been scraping and tearing at the ground, *grasped the choker around her neck.*

"......?!"

In that moment, Kyousuke recalled Reiko's words:

"Renko is planning to kill you. Now more than ever, I don't think there's any point in trying to persuade her otherwise... Will you accept her feelings or not? Either way, you'd better prepare yourself."

And then he remembered Renko's:

"If I unleash my Over Drive just one more time... Well, the next time could be the end *of me!"*

Memories of the half year that he had spent with Renko, and the feelings that had developed during that time, flickered like a slideshow through Kyousuke's mind. In the white light, Renko slowly collapsed. He had seen this before...but this time Renko did not get back up. She did not open her eyes again...

"—Ah."

Deep in Kyousuke's chest, he thought he could hear the sound of something breaking. And—

"Renko! That's enough, stop—"

"Stop it."

Suddenly, a purple-black figure flew into view, blowing right past Kyousuke before he had the chance to run to Renko.

—*Crack!*

A blue flash of lightning exploded in the air.

"Ngyaaah?!" With a deathly wail, Renko was thrown to the ground. She landed facedown, convulsing weakly.

"......................"

She stopped. Renko stopped moving, as if death had already taken her.

Fall in Love Equal Kill

DEATHBED PROMISE

TRACK SIX

Sweet Killing Engage

01. Limiter Removal (Intro)

02. Sanity and Satanity

03. Masqueraid

04. Carnage Anthem

05. The End of Heartache

06. My Last Nocturne

RENKO HIKAWA 1st EP

"..........................Eh?"

Kyousuke had no idea what had happened. He had no time to move or think. Before his eyes stood—

"Hyooo, look out, look out! Are you hurt, Kyousuke?"

—a massive suit of *purple-black armor*. It had an angular silhouette that recalled a bird of prey, and the wearer's face was concealed by a lustrous black helmet resembling a gas mask. Every inch of the figure before him was clad in thick protective plating, down to each and every individual finger. It looked mechanical, more like a robot than a person in a suit.

Opening and closing its right hand, the figure turned its head to look at Renko...

"...Geeeeeez. Didn't I tell you not to kill them? I can't use broken tools. You gotta be kidding me! Ignoring orders like that, come oooooon! They're not consumables like bullets—Kyousuke and his sister are one of a kind. I can't just replace them! You're out of line, stupid, stupid, stuuuuuupid!"

It was a husky, genderless voice with a familiar tone and cadence.

"...Board...Chairman......?"

"*Bingo! ♪*" the armored figure replied to Kyousuke's incredulity. "*It's meee! Good guess, that's my Kyousuke! And sweet Ayaka also looks safe, so it seems like you're doing all right, which is great, juuust great! Unfortunately, you won't be passing the exam after all! Kee-hee-hee!*" Origa snickered from inside the mechanical armor.

"Renko?!" Ayaka shrieked. "Pull yourself together, Renkooooo!"

Kyousuke snapped back to his senses. "...Eh?! That's right, Renko... Renkoooooo!" He frantically rushed over to the fallen girl, who was still lying senseless, facedown on the ground about ten feet away.

Ayaka was kneeling beside her. She looked up at her brother, on the verge of tears. "Kyousuke! Renko is— Renkoooooo..."

"Hey, Renko! What are you sleeping for, hey...get up! Open your eyes!" Kyousuke continued calling out to her in a daze.

Renko's eyes stayed closed. Her body was limp.

"*Ah, sorrrrr-yyy. Is she dead? I hit her at full power, sooo...*" Origa lumbered toward them, armor clanking and rattling. "*No matter how durable Murder Maids are, I guess this one just couldn't take it, huh? Her heart's stopped, hasn't it?*"

Crack!

The suit raised its right arm, and blue lightning crackled around its fist. Renko had taken a direct hit from that...and *was no longer breathing.*

"Renko!" Ayaka clung to her.

Kyousuke's mind was blank, as if the electric arc had fried his brain. "W-why—?"

I don't understand.

Renko was supposed to be the last member of the pursuit team. So why was Origa here participating at all?

"......Foul play." Ayaka, still clutching Renko's body, glared at Origa and screamed, "Foul plaaaaaay, you coward! Doesn't your team have too many people?! You're breaking the rules, so die! Diiieeeeee, you garbage-hole!"

"*No, no. I'm not breaking the rules at all!*" Origa answered indifferently. "*You're a bad listener, aren't you?*"

"You are just sooo—!" Ayaka shouted back. "Your team was only supposed to have twice as many people as ours! We had nine, so—"

"*Bzzzt. ♪*" Origa interrupted. Both armored hands were sticking out, mockingly. *"You didn't have nine... You had ten. Kyousuke Kamiya, Ayaka Kamiya, Naoki Kamiya, Sanae Kamiya, Fuyou Akabane, Kagura Akabane, Basara Akabane, Eiri Akabane, Maina Igarashi—"*

Origa bent one finger down at a time, and when the final remaining finger dropped, the left pinky—

"And Saki Shamaya."

"......?!"

That's right! Kyousuke thought. Shamaya had originally been on the pursuit team, but halfway through she had changed sides and joined the escape team. Which, in turn, had *increased the maximum number of people allowed on the pursuit team...*

"Meaning I got to come out and plaaaaaay! The surveillance cameras hidden all over the island catch eeeverrrything, you know? Mohawk also barged in all on his own, but even if we count him, there's no foul! No foul, even if we count him! I wonder if you understood that? Kee-heh-heh-heh-heh-heh-heh!" Origa cackled.

It was clear from the way Origa spoke that *Shamaya's double cross had been expected from the beginning.*

From the secret chairman's room, Origa could monitor all the cameras hidden throughout the academy, giving Origa access to information that even the other teachers didn't have—if Origa had known from the beginning and had chosen to keep quiet in order to catch them off guard, then...

"...So you're a professional killer, too?" Kyousuke asked as he moved to put Ayaka behind him.

"Bingo ♪," Origa chimed again. The arms of the purple-black mechanical armor opened wide, the voice within full of haughty pride.

"Morbid Angel—with the many secret weapons built into my armor, I'm the strongest killer in Purgatory! Compared to me, Kurumiya and Busujima and Barazono and Muguruma and Greyman—and of course the Murderers' Murderers, the whole lot of them!—all of them, eeeeeveryone is insignificant, you see? It's only natural, since I'm the chairman of the board—"

*   *   *

—Chiiiiiing!

Before the long monologue could be finished, a sword rang off the back of Origa's armor.

"...Hm?" By the time the chairman turned around, the attacker had already darted around, into the armor's blind spot.

—Ching, chin-ching, chin, chiiiiiiiiing!

Blow after blow rained down, faster than the eye could see. The high-pitched sounds of the blade colliding with the armor filled the air, one after the other.

"Aaahhh?!" Origa shrieked in fury. *"When your board chairman is speaking, listen to the end!! Listen to the end when your chairman is speaking!"*

The armor hunched over, and—

"......?!"

A cascade of bullets spewed forth from the armor's back. They spread out in a fan shape over a wide area, and the attacker—Eiri—leaped sideways out of the line of fire.

"How annoying..."

She slashed at the top of Origa's right shoulder. Origa swung back at her with an armored hand, looking irritated. Each of the armored hand's five fingers was tipped with a sharp claw the size of a combat knife. But the talon tore through empty space: Eiri was already flying overhead.

"You go on and on and on..."

A flutter of sword strokes collided with Origa's neck. No sooner had Eiri alighted on the opposite side—

"It's really irritating..."

—than she dodged the left arm that swept at her, slashing upward at the same time and then down again before quickly dashing away faster than Origa could follow.

"Your voice is really grating on my ears, so..."

Before the weapons on the back of the chairman's armor could fire, Eiri carved into them, her sword moving faster than a muzzle flash.

"Just...shut...UP!"

The back of the armor exploded, sending shards of broken metal and smoldering ammunition flying in every direction.

"Whoooaaa?!"

Eiri slipped into the armor's blind spot once again and raised her sword for another swing, when—

"Wait a minuuuuuuute!"

Origa raised both arms like wings, and the armor below the elbows instantly rearranged itself, long crimson blades slipping out from hidden gaps. Origa spun around, swinging the three-foot blades while turning. Eiri nimbly ducked under them, but—

"......?!"

—another set of silver-white blades extended from the armor's legs like spears. Eiri was forced to break off her counterattack and retreat some distance away.

The blade that had sprung from the left arm of Origa's armor quickly retracted. *"......Wheeeeeew,"* Origa sighed. *"You're too violent, Eiri... Who would have known you were so aggressive? You really should be more careful— Wait, heeeeeey?!"*

The chairman looked down at the chest plate before shouting hysterically with head leaned all the way back. "My precious angel has been damaged?! Wha...? No way, even though it's titanium alloy! I'm shocked. What amazing power! House Akabane is too scary. Hey, Kyousuke, Ayaka...is my back all right? It's not too bad, is it?"

Origa turned to give them a full view of the back of the armor. Kyousuke, who was hugging Ayaka to his chest to protect her, timidly looked up.

One part of the armor slowly opened, revealing a battery of guns that had been completely destroyed. A long, narrow gash ran from the right shoulder down to the left flank of the purple-black armor, but—despite how many times Eiri had attacked, that was the only place where the armor had been seriously damaged.

Eiri, for her part, looked puzzled. She checked her sword, then clicked her tongue. "...Tch. Is there something wrong with my sword? This armor is too hard. I can't seem to get through, even when I hit the same place over and over. And I don't see any gaps. What the hell is it made of...? Damn."

That statement finally helped Kyousuke make sense of what had happened. The long gash was where Eiri's sword had struck over and over in the exact same place, gradually wearing through the armor. Due to that, the cut on Origa's back was much deeper than the one scored into his right shoulder, where he had been slashed only once. Her skill with the sword was truly amazing.

"Kyousuke," Eiri, standing on the opposite side of Origa, called out to him. "...Stand down. I'll take care of this... You finish the exam, no matter what happens. As for Renko...forget her for now. This is no time to mourn."

"Eiri—"

"*You forget your place!*" Origa interrupted. The shoulders of the mechanical armor shrugged. "*Good grief. Eiri...you can't 'take care' of me at all! Even if you do manage to cut through my armor, you can't kill me. Besides, the metal is practically invulnerable, and the armor has no openings what-sooo-everrr! How can you possibly hope to fight me?*"

"I'll cut you."

"*...No, no. I toooooold you, it's impossible. This armor is made of titanium alloy—*"

"Doesn't matter," Eiri nonchalantly interrupted. She raised her sword, pointing it at her opponent's face. The silver blade flashed, but not as brightly nor as cold as her sharp, rust-red-colored eyes. "My sword will prove you wrong. That armor may be invulnerable, but I'll destroy all your weapons, until you're nothing but a big metal doll. I will never... I *could* never hand over Kyousuke and Ayaka to the likes of you..."

"*...Eh? I don't like this one bit. I don't like the way you're looking at me, girl... To glare at me with such a sour expression—do you think it'll make me feel hopeless? Do you think I'll just surrender?*"

Origa vigorously swung downward with the blade that extended from the armor's right arm. Red liquid spattered off of the deep crimson blade, showering the ground around him.

"............Eh?"

For the first time, Eiri stopped to examine the blade attached to Origa's armor, the blade that was dyed bright red with—

"—Blood?"

It was unmistakably fresh.

When Eiri took a moment to focus, she saw that the purple-black armor was dotted here and there with something that looked remarkably like blood spatter.

However, Eiri had not been injured. Kyousuke and Ayaka were also unhurt. And Renko had been hit by an electric shock, not by a blade, so—

*   *   *

—exactly whose blood was it?

"*Kee-hee...keh-hee-hee-hee...keh-hee-hee-hee-hee-hee-hee...whose blood do you think this is? Basara's? Bzzt. ♪ Fuyou's? Bzzt. ♪ Kagura's? Bzzt. ♪ Saki's? Bzzt. ♪ Maina's? Bzzt. ♪ Naoki's? Bzzt. ♪ Sanae's? Bzzt. ♪ All wrong! The answer is—*"

Even with the thick armor in the way, they could easily imagine the sadistic grin spreading over Origa's face.

"*The answer is all of them! The blood belongs to all of them! Ah-ha-ha-ha-ha-ha-ha! Basara Akabane and Fuyou Akabane and Kagura Akabane and Saki Shamaya and Maina Igarashi and Naoki Kamiya and Sanae Kamiya...I killed every one of them when they were on their way here! Kya-ha-ha-ha-ha-ha-ha!*"

"—Huh?"

Kyousuke's breath caught in his chest. He couldn't comprehend what had just been said. The shock had left his mind blank. Vacantly, he murmured, "......Killed...them...?"

"*Yep, that's right! Keh-heh-heh-heh-heh-heh-heh! I butchered every-one, eeeeeveryone! I sliced off Basara Akabane's heeead, and I pierced Fuyou Akabane's cheeest, and I cut Saki Shamaya in haaalf, and I carved Maina Igarashi into a honeycooomb, and I stabbed Naoki Kamiya ooover and ooover, and I chopped Sanae Kamiya into little pieeeces!*"

"..........Liar," Eiri muttered. She lifted her head and stared Origa down. "A story like that is definitely a lie!" she shouted. "There's no way you killed them... It's absolutely, completely impossible that those people would fall to someone like you! To be killed by you alone—"

"*That's right. All alone, I probably couldn't have taken them,*" Origa answered calmly. "*Buuut, by the time I got to them, each and every one of them was completely exhausted, you see. They were allllll exhausted and allllll in one place. And so it was easy to kill them! Because all I had to do was ambush them in the middle of a fight and take them down lickety-split. And then I gobbled up every last little tasty bit!*"

"......?! Y-you—"

"Oh? Oh, oh, oh? Could it be that just now you thought, 'I'll kill you'? Could it be, you worthless virgin assassin who can't bring herself to kill? Could it be, Rustyyy Naaail?! Hooray, you did it! Congratulations! Come on, come on—try to kill me! Try to kill me—let's go, let's go! Do your best! Avenge their deaths, Eiri! Let me be your first!"

"Guh—"

Origa advanced on the girl, who was gripping her sword and trembling. The bulky purple-black armor blocked Kyousuke's view of her face.

"Huh?" Origa titled his head. *"What's this—are you still holding back? What stiff resolve. Of course, that must be your papa's influence? You've got a father complex, Eiri! I read Mr. Busujima's report on you, you know?"*

"............"

Eiri stayed silent.

Origa leaned in close to her face and whispered, *"Thanks to the death of your beloved father, you can't kill anyone, making you useless, defective merchandise... When I learned that, I was teeeeeerribly shocked. It felt like my chest would burst open. Ah, poor Eiri, she's so pitiful...ah, and I......I'm probably the one that made her that way."*

Eiri's expression suddenly shifted. "...What did you say?"

Her voice was perfectly flat.

Origa's voice, on the other hand, was full of sadistic glee.

"It was the summer of six years ago, right? The one who killed your father, Masato Akabane...was me."

Instantly:

Chiiiiiiiiiiiiiiiiiiiiiiiiiiiiiiiiiiiiiing! A metallic roar filled the air as the head and arms and neck and chest and shoulders and legs and back and belly and fingers of Origa's armor were struck with slashing attacks one after another. However—

Chiiiiiiiing!

With a terrible wrenching screech, the blade of Eiri's sword snapped.

"Aaah," Origa muttered, *"you're swinging that with all your strength... Eiri, you're going a little overboard there."*

If Eiri heard, she did not care. She raised what remained of her sword above her head. "Die—"

As Eiri swung downward, Origa sliced through the remnants of the sword with his right-hand blade, sending it flying.

"—Ah?" Eiri was left clutching little more than a hilt. The shattered blade spun through the air before sticking into the nearby ground like a gravestone.

"......................What?!"

A tiny noise escaped Eiri's mouth. Still tightly grasping the hilt of her broken sword, she was frozen where she knelt.

Origa smiled down at her.

"*Keh-heh-heh-heh!*" A heavily clad left hand extended outward and patted Eiri's head. "*Wooow, you did so well! That was really very good just now! You felt the urge to kill and held nothing back. I think I would be one hundred percent dead if I wasn't wearing my armor! You caaaaaan kill someone if you really try, Eiriii. I mean, you couldn't kill me, but still... Hey, look here, look here! This weapon—*"

Origa held the blade extending from the right arm up in front of Eiri's eyes. The light reflected off of the edge as it moved.

"*This is* made from the blade that killed your father and snatched him away from you! *It's got incredible cutting power, it does... I wanted this Akabane secret no matter what, so I went out hunting for it. Completely by chance, I happened to run into your papa, Eiri. Sorry, sooo sooorrryyy!*"

Origa lightly tapped Eiri's cheek with the broad side of the blade.

"_____"

Eiri, her cheek now painted with the blood of Fuyou, Kagura, and the others, looked up at Origa. Her lips moved to form the word:

KILL.

"Aaaaaaaaaaaaahhh!"

With a howl of unparalleled ferocity, Eiri leaped forward.

"*Uah?!*" As Origa staggered back, Eiri pounded hard with her fists.

"I'll kill you! I'll kill you, you biiiiiiiiiiiiitch! Kill kill kill kill kill kill kill kill kill kill kill kill! I will, I will! Die die die die die die die die die die die dieee! Aaaaaaaaaaaaahhh!"

Eiri cursed madly. Soon curses changed to screaming, and screaming changed to wailing. Her nails split and broke, her fists cracked and bled, her throat grew hoarse, and tears poured from her eyes.

Origa gazed down. *"Kya-ha-ha-ha-ha-ha-ha-ha-ha-ha-ha-ha-ha! Oh nooo, this girl has become hysterical. How funny! You're too worked up—I can't understand a word you're saaayyyiiing.*

"You're too weak, though! Your punches are so weak—it's true! Sooo weeeaaak, and yelling, 'I'll kill you, I'll kill you,' seriously! You're not doing anything but crying! Punches like that won't get through this armor! You can try again in the next life, duuummy! Die now! Gya-ha-ha-ha!"

Origa raised his right arm overhead. The red blade, still covered in blood, was about to lop off Eiri's head—

"You're the one who's going to die."

"......Hm?"

Suddenly, a right straight punch slammed into the side of Origa's face. The chairman never saw it coming. Origa went flying, armor and all.

Finally, the loud, grating laughter stopped.

X   X   X

"...Kyou...suke......?" Eiri mumbled, her voice barely a whisper.

Kyousuke looked at her hands tattered from colliding with the armor and at her eyes drenched in tears, and he sighed. He unclenched his right fist, which had punched Origa—it was covered in a wine-red leather glove.

"Sorry. Is it okay if I take over for you now? Though I know I'm probably not strong enough...I also want to beat him up, you know," he said quietly.

Though he had lost important people, though Renko had been trampled and beaten, though Eiri had been injured, Kyousuke's mind was surprisingly calm. He did not feel the roiling churn of violent emotions. His passions did not burn bright. What Kyousuke felt was simply an absolute zero, a freezing-cold fury that numbed him to his very core...

"Whoooaaa...what was that impact just now? My head is spinning! What ridiculous physical strength you have! You're quite the oddity, Kyousuke! You're really something special, Kyyyooouuusukeee!"

As the young man approached, Origa continued to rant from a spot on the ground. *"And to do this unarmed, to do this with your bare hands...it's tooooo amazing! If you were trained properly, as a real professional killer, what kind of monster would you become? This is like if a level-one character with no equipment went up against a decked-out level fifty!! Incredible, incredible! So we were right to keep an eye on you— Gbuh?!"*

Kyousuke once more smashed a fist into Origa's face, interrupting the ceaseless squawking. Despite the weight of the massive armor, Origa was still sent flying. Kyousuke thought he had hit the chairman with all his strength, but he couldn't feel the least bit of pain. Could it have been thanks to the leather gloves he got from Naoki? That was just like his dad, and—

"Ngggh...effective, really effective punches! They don't hurt, but I could get sick from the vibrations...oioiii. It would be miserable if I threw up inside my armor— Gyah?!"

This bastard who had killed Eiri's father with his own hands—this disgusting imp made Kyousuke want to vomit. There was absolutely no need for restraint, leniency, or moderation. He could smash him to an absolute pulp.

"I'm going to beat you half to death. Until you're throwing up blood."

"...Keh-heh-heh, is half going to be good enouuugh? After all, it's your debut as a real killer, so don't you think it would be better to go all in? Keh-heh-heh-heh-heh-heh-heh-heh-heh-heh-heh-heh-heh— Egh?!"

Kyousuke wasn't going to let him raise his grating voice. Flexing his fists inside his father's leather gloves, Kyousuke punched Origa in the head again. There was no way that a few blows would be enough. Tens or hundreds or thousands might not be enough. The freezing-cold emotion coursing through his body and gripping his icy heart was unlikely to ever melt.

"Kyyyooouuuusukeee. Give it up already!"

—Wham!

"I mean, why not give up on going back to your old world and stay here in the underworld?"

—Wham!

"Wasn't your school life fun? It was comfortable, wasn't it? It wasn't that bad, right?"

—Wham!

"You fell in love with that homicidal maniac Murder Maid, so you can't hate killing that badly!"

—Wham!

"I'm right, aren't I? If you hate killing from the bottom of your heart, it's impossible that you would fall madly in love with a girl like thaaat. You have aptitude, Kyousuke. You of all people can kill!"

—Wham!

"Yes, welcome to the criminal underworld! Welcome, my dear! I'll take responsibility for you, Kyousuke, and make you a full-fledged killer! I'll turn you into a wonderful assassin! And so—"

—Wham!

"Shut up!"

Kyousuke continued pounding Origa's head, ignoring the taunts thrown at him between each punch. However, the chairman's armor was incredibly strong, and no matter how many times Kyousuke punched it, he couldn't break through. It was a one-sided fight, and his opponent was treating it like a joke. Origa was so sure that human fists could never break the armor, Kyousuke was simply allowed to keep attacking.

Unfortunately, that was right.

Kyousuke hit again and again, dozens of times, and in the end, the only things he broke were his own fists. Origa, meanwhile, was looking perfectly cheerful.

But so what?

Able to kill or unable to kill, it didn't matter. What mattered was whether he would not break, not yield to the opponent. Even if his arms broke, even if he fell to his knees or dropped senseless to the ground...

"Who the hell would go with you?!" Kyousuke shouted. "I'm going back, back to my world—or if not, *Renko will send me to the other side.* There are no other options."

"............*Hmm?*" Origa straightened up, stepping away from a tree that had been used as a leaning post. An armored right hand rose, and with a *crack!* blue lightning sizzled in the palm. *"Even though I*

killed the Murder Maid and destroyed the world you hoped to return to?
Kya-ha-ha-ha! I understand... If that's what you say, Kyousuke, then
I'll have to take even more away from you. I'll make you even more
hopeless!"

As he spoke, Origa turned to look at—

"Ayaka!"

—Kyousuke's little sister, still crouching near Renko, her back
turned to the fight.

Hearing her brother's panicked voice, Ayaka turned to look at him.

"...Yes, brother?" she asked cheerfully.

"What are you doing?! Run—"

As he was screaming at her to get away, Kyousuke noticed that
pressed to Ayaka's ear was a bright red...

"—Ah, you finally picked up! Hello, Crappura? You alive?"

A cell phone. One of the ones that Kyousuke and Ayaka had been
given by Fuyou.

"Wh-wh-what the...?" Origa sounded shaken. He was clearly surprised to see it. *"How d'you get something like that?!"*

However—

"...Hah! That's just like you, a stupid question, Offal Ayaka. Of
course I'm alive, and so is Lady Fuyou. *I just now decapitated one of*
our enemies. And Lady Fuyou has taken care of the other one, so—we're
headed your way now. I heard from my big brother as well—he's fine.
We've got twenty-three minutes until the deadline, right? Aren't you
already headed for the goal?"

The voice coming out of the cell phone speaker belonged to Kagura,
who had supposedly had her head crushed by Origa...

"Hey listen, Crappura... Will you let me ask you one thing? Were
you ever attacked by an assassin wearing something like black robot
armor?"

"Huh? What are you talking about? Lady Fuyou and I haven't seen
anything like that."

"......Eh?" "......Huh?" "Huuuuuuuuuuh?!"

Kyousuke and Eiri were at a loss for words, and Origa was looking
panicked.

Ayaka laughed. "...Is that so? Tee-hee. What's thaaat, it was all a liiie? Tee-hee...it was a made-up, bullshit story in order to distract us! Ah-ha-ha-ha-ha-ha-ha! Hey, little miss sister complex...someone made your beloved older sister cry, you know?"

"...*What did you say?*" On the other end of the line, they could hear Kagura's voice change.

"Hey, so, *you know the person who killed your papa?* We're being attacked by the board chairman, and we're in real trouble. He nearly took Eiri's first time, you know? My big brother prevented that, but he's fighting desperately! If you don't come soon, you're gonna be too laaaaaate!"

"............"

Silence. Kagura was speaking on the other end of the line, but her voice was too quiet to make out. She was probably telling Fuyou about the situation. Before long:

"*Hello? Can you hear my voice, Origa? If you can't hear me, please hear it from Ayaka. Right now—*"

Fuyou's voice was coming out of the phone's speaker.

"*Right now, we are coming to end you. I will annihilate you, drawing out the pain, suffering, and anguish, so...say your prayers and wait for me, all right? Well then, see you soon.*"

Even through the phone, her voice was tinged with a cold hatred that sent shivers down the chairman's spine...

Ayaka slammed the phone closed. There was a brief moment of silence before she laughed. "Tee-hee! Did you hear that, Board Chairman? Did you hear that the assassins of House Akabane, the ones you killed (ha!) are coming to kill yooouuu? At this point it seems like maybe you didn't kill Papa and Mama, either! Tee-hee! You're such a liar, Board Chairman, how uncool! What a bad look!"

"......*Shut up.*"

"Ah, but you should be all right, yeah? You're the strongest assassin in the Purgatorium (ha), right? Everyone, eeeeeeveryone's an instant kill (ha) for you, right? Ah-ha-ha, what the heck! It's all lies, ah-ha-ha-ha-ha-ha-ha!"

"*Shut up, you little munchkin—I'll kill yoooooouuu!!*" Origa's voice cracked into a falsetto; the chairman was clearly livid. Both hands, both legs, both shoulders, his back, his chest, his waist—each part of his armor shifted and rearranged itself as blades, hammers, drills, machine guns, rotating saws—a huge quantity of weapons—appeared from within.

"Ah, that's right! They're all lies, lies lies lies lies lies lies! But it's true that I butchered Masato Akabane and double true that I'm the strongest at the academy! I mean, even if it was a lie, it will become the truth after I kill everyone, won't it?! Bring it on! I'll destroy you... Yes, I'll kill you! You're first, Ayaka Kamiya!"

Aiming the gunport that had opened up in the armor's chest, Origa yelled, "You have no value! You're just a bonus that comes with Kyousuke! So—"

"Stoooooooop!"

Kyousuke launched a desperate attack, sweeping Origa's legs with a reckless kick.

Origa stumbled, but—

"Don't get in my way!"

—after managing to brace himself against the impact, immediately countered with a left kick. Bristling with spikes and blades, the legs of the armor itself were a mass of lethal weapons, and even though Kyousuke was only grazed lightly by the attack, fresh blood sprayed from his stomach, and his clothes were shredded.

Kyousuke fell to the ground, overcome by pain. Origa aimed again at Ayaka, who was running away with a panicked scream.

"Die."

The machine gun spat fire and lead.

Blood sprayed into the air.

"_____!"

A huge figure had stepped in front of Ayaka. Even as the flesh was torn and gouged, the massive form stood unmoving. Becoming a protective wall, the person defending her from the bullets was—

"............"

—Renji, who should have died when Eiri cut him down. Renji, who possessed superhuman resilience, had revived, and there was nothing too surprising about that. But...

"Huuuh?! Hey, what the hell...? Why is this Slaughter Maid moving on his own?! Nobody's given him any orders! You've gotta be fucking kidding me!"

...Renji did not act without Reiko's instructions. And yet, he had moved of his own volition and protected Ayaka. His steely muscles were strong enough even to stand up to machine-gun fire. Origa emptied all the ammunition into Renji's body without inflicting a single fatal wound.

"Aaaaaarrrh! This is bullshit, this is some serious bullshit!" he fumed. *"You're entirely out of line, damn iiittt! I'm pissed off, I'm really pissed off! If you want to die that badly, I'll kill you along with her! I'll kill you, right along with herrrrrr!"*

Yelling, Origa ran toward Renji, blood-soaked blades extended from both arms. Made from the sword that had once been carried by Eiri's father, they were sharp enough to cut through steel like butter. Using these and many other deadly weapons, Origa attacked.

"Hyah?!"

Renji lifted Ayaka's body into his arms with both hands. ".........Run away."

"Eh? Ah, hyaaaaaaaaahhh?!"

—*Whoooooosh!*

Renji *threw* Ayaka with all his strength. Her relatively light body flew high in the air, tracing a wide arc as she flew over the approaching Origa's head.

"Ayaka!"

"Big brotheeeeeer!"

Ayaka landed near Kyousuke, and he quickly moved to scoop her up into his arms.

"Kyousuke!" Ayaka shouted. "Renji said to run—"

"As if I'd let you two get away!"

Origa, who had been closing in on Renji, suddenly changed course. In his path, before Kyousuke's and Ayaka's eyes—

—spreading two tattoo-covered arms, a girl with silver hair was standing in the way.

"...Huh?" Origa slammed to a halt, and Ayaka cheered.

"Renko! Are you all right?! Th-thank goodness... Oh, Renko..."

"Heh-heh. Sorry for worrying you, little Ayaka. Looks like I was dead for about two or three minutes. Sorry to you, too, Kyousuke. Eiri, you've got mixed feelings, I guess? And—"

"Murder Maid... So you lived, you hunk of death-defying junk." Blue energy crackled in Origa's hands.

"Oh, shut up." Renko shrugged her shoulders. "It's not like I would let some boring *man* like you kill me, anyway. And what is with that ridiculous shell? Are you still hiding from the world, even in a place like this, you coward?"

"—What did you say?" Origa's voice was low and angry, downright incensed.

"Heh-heh-heh," Renko laughed. "I said you're a cowardly, timid creature. I mean, I'm right, aren't I? You're afraid to die when you kill someone, so you protect your body with armor like that—you fear the killers and assassins among your teaching staff, so you *barricade yourself* in an isolated stronghold. And you're as effeminate as you could possibly be!"

"Y-yooouuu..." Origa shook with anger—or possibly shame.

"Kyousuke!" Paying no attention to the frothing, Renko called out to her love. Her voice was so gentle that it was hard to imagine the murderous urges roiling around inside her head. *"Get on with it,* you two."

For a moment, Kyousuke didn't understand what she had said. "Eh?"

"Heh-heh," Renko laughed again, still facing the same direction. "Ah, I didn't mean it as 'get on with dying,' okay? I meant run away and"—her ice-blue eyes met his—"*live.*"

"........................Huh?" Kyousuke's breath caught in his chest at Renko's unexpected words. "W-what do you—?"

"I thought I told you I won't let you escape!" Origa, furious enough to be frothing, readied himself to leap at them, but—

"_____!"

"Uaah?!"

Renji crashed down from behind, smashing at the armored head with interlocked fists. Origa just barely avoided the full power of his wrecking-ball blow. With his limiter removed, the Slaughter Maid's physical strength was far greater than Kyousuke's, and even covered in protective gear, there was no way Origa could stand up to the full force of one of his attacks.

Origa grumbled and swung back with an armored arm—even while leaping out of the way. *"You're so annoying!"*

Renji avoided the black steel blade. On its heels, Origa fired a grappling hook from the side of his armor, but Renji dodged that as well, and—

"Nwaaaaaaaaaaaaaaaaaaaa?!"

—he grabbed the cable trailing behind the hook and gave it a mighty heave. Moving as if he were executing an Olympic hammer throw, Renji tossed the powered suit with all his giantlike strength. Origa went flying through the forest, leaves and branches snapping in his path. Renji chased after him as he disappeared into the distance.

"Kyousuke," Renko said when they were done watching the display, turning to face him. Slowly, she took a deep breath. "I want to kill you."

She closed her eyes and inhaled again. "But the mood is important...because I can't enjoy my love affair with you if there are other people in the way, you know? I tried hard to get high on a great melody, but it got interrupted in the middle, and I'm very angry about that. Extremely unpleasant noisecore, bad enough to drown out my feelings for you, is filling my head. Ah, it's really annoying, annoying, annoying..."

Keeping half-lidded eyes trained on the direction in which Origa had disappeared, Renko let out a fierce, guttural snarl from the back of her throat. "And so first, I'm going to eliminate everyone who's in the way. After that, I'm going to kill you. So be sure to stay alive until then."

"Well, in that case!" Kyousuke stepped close to Renko, clenching his broken fists. "Let me take them down with you, Renko! My hands may be a little worse for wear, but I'll be fine if I'm with you, and my legs are still fine. Let's hurry up and take them out, and after that we—"

"I'm sorry, Kyousuke. But you're also in the way."

They were unexpected words.

"...What?" Kyousuke froze, and Renko pointedly narrowed her eyes at him.

"What I'm planning to do now is not a fight or scuffle—it's *to kill*. Kyousuke, you are a normal, ordinary person, aren't you? You're no murderer or assassin, and you have no wish to be... If that's the case, then don't poke your head into other people's affairs anymore. Don't try to get involved. It's got nothing to do with you. Anyone who has decided to return to polite society needs to commit to that decision."

And that's why...

With a sigh, Renko cast her eyes down slightly. "You've got your eyes set on the daylight world, right?"

When she said that, he remembered; Kyousuke recalled the reason why he had been sent to Purgatorium Remedial Academy in the first place. Even if he did make it back to his old life, if he didn't change anything about himself, he would just end up repeating the same mistakes that had brought him here. None of this would have meant anything.

Even so, it would be a pain if, after saying that he would finish the exam with his own strength, he shut up now and let Renko save him...

"For now..." Kyousuke ground his molars in frustration.

Renko's expression softened. "Just for now, see? Even if you don't stay with me in the criminal underworld, even if *you feel like you want me to kill you now*, there's just no particular need to rush. It's all right to take our time, right? And besides, it's not like we're going to be separated right after the exam is over. Finish your exam, take a little time, and then you can get killed at your own pace. You don't have to rush death. There's no need to rush anything, all right?"

"......You..."

"Hm?"

"You think it's all right not to rush things?! This is serious, Renko—you could die at any moment! We have no time!! We can't afford to lose one minute or even one second—"

Suddenly, Renko grabbed Kyousuke's left wrist, pulled him close to her, and—

—pressed her lips to his.

Kyousuke was frozen in surprise. Undeterred, Renko wrapped one hand around the back of his neck, the other around his waist, and squeezed, pressing their bodies together as one. Their lips met more forcefully now, and—

"〰〰〰〰〰〰〰〰〰〰〰〰?!"

—Renko's tongue thrust out, parting her lips, to assault the inside of

Kyousuke's mouth. She slid her tongue around and entwined it with his, biting his lip gently as she did, and then caressed the inside of his mouth, sweeping over the back of his teeth and the inside of his cheeks. Renko's soft, warm tongue danced like a living thing in time to her murderous melody.

Kyousuke, dazed by the vigor and surprise, was completely at her mercy. Even after Renko's tongue retreated and their lips and bodies separated, he simply stood there, spellbound.

Breaking the gossamer string of saliva that she had pulled from the tip of his tongue, Renko smiled mischievously. "Okay, good, that shut you up at least."

Kyousuke...

Renko spoke his name as she stared at him. This close, Renko's eyes were pretty and clear, and they shone with a piercing intensity. Her pupils, like two deep, dark pits, were brimming with insanity.

"I could die any moment?! Don't say stupid things. Do you think I would die and leave you, the one I love so much, behind? Heh-heh, I'll be fine. Don't worry. I will absolutely come back to kill you. I won't let anyone else kill you, and I won't let anyone kill me, either! So shut up and go, Kyousuke. I want you to believe in my feelings."

"Renko..."

"You too, Ayaka." Renko shifted her gaze to the girl who was standing next to her brother. Ayaka, who had stared hard at their kiss, looked back at Renko vacantly.

Putting a hand on her head, Renko flashed her canines. "You'll be lonely if Kyousuke dies, so I'll be sure to kill you, too... Ah, but before that, let's do that thing, okay? Do you remember? Before summer vacation, we were planning a date, right? We made plans to go here and there, but in the end we couldn't do any of it, so after you pass your exit exam, let's make it happen! If I ask Mama, she should allow me that much."

"Renko..." Ayaka's vacant eyes began to shimmer, and her face crumpled and twisted. "Renko!"

Ayaka embraced her, burying her face in the older girl's abundant chest. "It's a promise—you promised!!" she shouted.

Stroking Ayaka's head as she sobbed and cried, Renko turned to the last person—the girl looking the other way with her arms crossed, sullenly pouting.

"Eiri—"

"Aaaaaaaaahhh, shut uuuuuuuuuuuuppp!"

Before Renko had the chance to speak to her, Origa burst from the forest. The purple-black armor was covered in so much blood spatter that it was hard to see the colors underneath, and the blades on both arms were entirely coated in bright red. However, no conspicuous new damage could be seen on the armor itself.

Venting all the pent-up fury, Origa sliced through the trunk of a nearby tree. *"Are you fucking kidding me, you traitors?! What the hell, Murderers' Murderers?! You're worse than useless… You're in my way! What the hell is with you, you pieces of junk…? Ah, geez, I don't know! I just don't know! I'm going to slaughter you… Every one of you assholes who defy me, I'm going to kill every single one of you and leave no one behind!! You're next, Murder Maid, ooooooohhh!"* He brandished his bloody blades like crimson wings.

"Eiri," Renko said as she gripped the choker around her neck, preparing to meet Morbid Angel's attack.

"I'm entrusting Kyousuke to you."

"……Huh?" Eiri's eyes opened wide. "Ah, don't tell me, you're—"

Without a moment's hesitation, Renko tore off the leather choker and invoked her second use of Over Drive. A torrent of invisible energy seemed to warp the air, and the temperature suddenly dropped.

Sensing the unusual phenomenon, Origa skidded to a quick halt, leaving some fifteen feet between them. *"Damn, so you used it! You've gotta be fucking kidding me—"*

Warily, the chairman began to back away.

"Renkooooooo!" Kyousuke snapped out of his trance in a fury. "You, what are…? Why are you doing such a stupid thing?! Don't you understand?! If you use that—"

"I won't die."

"Eh?"

"I told you, didn't I? That no matter what happens, I am absolutely coming to kill you…to take your life. So my body won't survive? No problem! It's a promise, Kyousuke." Renko was facing away from him, and her hair fluttered softly in the breeze. Her voice was soft but strong.

"After you finish this exam, even if I don't open my eyes…no matter how many days pass, no matter how many months pass, no matter how many years pass, no matter where you are, no matter where I am, no matter how far apart we are, I will come to you. I will absolutely come to reap you. Until that time, this is good-bye."

"……I…understand," Kyousuke replied and sighed. Honestly, he wasn't sure he really understood it all, but he felt as if he had no choice but to accept it.

"Ooohhhhhh, Renkooo…," Ayaka grumbled as her brother took her hand.

"…Tch. Well, I guess there's no choice, then! As if I wanted you to trust me, stupid Renko… You are really, until the very end…such an aggravating, offensive bitch. Hmph…you're better off dead!"

Kyousuke and Ayaka followed behind Eiri, who was pouring ill-omened abuse down on their classmate. Origa was screaming loudly for some reason, but they mostly tuned it out.

As they left, Kyousuke turned back and called out to her.

"Renkoooooooooo!"

"……?!"

The girl trembled, but either because she could not take her eyes off of her opponent Origa or because their parting was just too painful, Renko remained facing away from him. She did not turn to look as Kyousuke shouted:

"—I'll be looking forward to it, okay?! Some day, some month, some year—I'll be waiting always *for you to come and kill me!*"

*   *   *

He made his declaration and with it left behind any desire to stay there with her. He did not wait for Renko's response, though as he turned his back on her, Kyousuke thought he saw Renko starting to turn toward him. That was plenty.

Kyousuke and the others took off at a run, dashing furiously toward their goal without slowing or stopping even once.

And then......

Biiiiiiiiiiing, boooooong...
   Baaaaaang, boooooong...

"Big brother, wake up!"

It was a beautiful day. Small birds were singing, and spring sunshine was pouring through the window. Kyousuke's blankets were pulled away, stirring him from sleep.

"...Uunh."

Turning toward the gentle chirping, he felt as if he was hearing a sound from long ago. When he opened his heavy eyelids and looked, Ayaka, wearing a gingham checkered apron, was standing beside the bed in an imposing stance. Apparently she had come to wake him in the middle of cooking—she was still gripping a ladle in one hand.

"If you don't come soon, you'll be late!"

"...Late?"

He checked the time—it was a little bit past nine o'clock. If it had been a weekday, Kyousuke would have been completely late, but today was a holiday. He turned over, hoping to escape back into sleep.

"...Dummy. Today's a holiday—school's out. You may be up, but your brain's still half-asleep—"

"Stupiiiiiiiiiiid!"

Something solid cracked down on the back of his skull.

"Oww?!"

Ayaka glared down at her brother, brandishing her ladle overhead. "Geez! You're the one who's half-asleep!! Today sure is a holiday, but you've got more important plans than school! Don't you know that if you're late, you'll miss your chance?"

"......?! Oh shit—"

The moment she said that, Kyousuke's eyes shot open. Jumping up, he rushed to get ready. "Good grief," Ayaka said, exasperated, as Kyousuke threw his sweatshirt off and ran out of his room.

"Naoki, sweeetie! ...Ah, it's Kyousuke. Good morning, dear."

"Sanae, honeeey! ...Whoa, tch. Don't be a nuisance, ya damn brat."

"...... Morning."

On the sofa in the living room, today as always, his parents were making out. It was really irritating. He hoped they'd go back to work soon.

"How annoooying," Ayaka said, returning from Kyousuke's room after folding his sweatshirt. "I hope they go back to work soon." After voicing Kyousuke's exact thoughts, she started preparing breakfast.

Perhaps because Naoki and Sanae had already finished eating, they continued their games on the couch. Ayaka served up rice and carried over bowls of reheated miso soup, and brother and sister sat down to a happy table.

"How about it, Kyousuke? Are you used to *normal* school yet?"

Naoki briefly stopped making out with his wife to pose the question.

The abnormal school for student murderers—Purgatorium Remedial Academy. Already almost half a year had passed since Kyousuke and Ayaka had escaped it.

The family had moved away from their old place, sold the house, and were now living in a four-room condo in town. They had had their previous convictions expunged and had worked over their personal histories, and the two siblings had enrolled separately in a public high school and a private junior high school in April of that year.

And it was currently the beginning of May—

"Hm, let me see..." Kyousuke recalled, "I was confused by a few things at the beginning, but as you would expect, I think I've gradually gotten used to it?" He nodded. "I was always 'normal' after all."

The first week or so of school, Kyousuke had felt out of place everywhere he went. It was frightening to think about what he had gotten used to, but Kyousuke had felt as if his peaceful school life, without the abusive language, horrific violence, and constant threats to his very life, was somehow lacking...

"I'm able to enjoy myself every day. And I've made some normal friends, I guess? The girls talk to me like normal and aren't weirdly afraid of me."

"Slayer," "Megadeth," "Anthrax," "Metallica"...here nobody called Kyousuke by those nicknames, and he was not getting into any fights, so his daily life was one of unparalleled calm.

"—Ugly sows talking to my big brother? Hmm, is that so? Hmmmm?" With lightless eyes and an unnerving smile, Ayaka stabbed at the eyeball of a grilled fish with her chopsticks. She was as deeply jealous as always, and it gave him a chill to watch her...

Ayaka had also experienced daily life at Purgatorium Remedial Academy, and perhaps because of the experience, recently she had been spending more and more time with her new friends and distancing herself from him little by little. Even today, she had plans to go to karaoke in the afternoon.

Looking over his children, Naoki smiled, glad they seemed to be doing well. "...Is that so?"

Naoki and Sanae, who were still recovering from the wounds they had suffered during mortal combat half a year ago, spent most days at home now, even though the worst of their injuries had already healed.

"Sanae, honey, the kids seem all right, so how about we go back to work soon?"

"Eh? No, no, I want to get lovey-dovey some more! I want to make out with my Naoki some mooooooore!"

And so they continued flirting. Maybe because they had almost died, the two of them had become more lovey-dovey than ever. Kyousuke was already fed up with them; he yearned for them to show even a little restraint.

Averting his eyes from his lip-locked parents, Kyousuke, now finished with breakfast, quickly washed the tableware.

"Well, I'm going."

"Okay. Be careful, bro!"

He finished getting dressed and opened the entryway door as his sister saw him off. "Hey," he asked, just in case, "are you sure you don't want to come? You haven't seen her in a while, either."

"Tee-hee! I'm fine—I have other plans."

"...Don't tell me they're with a boy?" he asked suspiciously.

"Huh?" Ayaka looked back reproachfully. "No way. Are you stupid...? I've got you to take care of!"

"O-oh...is that so...?"

"It is. Really now. I'm telling you, Kyousuke, you—" Ayaka was exasperated and gave an exaggerated sigh. But after that, she smiled. "...Well, whatever. Tell her hello from Ayaka. And tell her I said, 'Let's go on another date together soon. ♪'"

"Got it—I'll tell her. See you later!"

"Mm. See you, big brother! And don't forget to wear a condom!"

...What was that about? She sure seems to be learning a lot about sex lately... Maybe it's the influence of that person she's been exchanging e-mails and calls with for the last six months...?

As he left the house, Kyousuke decided that he would follow his little sister's advice in that particular area, should the situation arise.

X   X   X

From the nearest station, Kyousuke had to make two train connections in under an hour. It was nine thirty when he left the house, so he would make it to the meeting at eleven with time to spare—or that's how it should have gone, anyway.

"C-crap...I'm totally late."

The train was delayed due to a suicide on the tracks and arrived just past eleven fifteen. Kyousuke rushed through the gates and headed for the meeting spot, thinking frantically about the apology he would have to give.

In a corner of the crowded station, standing near a bronze statue that was their meeting point, was—

"......*Fwah.*"

—a beautiful, listless girl with a rust-red ponytail and a slender figure who stood out even among the crowds of fashionable youths. A seasonal pink jacket, a white dress, and two-color sandals—wearing civilian clothes, she was toying with a sparkly cell phone and yawning with apparent boredom.

"Eiri! Sorry for making you wait—"

"Eh?! No way, aren't you just the cutest? I woulda thought there was an angel here, for real!"

"Fer real, fer real. Amazing, huh? Hey, where're ya from? Heaven?"

Just as Kyousuke was about to run up to her, two young men who looked like troublemakers sidled up to Eiri.

"You'd be better off dead," she answered flatly, never even taking her eyes off of her cell phone screen.

"Ehh?!" The pair recoiled.

"No way, aren't you just the scariest? I thought there was an angel here, but it was a demon, for real…"

"Fer real, fer real. Awful, huh? Hey, where're ya from? Hell?"

"…………"

Eiri completely ignored them. However, the two men didn't seem to get the hint and continued trying to start something with her.

"Hey, hey, hey? Don't play those games—how 'bout you come play with us?"

"Let's play, let's play. We'll pay you for your time. We'll lay down some cash."

"Say, say, say! Knowing you, bet you'd like to lay down more than that, huh? I won't allow it!"

"You won't allow it! What are you, her boyfriend? Naw, man, I'm gonna be her boyfriend!"

"…Huh? Who would go out with guys like you—?"

"*It's me.*" Kyousuke cut in before Eiri could finish snapping at them.

"…………Eh?"

The man whose shoulder he had put his hand on loomed over him. "—Huh?"

The other punk drew closer as well. "Hey, hey, hey! Who the hell're you? What a boring dude. You don't have the balls to go fishing for this girl!"

"Yeah, you don't have the balls! If you don't want to get hurt, you better hurry up and get outta my sight, you dumb bastard!"

"Is that so?" Kyousuke could feel the blood rushing to his head as his temper rose. He was about to reflexively return their threats, when—

"In that case, you've got your eyes set on polite society, right?"

—he recalled *her* words and the reason why he had ended up at Purgatorium Remedial Academy in the first place.

"…Ah, sorry. You're right—a guy like me could never score a girl like her, right? Ha-ha-ha…" Kyousuke gave a strained laugh. He relaxed his tense expression and scratched the back of his head.

"……?" The good-for-nothings exchanged glances.

Kyousuke immediately grew serious again. "…But that's got nothing to do with it. She's the one who gets to choose her partner. Not you guys. Eiri—"

He held out his hand and smiled at his friend, who was standing stock-still, eyes wide. "Shall we go?"

"Eh? Ah, aah…mm. Thanks, Kyousuke…" Eiri blushed and took his hand bashfully.

Kyousuke and Eiri left the station together, ignoring the two men mockingly shouting "You're better off dead!" behind them.

X   X   X

"……That surprised me," Eiri mumbled.

They entered a nearby fast-food restaurant, and Eiri settled in across from Kyousuke. She drank her strawberry shake as she spoke.

"Ha-ha-ha… It was almost a disaster, huh?" Kyousuke laughed, strained. "Well, there are lots of guys trying to pick up girls in the city, so—"

"Not them."

"…Hm? Ah, right. When you're as beautiful as you are, Eiri, you must already be used to it. Even when it's a pain in the ass…but I'm thinking about giving up fighting already. Before, I probably would have sent them flying without a second thought, but the fact that I can never seem to hold back is what got me tossed into that place—"

"Not that, either! Well, okay, I was surprised by that, too, but…" Eiri was looking down and squirming. Her face was red, and she kept her head hung low even when she looked up at him. "Th-that… When you came to help me, that thing you said? Y-you said, 'It's me'…'Her boyfriend is me,' you said. Those words……"

"Ah, sorry to surprise you… I just said that so I could help you—"

"I know that, stupid! Could you not go out of your way to explain things like that?!"

"S-sorry…"

He had made her angry. Though it may have been a split-second decision, claiming to be her boyfriend out of nowhere probably hadn't made Eiri feel very good. Kyousuke slouched and picked at a french fry while Eiri chewed her straw.

"…Hmph. So you haven't matured in that arena, huh? Not that I care…but, anyway, hello again. How is your life going? Has it calmed down?"

Kyousuke looked up at Eiri's face. It was the first time he'd seen her in half a year. They had exchanged e-mails and phone calls, but both of them had somehow always been busy, and today was their first time meeting since Kyousuke had dropped out of the academy. He spontaneously let out a smile.

"…Oh yeah, things have really calmed down for us. Before I started school, I tried to study up on all the things I hadn't learned like my life depended on it, and I'm getting used to normal school life, too… How about you? You don't have any experience living on this side. And you're living alone—"

"No problems," Eiri answered nonchalantly, unwrapping her shrimp burger. "…It's easy, really. My family is a great help. Two months have passed since I moved here, but so far I have no complaints. Maybe just that I can't fit all of my clothes in my closet." Eiri bit into her burger and smiled widely.

Eiri, who had just started living on her own in the city after leaving the Akabane manor, was currently an amateur model for a girls' fashion magazine. She had been scouted as soon as she had gotten off the bullet train, and she started the job a few days later—and despite the fact that the magazine had printed only two issues with her in them so far, her popularity was already through the roof. Several months earlier, she had wailed into the phone that her grades weren't strong enough to get her into the same public school as Kyousuke, but now she didn't seem to care about that in the slightest. She was making impressive and rapid progress.

"…Well, I can't make a living just as an amateur model, and if I paid for my own clothes I would go into debt…so recently, I've been studying for professional certification, too. For the technical skills trade test to become a nail artist."

Eiri showed him her nails. A black checkered pattern was painted on a red background, with a ribbon decoration on the ring finger. They were delicate and cute, done well enough to put a pro to shame.

"Wow, Eiri…you're really giving it your all."

"Heh-heh-heh, I told you! There are lots of things I want to do. Plenty more besides modeling and nail art! I went to the trouble of getting out of my parents' house, so I plan to have as much fun as I can."

"…Is that so? Yeah, that's right."

Kyousuke grinned at Eiri, whose smile spread across her whole face. Thanks to starting work as an amateur model, she sported a cheerful expression far more often now than she had when they were at that school. She seemed more lively—more alive.

Half a year ago.

Kyousuke and the others had passed the Deadly Exit Exam with flying colors. As they had arrived at the goal thirty-six minutes before the deadline, it had been decided that Kyousuke Kamiya, Ayaka Kamiya, and Eiri Akabane would be allowed to leave the academy.

There had been ten casualties during the Deadly Exit Exam. Basara had killed Abashiri, Takamoto, and Barazono; Kagura had killed Motoharu, Takakage, and Greyman; Shamaya had killed Kuroki, Kiriu, and Mizuchi; Fuyou had killed Origa...

After the armor had been destroyed, Origa had been chopped into pieces too small to recognize. On the other hand, Busujima, who had fought with Fuyou earlier, had been left heartbroken by the incredible slaughter that had killed each and every one of his dear pets; he had taken to secluding himself in his staff room. Kurisu, who had been stuffed with Busujima's pets and sliced open by Kagura, had somehow survived. Though her wounds had seemed absolutely fatal, she had apparently managed to escape death thanks to one of Busujima's hemostasis toxins, which she had administered to herself while the fighting went on.

After that, there were three others who had sustained serious injuries—Muguruma, Haruyo, and Shamaya. The incredible warrior who had taken all three of them out was...Maina Igarashi. In her absolute, frenzied panic, Maina had conjured up her usual whirlwind of hapless destruction, catching Muguruma and Haruyo, the two masters of the Assassin's Fist, and Shamaya, who had nominally been fighting on the same side, up in the haphazard tempest. All three had been laid out with multiple compound fractures.

After Kyousuke's class graduated, Maina would probably reign as the Accidental Assassin—or so he had thought. But—

"Last night, I got a call from Miss Reiko."

"—What?" As soon as Kyousuke broached the subject, Eiri's brow wrinkled.

Kyousuke rushed to continue. "Ah, well, it sounds like Maina and the others moved up to second year and started the assassination curriculum for real."

"......Ah."

Eiri's expression relaxed. Kyousuke lowered his voice so that the customers around them couldn't hear and told her what was going on.

Currently, at Purgatorium Remedial Academy, Reiko had replaced Origa as the board chairman. While alive, Origa had apparently been a key scientist for the Organization and had been provided with an extensive underground laboratory. That was where he had created the mechanical armor he had used during the exit exam.

Machines and living creatures. Though they had worked in different fields, as scientists, their approaches were similar. Therefore Reiko had been entrusted with the remainder of the lab, and her days were apparently very busy now. Among her new duties—

"It sounds like Maina's physical constitution is a matter of some debate at the academy. She's just too different, and they're not sure how to train her or whether she'll become unusable after training or something..."

"...I can believe it. Honestly, that girl's future is the hardest to envision."

"Yeah, well, because of that, they eventually decided to stop training her."

"—Huh? Well then, what is she...?"

"She's been made Miss Reiko's *assistant*."

"Assistant?!"

"Yeah. Keeping Maina by her side, Miss Reiko can thoroughly study her unique physiology, she says. She's doing things like making new poisons from food that Maina cooks..."

"H-huh..."

"The higher-ups apparently didn't have much choice in the matter. Reiko's keeping Maina at a distance from the other murderers. Maina doesn't want to kill anyone...but if they released her into regular society, there would be no way to know when she might slip up. Miss Reiko is keeping close watch and taking care of her, it seems."

Eiri's eyebrows rose. "Hmm, is that so?" She looked doubtful. "If that's the case, I suppose we can sleep a little easier..."

"Yeah. It sounds like she's able to go outside if she wants to, so if she has some time in her schedule, she might come hang out with us. Reiko even said she's going to buy Maina a cell phone soon!"

"...Eh? Not bad. I might have to give that old lady a little more credit."

After that, they chatted about the academy for a while.

About the fact that Mohawk, who was supposed to have died during the exit exam, had of course survived just fine and was pursuing Kurumiya even more fiercely than before, prompting Kurumiya to finally submit her resignation from the faculty. About how Reiko's diplomatic efforts to mend ties between House Akabane and the Organization had included giving Basara Akabane a teaching position at the academy. About the fact that Basara was making passes at all the female students. About the fact that this year, as always, had a new crop of dreadful freshmen. About the fact that Bob had joined the Public Morals Committee. About the fact that Chihiro had killed and eaten Michirou...and so on. Kyousuke shared the stories he had heard from Reiko, and Eiri shared what she had heard from Basara.

"Uh, hey, um..." Suddenly, Eiri faltered, casting her eyes down as if she had something difficult to say. "It's...about *her*—"

"Eiri!!"

The chatter in the restaurant instantly stopped. Kyousuke hadn't meant to shout like that. He felt everyone's gaze fix upon their table.

Since Eiri was looking down, he couldn't get a read on her expression. But it was clear that he had caught her off guard.

As they sat there in mutual silence, ten seconds passed. Then twenty, then thirty...

"Kyo-Kyousuke—"

"Sorry!"

Interrupting Eiri as she was about to say something, Kyousuke pressed both hands together. Trying to clear the oppressive atmosphere, he apologized.

"I'm sorry I yelled! And that I was late...so if you would let me treat you to everything from now on... Really, I'm sorry!"

"It's fine," Eiri grumbled nonchalantly and stood up, looking down at him. "...Don't worry about it so much. I'm the one who's sorry, Kyousuke...suddenly bringing up a strange subject. Please forget it."

"N—"

"But…" Thrusting her index finger at the tip of his nose, Eiri flashed Kyousuke a wide smile. "There are a lot of things I want to do today. Go shopping and buy lots of cute clothes and accessories, eat lots of delicious food, and have lots of fun experiences! That's all I want—don't forget. Stick with me right until the end!"

After they finished having lunch at the fast-food restaurant, Kyousuke and Eiri went all kinds of places and enjoyed all kinds of things. They window-shopped in the fashion building, performed an impromptu fashion show trying on clothes in a high-end fashion store, went around to a sweets shop that Eiri had checked out a long time ago, took a small break at a café, found odd products at a store that dealt in miscellaneous imports, played on the UFO catchers at a game center, marveled at the strange atmosphere in a Lolita fashion boutique… Along the way, Eiri was stopped by a number of fans asking for autographs, and when they happened to run into a friend from Kyousuke's high school and were cross-examined about their relationship, Eiri answered, "…I'm his girlfriend" and made that person scowl. Eiri smiled and said, "That's payback for earlier," but Kyousuke, whose friend had told him to "fuck off" in a serious tone, could not smile back. They spent the day together.

"Ah, that was tasty! As you would expect for something shown on TV."

"Yeah. It was super delicious!"

…*And super expensive*, Kyousuke added as he chased after Eiri. At least she was still in high spirits.

The restaurant where Eiri had made reservations was on the top floor, and despite the fact that it had cost a mind-boggling amount of money, Eiri didn't seem to care. She had simply paid her own and Kyousuke's tabs plus the luggage-holding fee with her debit card and walked jauntily out of the restaurant.

One thing that Kyousuke had come to understand very well this day was that Eiri had some strange ideas about money. Though since she had come from a family that was famous for its assassins, and since she had been raised by a doting mother, that was probably only natural…

Kyousuke, carrying a huge number of shopping bags on each arm, climbed the stairs, feeling a little light-headed. When they reached the top, Eiri leaned against the guardrail of the pedestrian bridge and stared vacantly out into space. The lights of the cars running past below illuminated her profile.

"............"

Eiri was wearing an extremely serious expression. Even when Kyousuke caught up to her, she didn't look as if she was going to start moving. Confused, Kyousuke was about to say something, when—

Suddenly, Eiri looked at him. Her gaze was resolute, as if she had made an important decision.

"Kyousuke..."

She called his name and slowly stepped away from the guardrail.

"I like you."

"......?!"

As she spoke, she pressed her lips against his.

The bags dropped from Kyousuke's hands. The noises of the city faded away, and his breath caught in his chest.

A soft feeling. A stiff kiss, like the peck of a small songbird. A moment passing that felt like an eternity.

"I—"

Eiri gently opened her mouth to speak. Only then did Kyousuke finally realize that her lips had left his. Looking directly back at the dumbfounded young man, Eiri continued:

"I love you, Kyousuke. I really love you, no less than Renko."

Renko. The moment he heard that name, a tremor rippled through Kyousuke's heart. It was a name that Kyousuke still believed in, had believed in for the past half year, the name of the monstrous murderer and crazy girl whom he still felt so much for.

As far as what had become of Renko, who had fallen into a coma after releasing her second Over Drive during the exit exam...Kyousuke had no idea. But—

"I know that you feel like you *can't give Renko up.* I know that you

don't want to give up on her, and that you also don't want to hear about her, and that even now you still love her and want to see her and want to be connected to her—I know all of that. I understand..."

"............"

"I'm not denying that part of you, and I'm not blaming you, either. If you love her, you love her, and you can go right ahead feeling that way. But I'm also not giving up!"

Eiri's expression held a resolve stronger than any he'd ever seen. She spoke with unwavering certainty.

"I'm going to continue pursuing my feelings without giving up, and someday I will absolutely win you over. We'll fall in love; you'll see. Before that girl Renko can come and kill you."

"Eiri...I'm sorry, I still—"

"Aah, just be quiet! I told you, I know. I said all of that knowing that right now you can't accept my feelings! Besides..."

...She entrusted you to me.

Muttering to herself, Eiri turned away. She pointed to the bags strewn out on the concrete of the pedestrian bridge.

"For now, though...would you carry those as far as *my bedroom*?"

She made it sound so casual.

"Eh? As far as...where did you say?" Kyousuke asked, dumbfounded.

She turned and gave him a sharp, half-lidded look. "I told you: as far as my bedroom. I can't carry this many bags all by myself...and you said you'd stick by me to the end, right? So, carry them with me?"

Picking up half of the shopping bags, Eiri smiled mischievously. Seeing her impish face, Kyousuke finally understood. She had been planning this course of action from the very beginning. That was why she had purchased such an enormous amount of clothing and accessories and trinkets and knickknacks and stuffed animals.

She would get Kyousuke to carry them to her room, and then—

"...Ah, don't worry—it'll be fine! My apartment isn't even thirty minutes' walk from here. Even if you come with me, you'll be able to get back home no problem. *If nothing happens on the way, that is.*"

—Is she planning something?!

Noticing the suspicious light shining in Eiri's piercing eyes, Kyousuke shuddered. He suddenly remembered both the words Ayaka had spoken to him as he had left the house that morning and the story of how Eiri's mother, Fuyou, had forced her husband to surrender with her passionate, carnivorous allure.

"............"

He trembled with fear, a feeling he had almost forgotten since returning to polite society and washing his hands of daily violence. Nevertheless, it wasn't as if he could leave Eiri and her bags where they were and just run away...

Hey, Renko..., he thought, *how long are you gonna sleep? You'd better hurry up and come for me. If you don't, then Eiri might do me in before you kill me...*

Joking to himself, Kyousuke looked up at the navy-blue night sky. He wondered if, in that faraway place, Renko was still fast asleep.

Or if she was already......

"Hey, Kyousuke, what are you just standing there for? Hurry up and come on!"

"Hm? Ah, sorry. I'm coming!"

Snapping back to his senses, Kyousuke quickly grabbed the bags and looked up. Eiri, holding the other half of the bags, had turned around to look back at him, and behind her—he could see a figure moving nearer.

—When asked what part of him she loved, Renko Hikawa had answered without hesitation, "All of him."

She loved his gentleness, she loved how he was awkward but honest, she loved how even though he seemed strong and masculine, he was actually fairly pure and sweet and therefore, she felt as if she had value by protecting him. And though she normally couldn't stand idiots, she even loved how he was a little dumb and charmingly pathetic. She loved all of him.

Even so, if she had to name just one quality...?

Finally, after puzzling it over, Renko gave this answer:

"I love the murderous melody that plays for him."

Renko's brain was somewhat unusual. Every single one of her emotions was somehow tied to the act of *murder.* Happiness and sadness and anger and distress, fear and impatience and longing and jealousy...

All of them mixed together into something confusing and bizarre, jumbled together in infinite variety to play the many diverse sounds of her murderous melody. Death metal, brutal death metal, techno death metal, melodic death metal, hardcore, metalcore, deathcore, mathcore, chaotic hardcore...though it was always a "murderous melody," there was some deviation in the genre. It was rough and violent, beastly music, and depending on the person, she couldn't suppress her emotions when she heard it. It stopped if she was wearing her limiter, the thing shaped like a black gas mask, but from the moment she had been born, she couldn't find even a moment's calm without the echo of background music, so even with her limiter on, she also always wore headphones that played the music that most closely resembled her murderous melody. No music, no life. To Renko, living was playing music, and playing music was killing.

So what Renko had initially been drawn to was not Kyousuke himself *but the murderous melody that flowed through her head whenever she thought of him.*

And she could never forget what had happened the night after she first exchanged words with him—what had happened when Renko took her limiter off in her room in the student dorms. Renko's whole world was shattered in one instant by the melody that filled her then. It was a magnificent tune, enough to make all the music she had listened to before seem like nothing more than annoying noise. And the more she thought of him, the more the melody grew deep and clear, and her emotional reaction to the music only made it even more powerful—on and on in a dreamlike spiral. The rushing torrent swallowed Renko up in the blink of an eye...

—and *dropped her into love.*

Well, she had probably fallen in love on her own first. It was the first time she had ever experienced love, and she had not been able to recognize her own feelings without the tune of her murderous melody playing. But why...why was it that she felt such love for him...? She had wandering thoughts like this every night. As she contemplated her love, the marvelous tune would play, and Renko would transcribe the score in a trance. She wrote lyrics for that tune, gave voice to them, and sang a song that contained her true feelings. She forgot time; she forgot herself and wallowed in her love.

And so it came as a terrible shock when he rejected her love, and she was assaulted by an overwhelming sense of loss and the feeling that her whole world had been swallowed up, even more so than when she had first fallen in love. The magnificent murderous melody ground to a stop, leaving her in anguish, struggling to breathe. For the first time since her birth, she knew the saltiness of flowing tears.

Because of the pain she had felt in the past, Renko was all the more insanely happy when she unexpectedly heard his words:

"Who the hell would go with you?! I'm going back, back to my world—or if not, Renko will send me to the other side. *There are no other options."*

This, however, had come after she'd been knocked comatose by a surprise attack at the conclusion of the Deadly Exit Exam, the conclusion of which would determine her future with him.

And those words had pulled her back from the brink. And even if she had imagined them, even if she was his lowest priority, she didn't mind at all. Renko was simply happy happy happy happy happy happy happy...

She was so happy, she had already stopped caring about what happened to her.

Caring about her own life.

Caring about her own happiness.

That was why—

"I'm entrusting Kyousuke to you."

Renko had said that to her—to the girl who was her foremost rival in love and also her best friend. She decided to entrust *everything* to her. Entrust his life. Entrust his happiness. She would ask that girl to handle everything.

If it was her, she could without a doubt protect his life in broken-down Renko's place.

If it was her, she could without a doubt carry the burden of his happiness in worn-out Renko's place.

"......Huh? Ah, don't tell me, you're—"

The girl's eyes had opened wide.

Oh good, she understands perfectly that's right, I'm planning to throw it all away. My own life and my own happiness, I'm planning to give it up for the sake of his life and happiness. Please help me. Please support me. Make up for my loss after I'm gone, Eiri...

She had tried to make these thoughts come through in her words.

But he probably won't understand, so...

"I won't die."

Renko had decided to lie.

"I will absolutely come to kill you," she had said. *"No matter how many days pass, no matter how many months pass, no matter how many years pass. No matter where you are, no matter where I am, no matter how far apart we are, I will come to you."*

Since it seemed as if her lie would be laid bare if she met his eyes, she had spoken those words in a strong voice, keeping her back turned to him.

I'm the worst. I'm a cruel woman.

No matter how often she repeated to herself that she didn't care what happened, the truth was that she was slowly filling with regret after throwing everything away several seconds earlier. The reason that Renko had lied was not to persuade him. It was to persuade herself.

There was not much left of Renko's life. That was a matter of course, since she had unleashed her Over Drive for the second time. She would die. She would certainly die. But there was no helping it. If Renko hadn't done it, Eiri would have been killed, Ayaka would have been killed, Renji would have been killed (perhaps he already had been?), and Kyousuke would have been turned into mad little Origa's plaything... That was no good. No good at all!

And although she had given up her own life, she had not quite given up all happiness, it seemed. The lie that Renko had told him was not entirely meant as a vow. It was also a curse.

The curse of the seed of promise planted in his heart, the promise that "Renko will come and reap me." The curse of fleeting hope had taken root. Even after she herself had passed away, he would continue to think about her. As long as he believed her promise and longed for her without giving up... If she had just this one small happiness, Renko could *finish out her life* with a clear heart.

Just the tiniest glimmers of painful regret remained, but that was fine as long as he had his life and happiness, she thought. She tried to think.

—And then it happened.

"Renkooooooooo!"

"......?!"

As she was leaving, he cried out to her. Thinking that her lie had been exposed, Renko trembled and shook. However—

"—I'll be looking forward to it, okay?! Some day, some month, some year—I'll be waiting always *for you to come and kill me!*"

In that moment, as he made that declaration, everything fell into place.

"…………Eh?"

The tune of the murderous melody that was reverberating around inside of Renko *changed*. It didn't lapse into irregular meter or shift keys. The music itself transformed. It evolved from melancholic progressive death metal full of pathos to sublime symphonic black metal full of hope and majesty—

"……Kyou…suke……?"

Despite herself, Renko had looked back, but he had already turned away and was running from that place. The elegant tone of the music, weaving together stringed instruments and harps, tore through the clouds that hung thickly over Renko's heart, allowing radiant light to stream in. It was more dazzling and filled her with more complex feelings than any murderous melody she had ever heard before. She was absolutely overwhelmed. It took her breath away and engulfed her heart, and the next thing she knew, Renko was—

"……Heh…heh-heh…ah-ha…ah-ha-ha-ha…ah-ha-ha-ha-ha-ha-ha-ha!"

—laughing. The obstacle in front of her had said something or other, but it had been completely drowned out by the fierce roar of music, and she hadn't heard a word of it. Layered on top of the savage riffs and harmonics of the guitar was a magnificent keyboard harmony, and a ferocious drumming kept the beat. That tune—rapture that was almost like fear—gripped Renko as she realized that this was the song of *true love*.

And while she felt joy and regret and heartache and sorrow and fear and despair and remorse and disbelief, one harsh and vivid emotion dominated all the others:

I want to kill I want to kill—

I want to kill him.

"………Ah, I'm sorry, Eiri! My murderous melody has changed, and I've changed my mind."

As she apologized, she gathered strength in all four limbs. Her blurred vision cleared, and the silhouette in front of her turned into a distinct figure. Trumpets played valiantly, as if they were signaling the start of a great battle.

"I'm going to keep my promise. He'll be waiting for me. To think, he feels that strongly for me…heh-heh… There's no way he would betray me, right?"

Renko clenched her fists, grabbing hold of a future that she had once thrown away and crushing the small happiness that she felt in her last moments.

Listening to the lovely murderous melody playing for her beloved, she thought—*I won't die. I absolutely will not die. And even if I do die, I'll come back. Even if I have to crawl up from the depths of hell, I'll open my eyes, and without fail……*

"Kyousuke, I'm coming for you."

Psycome 6: A Murderer and the
Deadly Love Affair / End

AFTERWORD   Master of Ceremonies

Hello, it's Mizuki Mizushiro. How did you find the final volume? This afterword contains spoilers about the ending, so please be warned if you're reading this first.

First, I'd like to say that I'm delighted to have finally arrived at the ending I imagined. Otherwise we probably would have had to accept the bloody and depressing ending of Volume 3, when Ayaka transferred in. The fact that it didn't end there and that I was able to finish the series is thanks to everyone on the production team, starting with Mr. Namanie, everyone connected to producing the books, and most of all the readers, who kept reading and supporting *Psycome*. Truly, truly, thank you!

Now, as for the "figure" that appeared at the end of the epilogue, even I don't know who it was. It might be Renko after she awakens, or it might be an unrelated passerby. Or it might be someone else… I wrote the kind of ending that allows each of you readers to imagine whatever ending you like best.

…However, even though I said this is the end, there is actually one more collection of short stories coming out. It hadn't yet been settled at the time Volume 5 was published, so it became something of a surprise for everyone. This book was somewhat more serious, so I hope that you can laugh and enjoy the final collection.

Mizuki Mizushiro
~Written while listening to Converge~

I'm happy that I could work on Psycome.
There's still a short volume to come, but good job, Mr. Mizushiro.
To the person in charge, the designers, and the readers, thank you all!